Praise for Kelly Rimmer's
Start Up in the City series

"Rimmer showcases her talent with this sweet, lively contemporary set in New York City.... The flow is as smooth as the transition of the relationship, and the characters are wildly entertaining. This will delight fans of extremely modern romance."
—*Publishers Weekly* on *Unexpected*

"Kelly Rimmer has written one of the most darling love stories I've read in a long time... If you are looking for a joyous look into a wondrous love story, *Unexpected* should be at the top of the must-read list. Guaranteed to please."
—*Fresh Fiction*

"*Unexpected* is a warm, charming book...[with a] terribly cute, sweet friendship-cum-romance between our leads."
—*All About Romance*

"A friends-to-lovers romance that tugged at my heartstrings."
—*Romance Junkies* on *Unexpected*

More praise for Kelly Rimmer

"An intense story of survival, hardship, and heartbreak, *The Things We Cannot Say* is sure to evoke emotion in even the most cynical reader."
—*New York Journal of Books*

"Fans of Jodi Picoult and Kristin Hannah now have a new go-to author."
—Bestselling author Sally Hepworth

"Kelly Rimmer has outdone herself. If you only have time to read one book this year *The Things We Cannot Say* should be that book. Keep tissues handy."
—*Fresh Fiction*

"A heartbreaking book about an impossible decision. Kelly Rimmer writes with wisdom and compassion."
—Luanne Rice, *New York Times* bestselling author

KELLY RIMMER

Unspoken

HQN™

ISBN-13: 978-1-335-50506-4

Unspoken

This edition published by arrangement with Harlequin Books S.A.

For questions and comments about the quality of this book, please contact us at CustomerService@Harlequin.com.

www.HQNBooks.com

Printed in U.S.A.

For Mindy

Unspoken

Part One

Friday

CHAPTER ONE

Paul

I'VE BEEN DEVELOPING a single software application since I was seventeen years old. In recent years, I've worked with some of the best developers on earth, but it's still *my* software. The sum of my life's work is seventy-four million lines of code which, in layman's terms, enables people to use the internet in a safe and efficient manner. I don't know all of that code by heart of course, but if you were to give me any portion of it, I could tell you what it does and why and how.

Code is knowable. Understandable. Infallibly rational. Opening my compiler is like wrapping myself in a warm blanket on a cold day. Code is safe and familiar, and I am completely at home and completely in control in that sphere, which is pretty much the polar opposite to my feelings about other humans. People are unfortunately illogical creatures, and today, *people* are ruining my day.

Well, one person specifically.

"Hello, Isabel," I say to my almost-ex-wife. Her sudden appearance is as unfortunate as it is unexpected. Whenever we find ourselves in the same room these days, the tension is untenable, but it's certain to be even worse today, because *this* room happens to be in the very vacation home we spent most of the last year squabbling over as we negotiated the separation of our assets.

"*You* said that I could keep this house—" Isabel starts to say, but I really don't like to be reminded that if the divorce was a cruel game, there's a clear winner, and it's *not* me.

That's why I cut her off with a curt "my name is still on the title for four more days."

Her nostrils flare. She makes a furious sound in the back of her throat, then closes her eyes and exhales shakily. Isabel is trying to keep her temper in check.

I lived with Isabel Rose Winton for four years, one month and eleven days. She likes almond milk in her coffee because she thinks it's healthier, but she masks the taste with so much sugar, she may as well drink a soda. She sleeps curled up in a little ball, as if she's afraid to take up space in her own bed. She resents her mother and adores her father and brothers. She loves New York with a passion, and she has an astounding ability to pluck threads from a city of 8.5 million people to weave them into a close-knit village around herself. Isabel makes friends everywhere she goes. She never forgets a name and people always remember her, too, even after meeting her just once. Everyone adores her.

Well, *almost* everyone. I can't say I'm particularly fond of the woman these days.

"You're supposed to be on retreat with your team

this weekend." Isabel flashes me a look, but it passes too quickly. I don't have time to interpret it.

"How do you even know about my retreat?" I ask, but then I sigh and we both say at the exact same time, "Jess."

Jessica Cohen has been my friend since college and she's been my business partner almost as long. Isabel and Jess are friends, too, and they still see each other all the time. But Jess popping up in this conversation makes me uneasy, because she's the reason I'm at Greenport today. And Jess does so love to meddle...

I'm distracted just thinking about this, and that's when I make a critical error: I forget that there's a reason I've been standing at a supremely uncomfortable sixty-degree angle, with my lower half hidden behind the wall which houses the stairwell, my top half leaning into the living room where Isabel is sitting. As soon as I shift position into something like a more standard posture, I see Isabel's gaze run down my body. The scowl on her face intensifies, and mortifyingly, I feel myself blushing.

"Why are you naked?" Isabel demands.

That's not why I'm blushing; after more than four years together, I'm certain Isabel is at least as familiar with my junk as I am. And my current state of undress is actually easily explained. I arrived here ninety-four minutes ago, immediately went for a very long run and then took a very long shower. Everything was fine until I reached for a towel and discovered that Isabel's scent was all over the soft cotton.

That made no sense, because my assistant Vanessa was supposed to arrange for the cleaning service to refresh the house before my arrival here today. I was headed downstairs to see if Vanessa had at least managed to stock the fridge with food and booze when I heard the sound of footsteps in the living room. It seemed a safe assumption that if someone *had* broken into the house while I was in the shower, it wouldn't be someone who was already well acquainted with my nether regions, so I was careful to stick only my head around the corner to investigate.

That was when I found Isabel herself, sitting proudly on the sofa as if it was her throne, firing death glares in my direction.

Which, for the record, she is definitely still doing. I might not be super skilled at reading body language, but even I know a stink eye when I see one. And this particular stink eye is focused with laser-like intent on the fourth finger of my left hand.

That is why I'm blushing, because what she can see there is not nearly as easily explained as a casual spot of midday nudity.

"Why on earth would you put your wedding ring back on *now*?" she asks me stiffly.

The thing is, I never really took it off; I'd just slide it into my pocket if I knew I was going to see her. It wasn't all that difficult to hide the fact that I'm still wearing the ring—I've only seen her in person ten times since she walked out of our Chelsea brownstone ten months ago. Once at our one and only attempt at marriage counseling. Once at Jess's legendary and, this year, somewhat awkward New Year's Eve party. Once at the engagement party for our friends Marcus and Abby.

And seven times at mediation sessions, each one more heated than the last.

Isabel obviously noticed I wasn't wearing the ring during those encounters, although it seems she missed the way I constantly rubbed the empty space on my finger, endlessly aware of its absence, just as I'm endlessly aware of her absence in our home in Manhattan. I'd inevitably have felt her missing in this house today. If she wasn't here, that is.

I've tried to stop wearing the ring and I find I just can't break the habit, although if anything is going to cure me, the mortification of *this* moment might just do the trick.

"I thought I was here alone," I say. Suddenly, my future happiness all seems to hinge on Vanessa... Specifically, Vanessa having at least managed to get the fridge stocked with a shitload of beer. It's only just lunchtime, but I tell myself it's got to be 5:00 p.m. somewhere, and besides, if there's ever any circumstance where day-drinking was permissible, this is surely it. I walk toward the fridge, ignoring both my nudity and Isabel's huffing and puffing, and pull the door open.

Vanessa clearly has not followed any of my instructions and that's as confusing as it is depressing. There's no food at all in the fridge—although there is beer. Isabel usually prefers wine, so this is probably the beer I left here last time I visited—which was well over twelve months ago, but I'm willing to bet it's still drinkable. I withdraw a bottle and offer it to Isabel, only for her to gasp in indignation.

"Don't you dare make yourself comfortable— you're *not* staying."

"Well, I'm not fucking leaving." I shrug, then I carelessly think aloud, "That's your thing, not mine."

Isabel's eyebrows dip again, a deep crease forms between her eyebrows, and this time, her nostrils flare wildly. I drop my gaze to study the label on my beer.

"The season hasn't started yet. The village will be empty, just go find another room for the night. What difference does it even make?" she demands.

"As of next week, this place is no longer mine. This is my *last* chance to stay here. Why don't you go find somewhere else to stay? You can come any-time you want." I look up at Isabel as I add with de-liberate emphasis, "After next Wednesday."

"I'll call the police, Paul," she snaps.

I take a moment to think about how to respond, savoring a long sip of my beer, then running my gaze toward the water of the Long Island Sound, sparkling beyond the deck that bounds the living room. I stare into the distance until I've formed a response, then I drag my gaze back to Isabel.

She's looking down at the floor, blinking rap-idly, but the shine of tears in those big blue eyes is unmistakable.

This year, Isabel has called me variations on

heartless or *soulless* fourteen times—seven times via email or text during the three months we spent trying to negotiate our financial settlement, seven times on the phone or in person. I didn't want to count those insults, just as I desperately tried not to count the days and hours since I last saw her.

I glance at the clock on the wall above the sofa, and as I read the time, I automatically calculate that we filed out of that last volatile mediation session in stony silence five months, twenty-four days, twenty-two hours and forty-three minutes ago.

Give or take a few seconds.

When I look at the collective evidence of all of the comments Isabel has made about my apparent lack of a soul, there is no doubt in my mind that she believes me to be some kind of robot, incapable of typical variations in emotion. Actually, I know she thinks I'm a robot because she called me that, too, at the third mediation session.

The worst thing is that she was almost right about my lack of emotional depth, at least the version of me that existed before we met. Before her, I didn't really experience too many extremes when it came to my moods. There were exceptions to that rule, of course. I felt overwhelmed by grief when my mother died, elated at my college graduation, triumphant the day of the go-live for my software.

But around those times? I lived a lot of perfectly static days that might accurately be graphed as a flat line. I am, above all, a stable person. Life tends to happen around me; it doesn't sway me emotionally all that often.

Well, it didn't, once upon a time.

It does seem that love has a way of opening a person up. Love burrows deep inside and it wiggles around to carve a space out for itself, stretching and expanding as it goes. And now, even after the love has gone, the cavernous space it etched out inside me remains. Maybe that's why, in this moment, the shimmer of tears in Isabel's eyes leaves me feeling a depth of shame and misery I'm pretty sure I wasn't even capable of when I met her five years ago.

My gaze shifts to the clock on the wall again, because it *wasn't* just five years ago, and it bothers me to even think in such imprecise terms.

"Call the police, if you feel you have to," I say. My tone is flat, and I suspect that to Isabel, I appear to be resigned or unaffected. The truth is, I feel almost crushed by confused regret. I can name the emotion these days—I've worked hard on that this year—but I'm still trying to figure out how the fuck I'm supposed to deal with intense feelings like this. Showing Isabel how I feel right now would be to make myself vulnerable to her, which is difficult enough for me at the best of times—let alone when I'm as exhausted as I am today, and *especially* after the hurricane of fury she's unleashed on me since she gave up on our marriage last year.

No, I can't let down my guard right now, so instead, I try to point out some very logical reasons why she should not, in fact, call for backup. Isabel is an emotional person, but she's also very intelligent. I know she'll see sense here.

"You'd probably just make a scene. It's going to be pretty difficult to convince them to manhandle me out of here given I still own the place."

"Well, I'm not leaving either," she says, then her voice rises dramatically as she adds, "So if you're not leaving and I'm not leaving, you'll have to stay here with me. Do you even want that, Paul?"

It's the last thing in the world I want. I'd never admit it aloud, but I badly need to put a lid on all of the pain and frustration that lingers in the wake of Isabel's decision to leave our marriage. I'm adrift at the moment, and it's affecting my whole life…even, it seems, my work. This house has been a haven to me since I purchased it with an inheritance that matured on my twenty-first birthday. That makes it the obvious place for me to do some rapid-fire recuperating.

While I can't lick my wounds with Isabel stomping around, the thought of letting her win this final battle is infuriating. I'm so fucking frustrated with her that I want to tear my hair out every time she's in my field of vision. We were great, once upon a time, and we could have been again. If she'd bothered to let me know she was unhappy, I'd have found a way to fix it—no matter what it took. I might not be great with flowery declarations, but Isabel Winton was my sun and my moon, and it seemed a safe assumption that she understood that.

Turns out I was wrong about that.

Looking back on our life together now, I was

probably wrong about a lot of things. And these days, the only thing I'm really sure of is that Isabel can't stand the sight of me. That's why I'm pretty sure she's bluffing about staying here this weekend.

At least, I hope she's bluffing.

"If you really want to stay…" I shrug "…I'm sure we can keep out of each other's hair."

She gives me *that* look—the one I'd first seen her wear the night she told me she was leaving. I'm familiar with components that comprise this facial expression now…the flare of her nostrils, the way her gaze narrows, the scornful curl of her lip. It's taken me a long time to realize that the emotion displayed on my beautiful wife's face when she looks at me that way is something deeper and darker even than anger…something past resentment even, an emotion closer to disdain.

Observing *that* look again now, I wonder yet again how I can possibly be a "genius" if I really was stupid enough to fuck up the most important thing in my life this badly. Whatever went wrong between us didn't just break our relationship; it also broke Isabel and turned her into a completely different and far less likable person.

"Fuck you, Paul," she says now.

I'm about to echo the curse right back at her, but the sound of my phone buzzing on the dining room table distracts me. I know I set the phone on Do Not Disturb mode, so it's got to be one of my favorite contacts calling or my cell would have automatically silenced the call.

So that means it's one of my business partners or Dad or my brother Jake or…Isabel herself, because even though I haven't called her in five months (well, four months, twenty-five days and around thirty-four minutes), I've yet to delete her entry.

It's fair to say that embracing change isn't exactly one of my strengths.

"Some people would say it's rude to answer the phone in the middle of a conversation." Isabel stands.

I think about that as I cross the room to pick up my phone. What a strange thing for Isabel to say. There are 7.2 billion people in the world, and some of them talk constantly. It stands to reason that *some people* say just about every permutation of words, each and every day. I'm not at all sure why Isabel felt the need to point that out now.

I pick the phone up just as the call ends. It was Marcus Ross, my other business partner. I unlock the screen and move to return his call, but I'm distracted when Isabel growls behind me.

I turn to face her, and she shoots me *that* look one last time, grabs the handle of her suitcase and storms toward the smaller of the guest rooms—the one on the ground floor, directly below the master I've already claimed for myself. She closes the door behind herself, then opens it and closes it again—the second time, managing a much louder and I assume a much more satisfying slam.

The gentle, sweet woman I was married to never slammed doors or raised her voice. The shrew I'm currently divorcing raises her voice and cries in front of our attorneys when it suits her, so I barely even blink as the sound echoes through the house.

It seems I've managed to get caught up in the world's most depressing game of chicken, and I'm already starting to regret my bravado. Am I really going to stay here with the new and not-improved version of Isabel lingering in the house?

Apparently, the answer to that question is yes, because the alternative would be to give Isabel what she wants, and I've done way too much of that already since she stormed out of my life.

CHAPTER TWO

Paul

WHEN I RETURN his call, Marcus greets me with a booming, "Gollum! Glad to hear you're still alive."

"I told you to stop calling me that, asshole," I say.

"Gollum won't take off the precious," he rasps, but I can hear the laugh he's trying to stifle. This is not a new joke; he's been giving me shit about the wedding ring for months now, and I know he's trying to cheer me up. I'm well aware that it's absurd that I'm still wearing the ring, so his strategy actually works most of the time—hell, it probably would have worked ten minutes ago, but it's not going to work now, not now that Isabel is here. I can all but see the dark clouds of a bad mood gathering around my head. "Where the hell are you, Paul?"

"Didn't you check your email today?" That hardly makes sense. Marcus is *always* on his email.

"Uh…" There's a pause, and I can hear his mouse clicking, then he says tentatively, "Nope. Sorry, no emails from you since that one about that API request, and that was just…" He sighs heavily. "Paul. You sent it at 3:00 a.m. That's late, even for you."

I jam the phone between my shoulder and my ear and slide my laptop out of its satchel. The battery is critically low, but there's enough charge for the screen to flicker to life, so I quickly navigate to my email client.

I did work crazy-late last night, trying to clear the decks to give my team a fair chance of success with the mountain of work they need to tackle this weekend. At 4:16 a.m., I hadn't yet reached the "letting everyone know about me disappearing for the weekend" part, but I was so tired I was making careless mistakes, so I decided to stop just to rest my eyes. Perhaps unsurprising, I fell asleep over my keyboard and woke to the sound of the driver mashing the doorbell at 7:01 a.m.

But I did write that series of emails explaining my absence. Sure, I sent them later than I intended, but I had well and truly finished by the time my colleagues would have been arriving at the office.

My email client opens now, and the bold 13 beside my outbox jumps right out at me. Did I connect to the hotspot on my phone when I was working in the car? I can't even remember, and it doesn't matter now. All that matters is that the emails I wrote this morning went nowhere.

I watch as the laptop starts to search for an internet connection, then I reach forward violently and flick the computer into airplane mode to stop it belatedly sending the barrage of now irrelevant messages.

No wonder Vanessa didn't get the house ready— she didn't get the email I sent her asking her to do so. The linen and towels in my bedroom haven't been changed, and it's clear that Isabel has been here since my last visit. I don't relish the idea of sleeping in sheets that my ex-wife likely slept naked in recently, but the linen is the least of my worries right now.

I scan down the outbox, every email is more important than the last. The email to Vanessa. The instructions to my documentation analysts. And the testing manager. And my senior engineer. There are pages of detailed notes for Audrey, my senior developer and the unlucky woman I intended to task with holding the whole team together this weekend.

"Just an FYI, Paul, Audrey doesn't look so good. She's..." I hear Marcus shift, then he whispers into the phone, "She's watching me through the window of my office, and she's gnawing on her fingernails."

"She does that when she's stressed." I'm familiar with the habit, even if I didn't think to ask *why* she does such a thing until a few months ago. "If it bothers you, send someone out to get her some Twizzlers and give her those to chew on instead."

Six months ago, we announced that a new version of our browser would be released in May, which is now next month. The new version has a whole new interface. That's done, and it's awesome if I do say so myself. The problem is we also announced some exceedingly complex internet security capability and Marcus's team has been selling it hard. The whole industry is excited about the new features, so there's been heavy media coverage, and our corporate subscription clients are chomping at the bit for it but...

It doesn't actually work yet. At least, not reliably, and reliability is pretty fucking important when it comes to corporate software. There are a handful of catastrophic bugs lingering in the current code that we *need* to fix before we can move to testing, and it needs weeks of QA before we can even think about moving toward release. Hence the emergency "retreat" this weekend.

We call this kind of work session a retreat because everyone stays at the office until the work is done, but it's an ironic term, because there's no yoga or day spa treatments or rest at all. This kind of retreat represents a last-ditch effort to meet a deadline. It's an immersive marathon of work that only ends when the plan changes or the work finishes. The carrot on the end of the development team's stick is the big, fat bonuses they will all get if we find a way out of the mess we're in right now.

Audrey really needed to know before now that she was responsible for handling this weekend. That's why I sent her a very long, very detailed explanation of where I was going and everything she needed to do in my absence, starting with an announcement and quasi-motivational-speech to everyone else right on 9:00 a.m. this morning, before the team had time to panic about my absence.

"Why didn't someone call me when I didn't show up for work?" I've never so much as taken a personal day, let alone disappeared without an explanation.

"Well…I'm calling you now," Marcus points out,

then he hesitates. "And how do I say this diplomatically…"

"If you're asking me for advice on how to say
something diplomatically, you're screwed."

"Paul, you're not playing your A-game at the moment. Ever since you and Izzy agreed on that settlement, you've been…off," Marcus says, very gently.
I appreciate that gentle tone, but it doesn't stop the
words from hitting me with the force of a sledgeham-
mer. "Just look at today. As far as I can tell, you've
been coding since before you learned to talk, and
suddenly you can't even figure out how to send an
email?"

I know he's right and I'm embarrassed as hell
about it. I hate acknowledging even to myself that
my heart isn't in it anymore. It takes an awful lot of
motivation to work the way I used to work. I'm not
that guy anymore, but that's not even the real problem here. The issue is that I've yet to figure out who
I am now.

"I'm sorry." I sigh. "I know. I'm trying to get my
head back in the game but…you're right. Things
are shit. That's why I needed—and that's why I'm
taking—some space."

"Totally fine, Paul. Jess and I talked about it first
thing and we just figured with everything on your
plate this week, you were just resting up before the
retreat and we thought it would do you a world of
good. But…well, it's lunchtime now, and I was worried. Are you okay? Where are you?"

I pause, thinking back to Jess's determined insistence two days ago that I absolutely needed to be at the retreat this weekend.

I know your divorce is finalized next week. I realize it might be tempting to slink off somewhere to lick your wounds this weekend—were you planning on going to the house out at Greenport one last time? Well, don't even fucking think about it. I need you at this retreat—your team has to get back on top of this release. Got it?

Even at the time, the conversation struck me as odd. Not because Jess had caught me out on my plans to skip out on the most important weekend of my team's working year…quite the opposite, in fact. It hadn't even occurred to me that I could or should want to take this weekend off, not until that very conversation. And Jess can be a tough taskmaster, but even so, she'd never spoken to me like that before.

Her little speech grated me, and things that grate on me tend to stick in my mind. I've known Jess since my second year of college. Hell, I lived with her for two years, in a tiny, one-bedroom apartment that she, Marcus and I used as both home and office until we had the first version of our browser finished and we'd secured enough capital to start paying ourselves salaries.

Jess knows me better than almost anyone. She knows how to push my buttons and she's not afraid to play people like pieces on a chessboard when she wants something. Jess knew that if she irritated me with that autocratic speech about staying at the office this weekend, I'd do exactly the opposite and leave.

By the time I left the office last night, taking the weekend off no longer sounded like a crazy idea at all. I have been underperforming lately, but I still have a terrible habit of micromanaging, and that managerial flaw only intensifies when I'm under pressure. I eventually concluded that the team will actually be better off tackling the mountain of work ahead of them without me there.

I don't think I'm ready to admit this aloud just yet, but I'm starting to suspect that the reason my team is running seriously late for the first time ever is that *I* can't get my head in the game.

"I'm at Greenport," I tell Marcus. "I'm not coming in for the retreat this weekend."

"What?" Marcus shrieks like a panicked kid, then clears his throat and deepens his voice as he says carefully, "Uh…Paul…"

"Audrey is ready for this," I say, with complete confidence, but then I hesitate. "At least, she will be once she actually knows she's running things, anyway. I'll call her when we hang up."

"Maybe you didn't understand when I said she was chewing on her fingernails. I mean, she's really going to town on them. Frankly, it's disgusting."

"She's nervous, Marcus. Have a little sensitivity."

He laughs, because we both know I'm the last person in the world to lecture anyone about sensitivity, let alone Marcus, the most emotionally intelligent guy I know. At our office, it's always been me making the social faux pas. I'm the guy who congratulates the woman on what's inevitably not a baby bump, or asks after someone who recently died, or who dismisses someone's legitimate concerns too swiftly or even misses their concern altogether because I've got my head stuck in a fucking reference guide and I'm not actually listening while they beg me for help.

I've almost made a career out of stomping on other people's feelings, not because I don't care, but because I often don't even realize I've done it. That's why I'm not offended that Marcus is laughing at me right now. This is the pot calling the kettle black, and it's another moment that would be funny under just about any other circumstances.

"Why don't I conference Jess in?" Marcus suggests.

"I really need to cool down before I speak to her." I'm pissed at Jess, but she's still my business partner, and as CEO, technically my boss. What she's done here is messy and manipulative and I'm furious with her that she messed around in my personal life, but particularly because she did it via a conversation at work. Even so, I can't let my frustrations with her spill right back over into our business life. Things are complicated enough for me there already.

"Cool down?" Marcus repeats blankly.

"She tricked me into coming here and now that Izzy has turned up, too, I'd say Jess has some kind of master plan underway. Jess Cohen is like some fucking puppet master, manipulating people like… like…" I'm momentarily lost for words, and it's frustrating as fuck. "Like puppets!"

"Paul," Marcus says, cautioning me, then he draws in a breath. "Seriously, man. I'm worried about you."

"I'll call Audrey and apologize, then I'll run her through everything she needs to know for the weekend. Then I'm going to go right back to avoiding Isabel."

"Izzy's actually *there*. At the house."

"Yes."

"And you're there, too."

"Yes."

"In that tiny house."

"Tiny? It's 2,200 square feet, Marcus." It's a humble house, built in the 1940s and in need of some remodeling, but it's nothing like tiny—not by the Manhattan standards Marcus and I are accustomed to.

"That's tiny if you two are going to be there for the whole weekend, especially without some kind of referee or alligator-infested moat to separate you. Are you seriously both going to stay?"

"I guess you could say we're both too stubborn to leave." My gaze drops back down to the laptop, and the grayscale icon that shows the Wi-Fi is still deactivated. I prop my phone next to my ear against my shoulder, an idea surfacing as I plug the laptop into the power.

I know exactly what Isabel is doing in that guest room. She'll unpack her clothing and toiletries first, because that's always the first thing she does when she goes anywhere. Next, she'll crank up the AC in the room, and she'll do that because her next move will be to pull the duvet right up to her chin even though it's unseasonably warm today. When Isabel is flustered, she always retreats under blankets to binge-watch canned-laughter sitcoms.

And to get to one of those shows, she's going to want Netflix.

Once upon a time, Isabel would barely have reacted to something like nonfunctional Wi-Fi, but this year, her anger has somehow become permanently set on a hair trigger. I have a feeling that if I cut her comfort-binge off at the source, she's going to overreact. Maybe she won't be pissed enough to leave, but she'll definitely be pissed enough to get flustered and to come seeking another argument. She'll yell at me, because although we were never really the type of couple to argue, all that changed the day she walked out. It's like her temper was dormant for thirty-three years and then our marriage ended and a sleeping beast within her awakened.

I ponder this for a moment as the laptop screen brightens again as the current flows into it. A prank like this won't win me the war. The truth is, I lost that, probably some time ago. But a simple thing like switching out a Wi-Fi password might just get me another shot at this final battle between us: the battle for the last weekend at *our* vacation home.

"I have to go," I say abruptly.

"You'll call Audrey?"

"As soon as I hang up."

"And Jess?"

I snort. "When I get around to it."

"Fine." Marcus sighs. "I'll fill Jess in. You should probably answer if she calls you, though."

"She won't call me." I'm certain of this. Jess has set the game in motion. Now she'll just sit back and wait for it to play out. What I'm not yet certain of is her end goal. Does Jess seriously think that Isabel and I could ever get back together?

No, that's not it. Jess has been right at the sidelines this past year. She knows that whatever Isabel and I shared is long dead. And cremated. And then scattered on the wind.

"Are you sure you don't want to just come back to the city?" Marcus asks quietly. "Before... I don't know. Before things get any worse."

"Trust me," I say. "I know what I'm doing."

"Good luck, Paul."

"I don't need luck."

"You definitely need something," he laughs weakly.

I hang up the phone, log into the router, and get to work. It takes no time at all to change the password on the Wi-Fi network—and by the time I finish my handiwork, I've also finished the beer, so I wander back to the fridge for another.

But there's a spring in my step and a smile on my lips, because there's something surprisingly satisfying about knowing that for the first time in an entire year, I'm one step ahead of Isabel Winton.

CHAPTER THREE

Isabel

OF COURSE PAUL is here. It makes perfect sense. When we were married and I actually needed him somewhere? He was guaranteed to turn up late or on the wrong day or at the wrong place. But this weekend, when I just need him to be *anywhere else on the planet*, of course he'd show up here.

Since I stormed into the guest room, Paul has been on the phone in the living room. Irritation prickles along my skin, the sound of his voice through the wall a constant reminder that he is in my space. Just when I think maybe I can't take it after all and I might actually have to leave, I hear the creak of footsteps on the stairs and the sound of the door to the master bedroom closing above me.

Finally, the house is silent.

For a heartbeat, I almost convince myself he's left altogether…but then I hear him walking around up there, and now he's talking again—almost certainly another work call.

Because Paul Winton is all work, all the fucking time.

But this is actually the first time he and I have been alone in ten months and it turns out, I'm still maddeningly aware of his proximity. Maybe it's even worse today, because he was parading out there naked as the day he was born, and that meant I couldn't miss all of the ways his body has changed since I left him last year. Paul is tall, and he was always lanky—he's always looked like the middle-distance runner he is. He's gained a lot of muscle this year, and I have to assume he's made drastic changes to his exercise regime. Which is curious, because if there's one thing Paul doesn't like, it's change.

Stop thinking about him, Isabel.

My self-talk fails miserably. He's pacing upstairs, right above me. His voice is a steady, constant drone, and my body refuses to let me forget that he's still here. Once upon a time, I marveled that Paul and I shared the kind of chemistry that hums in the background even when you're in separate rooms, driven by the potential of an encounter. If sex was enough, Paul and I would still be together. Hell, if sex was enough, Paul and I might never have left our bedroom.

Sex wasn't enough, but I've wasted a lot of time convincing myself that it is. Sex is powerful and potent, and it lies. It says, *It doesn't matter that this is the only way we connect.* It says, *It doesn't matter that the friendship we once had is long dead.* And even now, if I strain hard enough to hear it, sex is still whispering to me. It says, *It doesn't matter that we're getting divorced on Wednesday.*

I've berated myself for believing those lies in the past, and right now, I hate myself for how tempted I am to believe them again.

Up until Wednesday night, I was going to stay in the city this weekend, and I wasn't going to take any time off even as the milestone of our divorce looms. I love my job and it's been an important distraction from the clusterfuck of my personal life this year.

But at our regular weekly dinner after my Wednesday night Pilates class, Jess suggested I take some time out to give myself some space to grieve. And like she said, where better place for a weekend of reflection than here?

I couldn't sleep that night, thinking about the enticing possibility of a weekend of R & R. The next thing I knew, I was in my boss's office at the gym, trying to figure out how to request five days off, literally at the last minute. I reminded him that I haven't missed even an hour of my rostered time at the gym throughout the debacle of my separation this year. I also pointed out that the Pilates and barre classes I teach are just a side gig around my real role at the gym; I'm the senior exercise physiologist there and have been for almost ten years now. Over the past year I've put in extra hours and extra effort, working my ass off to establish a new senior's health program. I reminded him because of that project alone, Nick's gym has welcomed dozens of new clients.

"Isabel," Nick eventually said, with obvious exasperation, "I can't tell if you're about to ask me for a favor or if you're putting on a ballet production—you've been dancing around something ever since you came in here. If you need something, just *ask* me."

I could tell he wasn't thrilled about it, but he did grant me the last-minute leave, and here I am. At my vacation home for a luxurious five days to mark the end of my marriage. With my almost-ex-husband right here to watch me sulk.

Dammit.

Jess and our friend Abby are not going to believe this latest development. My fingers are trembling as I formulate the group text and I'm not sure if that's adrenaline or anger or something else altogether. At the very last second, I hesitate, curse the awkward work connection between Jess and Paul and delete her name from the text.

I want sympathy and support, but not so much that I'm willing to whine to Paul's CEO about what Paul is choosing to do with a rare day off. Navigating the interconnected network that is our friendships and Paul's working life has been complicated this year. I hate him, I'm angry with him and I resent him, but I also apparently hate the idea that our personal drama might somehow spill into his working life.

Guess what? Paul was already here when I arrived. And guess what else? Turns out we're both too stubborn to leave.

The phone rings about three seconds after I hit Send. "Marcus just texted me. He said I should make sure you're okay because Paul sounds really upset," Abby says, without wasting time on a greeting. She's Marcus's fiancée. See what I mean? Every significant person in my life, outside of my own family, seems to have some connection to Paul.

"Paul doesn't get upset," I mutter. "Robots don't get upset."

"Well, he simply has to leave. Have you called your attorney?"

"I don't need to pay her hundreds of dollars an hour to tell me there's no point," I say. "The property *is* still in Paul's name. He's even paid the taxes this year. Technically, he has every right to be here."

"That…"

"…rat-bastard?" I finish the sentence cautiously when *she* hesitates a little too long, but I'm never really sure how Abby feels about Paul, because I know he's still technically her friend, too. Abby listens to me rant and she says all the right things, but I know her loyalties are divided here.

I guess her pregnancy hormones are swinging in my favor today, because Abby surprises me by growling and asking, "Should I look up the train schedules? I can be there in a few hours, and I promise you, I could mess his nose up real good. *Real good,* Izzy. Just think about it."

"And how exactly are you going to explain to Marcus why you've been arrested for assaulting his business partner?"

"You know how pregnancy mood swings can be,

and I've got twins on board so I'm twice as moody. I have a ready-made excuse, let's put it to work."

"Thanks for the offer, Abby."

"I'm really sorry this happened."

"The divorce, or the awful weekend I'm about to have?" I ask her wryly.

"Both."

I sigh, then answer her honestly. "Me, too."

We fall into a not-quite-comfortable silence, then Abby asks cautiously, "So, if you're really going to stay, will you try to...talk to him?"

"Talk to him?" I give a confused laugh. "More talking? What on earth could there be left to say?"

"It's just... I mean... I don't know, Izzy." She's clearly gearing up to drop a truth bomb. Given how long the pause is before she speaks, I have plenty of time to brace myself. "I do get the impression that he was kind of blindsided when you left."

I blink, bewildered. This is the *last* thing in the world I expected her to say.

"Are you kidding me? I gave that marriage everything I had," I gasp. "And even after I left, Paul didn't even try to convince me to come home. Maybe he's never said it explicitly, but the fact that he just watched me walk away surely proves that he was unhappy, too." I wait for Abby to comment. When she doesn't, I add a little defensively, "Besides, it's just too late to try to clear the air. There's so much bitterness between us now after that awful mediation process. Every time we do talk, we end up shouting at each other. Especially me." I clear my throat. "It's embarrassing, actually."

Abby is silent for a moment as she ponders this. "I can't imagine you doing that. You're so quiet. Gentle."

"I've never felt anger like this before," I admit. My throat is tight, and my eyes sting with tears I refuse to shed. "Paul is so different when we're alone together, he always has been. In the early days he was gentler…softer. But the last few years…he's just too arrogant and driven and cold and pigheaded. It's like he wanted to push me away, and if that was what he was trying to do…well, it worked."

"I've seen his arrogance. I've seen his gentleness," Abby says quietly. "I've never seen this mean, angry version of you. I can't even picture it."

"Trust me, Abby. Even now, I just want to go scream at him some more."

"It doesn't even sound like you want to be there, other than to annoy Paul. Come home and we can meet up with Jess at some five-star hotel, you guys can drown your sorrows in bubbles and I'll guzzle organic apple juice. Tomorrow morning when you're hungover and I'm fresh as a daisy you can send me out for coffees. You can still grieve or sulk or do whatever you needed to do this weekend…you can just do it with us instead."

"No," I say, blinking the tears from my eyes. "Paul doesn't want to be here with me any more than I want to be here with him. No way am I letting him win."

When Abby speaks again, her tone is heavy with uncertainty. "And you're sure about this?"

"I am."

"Okay." She sighs. "You promise me you'll ring me if you need anything?"

She's clearly hesitant, and I'm actually quite touched by her concern. I soften my tone as I promise, "I will. You don't need to worry about me."

"Just…please be smart about this weekend…"

"Abby," I laugh weakly. "I'm not going to do anything stupid."

"I know but…" She still hesitates, then she says in a rush, "It's just that you're vulnerable at the moment. You *both* are, despite what you may think about Paul. He's seemed so different lately. Emotions are running high—don't get sucked into anything you'll regret later. It's all over next week, so just try to be careful until then, okay?"

I close my eyes. It's all too easy to picture Paul and I spending the entire weekend snapping at each other. Breaking for lunch. Fighting some more. Sleeping. Then snarling our farewells and going off to live separate, angry lives.

I hate that picture just enough that for a moment or two, I second-guess my decision to stay. I force myself to imagine what it would be like to walk away right now. No fireworks. Just slipping from Paul's life all over again.

But I can't.

Mostly because I simply cannot bear the thought of the quiet triumph on his face when he hears the door close behind me and realizes he's won. It's stupid and it's petty and it's not at all the way I thought things between us would be when I decided to leave him ten months ago, but there you have it.

I'm staying because the alternative is to go, and that's what Paul wants me to do.

There's a big part of me that's deeply ashamed of how much of my behavior this year has been driven by such childish impulses.

There's an even bigger part of me that just wants to lash out at him. First, because he promised me he'd love me until his dying breath, and within no time at all he just sat back and let our marriage shrivel up and die. Of course that hurt, but I wasn't actually angry when I decided to leave him. On some level, walking out that door was just a desperate cry for help. I'd tried everything to get Paul to notice how much distance had grown between us, but I still thought he loved me, and I certainly still loved him. Leaving him was drastic, but I couldn't figure out what else to do.

The fury came later—starting with the brittle conversation he and I had on the sidewalk at the front of our brownstone while I waited for my car after I told him I was leaving.

We should talk about this, Isabel. We should have a meeting.

I still can't believe I *left* the man and instead of pleading with me to stay as I'd hoped he would do, he reacted as if I'd made a poor business decision. I remember staring at him in shock while that first, alien burst of anger surged inside. It's grown exponentially at every encounter Paul and I have had since then.

In the end, this vacation house and a small cash settlement are the only things I walk away from our marriage with, other than a few early wrinkles and a newfound distrust in the male species. I needed this weekend—I needed the space to think and to do some self-reflection because I don't like or even understand who I've become this year. Yes, Paul hurt me very deeply, but this vengeful ex-wife thing is really not me.

And yet somehow it is, because even now, even thinking all of this through, all I really want to do is go up there and fight with him some more. Just like that, Abby's concern about this whole long-weekend situation suddenly makes a whole lot of sense.

"If it gets too intense, I'll come home," I promise her.

"Good." She sounds supremely satisfied by this, and that makes me laugh.

"Listen to you. Your mommy instincts are kicking in already."

I hear the echo of her chuckle over the phone. "That's right." She adopts a mock-stern tone. "Don't make me come over there."

"Talk to you soon?"

"You keep me posted, Izzy. I'm here for you."

CHAPTER FOUR

Isabel

As I TRAVELED here today, I imagined myself sprawled on the sofa in the living room in my pajamas all weekend, ordering in takeout and watching soppy movies from a nest of used Kleenex. I figured I'd be comforted by long stints on the deck in the sunshine, reading or quietly contemplating the waters of the Long Island Sound. I hoped I'd be soothed by the rest and healed by the peace and quiet.

On Wednesday afternoon, I'd emerge from the cocoon of my grief a beautiful butterfly, ready to move on to the next phase of my life.

Okay, maybe that last bit was a little optimistic, but I really wanted to do some heavy-duty sulking this weekend. I'm sick of being brave. This year has been *awful* and I wanted a few days to lick my wounds before the divorce becomes final. I haven't really let myself do that until now. Once I finally accepted that our marriage really was over, I set a stiff upper lip and I forced myself to keep looking forward.

No regrets.

No second-guessing my decision to give up on our marriage.

My mantra was an endless loop of *you can't change the past so keep moving forward.*

The only problem with this approach has been an inexplicable and somewhat inescapable sense that I've forgotten something. It's just like when you go on vacation and you're traveling to your destination and the whole time you're mentally running through the contents of your suitcase, convinced you've left something vital at home.

That's exactly how I feel all the damned time, and it's exhausting.

I fumble for the remote and try to find something to watch on the TV, but the Netflix app immediately throws an error. This was once Paul's domain—the kind of situation I dealt with by calling, "Paul, Netflix is broken," and kicking my feet up with a glass of wine while I waited for him to fix it. But I'm no longer the wife of a genius software developer, and I've adjusted. Tech stuff is never going to be my strength, but I'm almost used to sorting these challenges on my own again after ten months of living alone in my shoebox in Soho.

I navigate to the Settings page on the menu of the TV, and I'm feeling confident as I diagnose a Wi-Fi issue. The network is still there, but the TV can't connect. I was just here two weeks ago and it was working fine, so at first, I'm confused about why it's broken now.

Until it occurs to me that the password has probably changed.

Likely in the last ten minutes, while a computer genius was out in the living room fuming about my surprise arrival. I should have known he'd turn our technology against me.

I try to guess the obvious options for a new password, but variations on IsabelIsABitch, GoHomeIsabel and IHateIsabel all fail. I set my phone down on the bed and take some deep, cleansing breaths while I talk myself down from what I know could very easily become a rapidly escalating war of childish pranks.

Don't do anything hasty, Isabel. Stay calm. Don't overreact. It's just the internet. Who needs Netflix, anyway? You were just going to waste the afternoon watching old episodes of Will & Grace. *Don't let him goad you into a reaction this easily.*

My very sensible self-talk fails miserably. I slide off the bed and walk out into the living room, planning to head for the staircase and spoiling for a fight. As soon as I leave the bedroom, though, just a hint of Paul's lingering scent on the air has memories bubbling up rapid-fire in my mind. This isn't just a living space right now. It's somehow become the museum of *us*, filled with things that were furnishings and decor mere seconds ago, but those objects have now become installations to take me back to another point in time.

We cuddled on the couch so many times—so many nights when I'd ask him to watch a movie with me, and he'd always agree...but he'd also al-

ways bring his stupid laptop so he could work. But
there was also that night when he was so tired after
a particularly long week at work that he fell asleep
with his head in my lap, and I stared down at him
as he rested, and the love and affection I felt for him
seemed boundless.

And then there's the kitchen—how many times
was I relaxing out on the deck with a book and Paul
would get hungry and I'd hear him open and close
the fridge, then he'd ask me what I wanted for dinner, a not-so-subtle hint for me to *organize* us some
dinner, without a trace of irony or apology in his
tone? That very same space could also play host to
so many surprisingly sweet moments, like the time
he sneaked out of bed early to make me waffles and
he did such an astoundingly good job on the recipe
that I was convinced they were takeout. He eventually admitted he'd been practicing at home when I
was at work because he wanted to surprise me on
our long weekend out here.

He really did surprise me that time, not just because of the waffles but because it was the anniversary of the day when we met. I hadn't even realized
he'd marked that date in his mind.

We sat at the dining room table for so many
meals—even our first meal together, when Jess
and Marcus and Abby and even Paul's brother Jake
were all here for the kind of noisy, wine-soaked long
weekends with friends that most twentysomethings
know all too well. I'd known Jess for a while by
then, after she started coming to my advanced Pilates

class, and we'd quickly formed a close friendship outside of class, too. She invited me to join her other friends for a long weekend out here, and I didn't realize that agreeing to that trip was going to change my entire life.

That was the first time I'd ever laid eyes on Paul, and I could scarcely convince myself to look away. He was utterly intriguing, brilliant and intense. He was also just a little too arrogant and awkward to be easy company, but intriguing nonetheless.

But I remember, too, that last dinner we had here, when it was just the two of us, and we sat in bitter, impenetrable silence. Paul's eyes kept drifting to his laptop, and I knew his hands were itching to hold the phone I'd snatched from him when we sat down at the table. Halfway through dinner, he pushed back his chair, scooped the laptop up and went upstairs to work. We were supposed to stay another few days, but the next day I sobbed as I packed my bag. He actually caught on for once and packed his, too.

"What's wrong?" he'd asked.

"Nothing!" I'd snapped, as I folded the new lingerie I'd packed for the trip but never actually worn.

I've been here over a dozen weekends since I left Paul—this house has become my haven when navigating life in the city alone becomes bewildering and exhausting. The first few trips were difficult, but I've never felt overwhelmed like this, and suddenly, the house I fought tooth and nail for is the last place on earth I can bear to be.

I step hastily back into the bedroom, scoop up

my wallet and all but run from the house into the street. I wander idly toward the village center— almost a mile from our house, but it's a pleasant walk down streets filled with much-loved family homes. It's warm for April today. The air is heavy with the humidity I know is only going to build over the coming months; the sun is hot on my shoulders when I step between the shade offered by the trees that line the street.

With every step away from Paul, I feel the chaos in my chest settling. By the time I reach the village center, I'm almost calm again—but I'm in no rush to go back to that house. That's why I linger, ducking and weaving through the stores without purpose or the desire to actually do any shopping.

It's the kind of spring afternoon here where the whole world seems fresh and new. On days like this, I used to joke with Paul that we should pack up in the city and move to Greenport permanently. I wasn't always joking. Most of the time I love the city, but I almost always loved *us* here. Every now and again when we stole a weekend away together here, I'd catch the full force of Paul's attention for a few hours. Even in those last lonely months, I'd remember exactly why I fell so deeply in love with him in the first place. In work mode, Paul is focused and obsessive and cold. He'll always be an intense man, but here at Greenport, the intensity was sometimes irresistibly focused on me.

It's hard to admit, even to myself, that I still really miss those moments.

When I tire of my rudderless voyage, I wander to Marie's, my favorite store here in Greenport. It's a quirky mix of homewares, flowers and food, tucked inside a remodeled Colonial house on Front Street. When I step through the front door, a blast of floral-scented air greets me, and Marie herself calls from behind the counter.

"Isabel! Back so soon? Weren't you just here last weekend?"

It took three or four visits alone to this café before Marie stopped asking after Paul. I haven't thought about that for a while, but I'm suddenly very grateful that she did eventually catch on. If she asked after him today, I think I'd burst into tears.

"It was a couple of weeks ago. And I'm already due some more Greenport peace and quiet," I explain, offering her a weak smile.

"Large iced coffee on almond milk, extra cream, extra caramel syrup, right?" she smiles, and I laugh and nod. I curl up in a bucket chair by the window of the café and begin flicking through a gossip magazine someone has left on the table, but I'm quickly interrupted by another familiar voice.

"I know we said we'd have coffee next time you're in town, but I didn't realize it would be this soon." I look up to find my friend Darby Whitlam sinking into the seat opposite me. He offers me a somewhat cheeky smile, which quickly fades as he surveys my face. "Oh, Izzy. Are you okay?"

"I'm fine," I lie, then explain, "This visit was kind

of a last-minute impulse. I didn't plan to be back so soon."

"I was just joking around with you. I actually have a client shortly. I felt my energy levels starting to fade so I sneaked out for a caffeine top-up. Nothing worse than your therapist falling asleep while you pour your heart out to him, right?" Darby gives me a little grin.

I met Darby at the little gym here in Greenport late last year. He's a super-friendly, happily divorced guy in his late thirties, and apparently the main driving force behind the gym's thriving social club. Greenport is a pretty intimate place in the off-season, so I've run into him plenty of times over the last few months. His office is over a store just down from the café, and we've caught up over coffee together here at Marie's place a few times now, most recently when I was here two weeks ago. I've joined the gym's trivia team for the Sunday night competition at a local bar at his invitation, but I've always declined his offers to take me out for dinner. I can tell that Darby is interested in something more than a friendship with me, and I really don't want to lead him on. I'm months, maybe years away from being ready to date again.

Plus…I feel absolutely nothing when I look at Darby, even though he's attractive. He has a thick head of blond hair and warm blue eyes, and he's kind and thoughtful and sensitive. He's exactly the kind of guy I should've been with all along.

"Listen, if you need to talk, you've got my number, okay?" Darby says quietly. That's when I know I must look awful—he's never directly offered a shoulder for me to cry on before.

I'm relieved when Darby quickly moves the conversation on. "We can catch up for a drink this weekend if you find you're up for some company. Or come along with the gang for trivia again Sunday night… you're always welcome to join us, and it's always handy having someone on the team who knows both sports and anatomy."

Jess might tell me to meet him for trivia, or better yet, to go out for dinner with him beforehand. She's been asking me why I'm not playing the field again, given the divorce was my idea and it's almost finished now. She even suggested she could set me up with her best guy friend, Mitchell, whom I've met quite a few times now and do genuinely like. I told her I just wasn't ready, and I guess that's true. What's also true is that the idea of dating anyone makes me feel like I'm cheating on Paul.

Paul. The man I'm quite certain I feel nothing but anger toward these days. It doesn't make sense that I still feel I need to be loyal to him, too. I'm in limbo, and that's part of the problem. I don't feel married anymore, but I sure as hell don't feel single. I can't help but think that part of the reason that I can't move on yet is that so much of my energy is still tied up in thoughts about Paul.

I glance up, and Darby smiles at me again. He has such a lovely smile, and I actually wish I could feel it in my chest the way I can see it with my eyes.

"I was thinking I might take a class at the gym tomorrow," I say lightly. "Will you be there?"

"Never miss 7:00 a.m. barre on Saturdays." He winks at me, and just then the barista calls his name and he rises. See? Perfect for me. He even does barre, for God's sake, my favorite of all of the classes I'm certified to teach. "You take care of yourself, Izzy."

"You, too."

I did the right thing leaving Paul. I'm sure of it.

I just wish I could understand why I still can't move forward, even though I now find myself stuck at a place I *hate*.

WHEN I'VE FINISHED my iced coffee and I've almost convinced myself to go back to the house, Marie hands me a bouquet of purple tulips.

"Oh," I say, surprised. "What are these for?"

"From your not-so-secret admirer," Marie tells me, then she gives me a knowing wink. I flush and leave the café in a flustered hurry, only finding the courage to open the little card on the tulips when I'm outside.

I hope these brighten your day. Darby xo

The tulips are beautiful, a generous gesture from a man who has shown me nothing but kindness in the months that I've known him. But they feel heavy in my arms, and I'm actually conflicted about taking those tulips back into the very house where Paul waits. A sudden, sharp thought prickles my consciousness.

If Paul had bought me flowers, even just once or twice, then maybe we wouldn't be in this situation.

I'm taking the tulips home. I hope he sees them in the vase on the dining room table and I hope he wonders if another man bought them for me. I fish my phone out of my pocket and send Darby a text.

Thank you, my friend.

To which he replies almost immediately:

It's my pleasure. I hope the flowers put that beautiful smile back on your face.

What is *wrong* with me? Darby is perfect. Why can't I just let myself feel something for someone who might actually feel something for me in return?

I stop at the grocery store on my way home to pick up some fruit and some almond milk for my coffee back at the house. I hover at the half-and-half, knowing that's what Paul would want for his own coffee, unsure whether or not I should pick some up for him, too. At the last minute, I scoop up a small carton and dump it into my basket, but I don't let myself think about the gesture too much. It's not a white flag, and knowing Paul, he probably won't even notice I made the effort.

I'm dragging my feet by the time I climb the steps to our front porch, but the flustered urgency of my anger and confusion has burnt itself out. Now, I'm just resigned to an awful, awkward weekend, and I decide to leave Paul well enough alone and return to my room to read.

My good intentions last exactly long enough for me to open the front door. Because as soon as I step inside the house, I see that Paul has left his laptop downstairs. It's sitting right there on the table, charging.

If there's one symbol of every single thing I came to loathe about my husband, that laptop is surely it. It's ridiculous to feel jealous of a device, but that computer certainly enjoyed more care and attention than I did during the last year of our marriage. I guess that's why the mere sight of the thing feels like a red flag to a bull.

He locked me out of the Wi-Fi. He must realize I'm going to take revenge for that somehow. He left the stupid laptop down here. What did he actually expect?

Locking me out of the Wi-Fi was stupid but essentially harmless—the kind of prank that, a year or two from now when I'm no longer feeling quite so miserable, I'll probably be able to chuckle at. It's so childish…almost playful, and that's so out of character for Paul, at least these days. Sooner or later, maybe, I'll enjoy the wry humor in the prank.

But I'm not thinking of delightfully playful pranks right now. I'm imagining myself dropping the laptop. Or throwing it. I could run down to the rocky little beach off the deck and throw it into the water. I could take it out onto the road and throw it in front of a passing car.

I could go *rent* a car and run it over myself. I'd drive over it, then reverse, and drive over it again and again until it was just a road mosaic of smashed plastic and metal.

But I understand how much of Paul's work life revolves around that computer. I can't even pretend I don't. If I was to return fire for him changing the Wi-Fi password by physically damaging the device that all but runs his business life, could I honestly say it was tit for tat for *his* prank?

I couldn't.

Besides, I'm angry and scorned, but I'm not the kind of person who'd deliberately damage someone's property.

My heart rate is returning to normal because I know I've made the right decision to ignore my childish impulse. I feel somewhat smug as I slip the half-and-half into the fridge for Paul. I arrange the flowers in a vase, and then wander over to the dining room table to set it down. It's only then that I focus again on the laptop.

I find myself staring down at it. Why is it here and not upstairs with Paul? Why isn't he working? That doesn't seem right at all, unless he has two laptops now, and he's working on the other one upstairs?

This laptop is open, although of course it's locked. The password screen blinks up at me, his username already filled in, the cursor in the password field. Paul once admitted that he had a system for his password, and when I pushed him to tell me what it was, it turned out to be unexpectedly sweet. He's understandably pedantic about computer security so he changed the password every week, but it was always some complicated combination of *my* name and a random number he calculated with some top-secret algorithm. That whole algorithm business seemed unnecessarily complicated to me, but Paul's mind for dates and numbers is extraordinary, and to him, it somehow just made sense.

There is a sudden creak of a floorboard from the master bedroom. The sound comes out of nowhere and I'm so lost in thought that it startles me. A little water sloshes over the side of the vase, and because the universe hates me, lands squarely in the middle of Paul's keyboard.

I'm too stunned to react at all at first. I stand in frozen horror, still holding the vase over the laptop as the water spreads between the keys. When the panic hits, I'm so flustered I spill *more* water as I try to set the vase safely down, swearing under my breath as I try to mop the moisture up with the only absorbent thing within reaching distance—the bottom of my tank top.

That effort is a complete failure, and soon I'm flapping my hands hopelessly as the password prompt on the screen flickers once…twice…

There's another sound from the master bedroom upstairs, and this time I hear movement—more floorboards creaking and this time footsteps are stomping and *oh God,* is he walking out to the little balcony up there, or is he walking to the stairwell to come back down to get his goddamned laptop?

Cursing under my breath, I slam the computer closed and sprint across the living room back to the guest room.

This time, I pull the door closed behind me as quietly as I can.

CHAPTER FIVE

Isabel

FOR A WHILE, I half watch stupid cable dramas and try to convince myself the laptop is fine…then I start channel surfing and instead try to convince myself that Paul actually deserves for the laptop to not be fine.

Then I give up all pretense of watching TV and spend several frantic minutes convincing myself that the laptop is *not* fine, Paul did *not* deserve the laptop to *not* be fine, and even if the water spill was a genuine accident, it was exactly what I had fantasized about in the first place, so maybe I got what I subconsciously wanted all along.

Finally, belatedly, I reach for my phone and do some research to see how much damage I've actually done. And *oh my God,* I've screwed up so badly here. It turns out the problem isn't just the liquid, but that by leaving it to soak while it was charging, I've probably fried the rotten thing.

I run out to the living room, knock the plug out of the outlet and try to turn the laptop on. It's officially dead as a doornail.

I spend *another* thirty minutes hiding in my room again, trying to figure out how to explain to Paul that, yes, I destroyed his laptop, but despite how unlikely this is going to seem to him, it really was an accident. It's now late afternoon and there's a pregnant silence in the house. I'm running out of time because sooner or later, Paul is going to want to work and to work he's going to need his laptop. I start to rehearse my confession in my mind.

So, Paul, here's the thing. I was going to do something mean to your laptop because I really wanted to watch Netflix and it seems you messed with the Wi-Fi which was probably kind of funny but also really mean. But then I decided not to do it, but also I was still thinking about it, but then I accidentally spilled water all over it anyway, and I know this is going to sound a little too convenient but I really do promise that it was totally an accident.

Then I panicked, and I closed it and walked away and did nothing for several hours. But I did eventually Google it to see if that would have done any damage and only then did I realize that I should have told you right away so you could unplug it and drain the keyboard.

But you're freakishly smart, so I'm sure you have backups and stuff. That's what "the cloud" means... right? And you guys make internet software so you're all about "the cloud" these days, aren't you?

I finally gather the courage to climb the stairs to the master bedroom, but I pause at the door and take a fortifying breath before I force myself to knock and call his name. There's no answer, so I call again as I push the door open just a little. The room is empty, but I can see that at the edge of the wall-length windows, the drapes are billowing gently, which means the door to the balcony is open. I walk toward it hesitantly.

I find Paul sound asleep on the sun chair, the one on the left—the one he always took when we were here together. He is such a man of habit—always taking the left side when we sat or slept. Left side of the sofa, left side of the bed, left side if we were seated side by side on the subway. Left side when we walked or jogged together? No…actually, that's maybe the one exception to the rule, he'd always shift so that he walked on whichever side was closest to the traffic. Was that a protective thing? I barely noticed at the time, so I never thought to ask him.

Were there other things I didn't appreciate about Paul? By the end, I didn't really appreciate much at all. He was just the stranger who slept in my bed.

He's sitting in the very sun chair he was sitting in when he asked me to move in with him. We'd only been together for a couple of months, but we'd barely spent a night apart since we met. After an afternoon of making love, drinking wine and napping, we'd come out here for the sunset and he looked over at me and he said ever so casually, "You know, you may as well move in with me," and I thought my heart was going to beat its way out of my chest.

He proposed like that, too, without pomp or ceremony, throwing the words out as a statement, not a question. None of that mattered to me. I simply couldn't wait to say yes.

These are the kinds of memories I haven't let myself dwell on this year. It hurts too much to remember us back then. It hurts far too much to remember how optimistic I once was about our future. Paul was forever telling me that things at work were going to settle down for him soon. One more sprint. One more retreat. One more release. A few more weeks. We fell into a pattern where I was always chasing after him trying to connect, and he was always putting up barriers between us through his business.

The sunset would have been magnificent out here an hour or so ago, but now darkness is falling and there's a definite chill in the breeze—the days have warmed up early this year, but it will still be weeks before the nights catch up.

Paul has one arm over his eyes and the other is curled over his torso. Other than the throw blanket tangled at his feet, Paul is still naked and he must be uncomfortably cold now that the sun is going. I don't feel sorry for him. I have a sneaking suspicion the only reason he's still naked after all of these hours is to irritate me.

And if that was his goal, he's succeeded. The sight of all of that bare skin right now is maddening, and that's *my* damn throw blanket around his ankles. It's a chunky knit and soft and so lovely, and I could have been cuddled under it on the sofa in front of the huge TV in the living room if Paul wasn't here. But if he's been lying under it at some point, it's going to smell like him, and that's not exactly going to comfort me, is it?

I have half a mind to snatch it off him and run back to wash the damn thing and keep it for myself, but then my eyes sneak just a little past it, to Paul's calves, and then I'm on a roll as my gaze travels across that expanse of bare skin. I survey the landscape of Paul's body, and forget all about my throw-blanket rage.

Paul was never a guy with corded biceps or prominent hip flexors or well-defined pecs. Now he's walking around in the kind of body that only comes from long hours at the weight bench.

"Are you just going to stand there staring at me? The least you could do is pull the blanket up." His voice is rough, and there's a thick slur to the words. "Surely you owe me that. At least that. I let you keep this house, and *you know* that made no sense at all."

These are the ramblings of a man who's clearly very drunk, but I can't deny there's some truth to that last statement. I knew right from the outset of our settlement negotiations that I had no legal claim to this place. Paul owned it when we met, and New York is an equitable distribution state—property purchased before marriage is technically off-limits in a divorce. He'd made a lot of money during the years we were together, much more than I did, but I didn't want alimony or to accept even what I was due. My original plan was to accept a small, one-off cash settlement—just enough to set myself up again, given I left most of our furniture and belongings with him.

It's just that when I sat down with my attorney to talk assets and I mentioned this place in passing, I started to wonder. Paul does love our brownstone in Chelsea, and I suspect that house is actually more to his tastes. It's plush, modernized and stylish.

This Greenport house has water frontage, but it's simple and a little dated. It really needs to be remodeled but we just never found the time. On paper, at least in its current condition, location is about all this house has going for it. And whenever we came out here during our marriage, it was generally my idea.

I know Paul bought it with an inheritance that matured when he turned twenty-one, but I never understood why it was *this* house in *this* village. It's hardly the kind of beachfront bachelor pad the average twenty-one-year-old might dream of. Once I really sat down and thought about it, I decided there were only two possibilities: either Paul no longer liked the Greenport house, and thus would be quite happy to give it to me, or that there was some appeal to him…one he was never willing to explain. I had asked him why he bought it over the years, but he always brushed the question off or changed the subject.

My attorney told me I could ask for the house but that Paul might simply say no and I'd have to accept that. My plan in the beginning was to do just that. So we sent off the proposed settlement via my attorney to Paul's, and my phone rang later that afternoon—the first direct contact between Paul and me in weeks. He was almost speechless with rage—the call punctuated by fierce half sentences and long periods of angry silence.

I'd never actually seen him so passionate about anything. I'd certainly never seen him so *moved*.

I guess that once I realized how desperately he wanted this place, all I could think about was winning it myself. My attitude of "let's go our separate ways but we'll keep this polite" became "I'm going to be completely unreasonable and refuse to give up my hold on the one asset we all know I have no right to."

In the end, we bickered and squabbled our way through seven mediation sessions before the mediator informed us that he had reached the conclusion that we'd never agree on the terms of our divorce, and he was referring us to a judge.

I knew that meant I wouldn't get the house. After all, my attorney had told me, time and time again, that the law was clear. I wiped my eyes, blew my nose and was about to withdraw my request for it to save us going to court, but Paul beat me to it.

"She can have it," he said flatly, while our attorneys and the mediator gasped and stared at us in shock. I've had six long months to think about this since then and I still don't understand why he changed his mind at the very last second.

"Wake up," I say impatiently. "We need to talk."

"Talking is overrated," he says, but his eyes remain stubbornly closed. He's clearly awake enough to hear me, so I nudge him again.

"Are you drunk?" I ask, and the arm over his eyes flops back to rest behind his head. He stares up at me in the semidarkness, then gives a slow blink and a subtle shake of his head, as if he can't quite focus— or maybe he can't believe what he's seeing. I don't blame him if it's the latter. I still feel a little like that myself. This afternoon has been a bit ridiculous.

"Maybe I am drunk," he says after a while. "It's a bit hard to tell just at the moment. Ask me again in a few minutes when the ground stops spinning."

I walk briskly to his feet and pick up the throw blanket, then dump it unceremoniously over his body as I sink down to sit on the chair beside him.

"Better?"

"Much. Thanks. That was so kind of you. That's the Isabel I knew and loved," he says. He's really slurring now, and then he closes his eyes and it looks like he's fallen asleep again. Great. I reach across and push his bicep to try to rouse him. This is definitely not an excuse to touch him, and I am definitely not at all impressed by the strength and the bulk he's added there. Also, even if his arm does feel absolutely fantastic beneath my fingers, I need to stop touching him and keep my damn hands to myself.

I snatch my fingers back and tuck them under my thigh, as if that will aid my self-control.

"Paul…ah…" I have to tell him about the laptop, but he does seem pretty out of it, and I'm not really sure how to convince him this really was an accident. Plus, what if I tell him, and he forgets, and I just have to tell him again tomorrow when he's hungover and even grumpier than usual? I slump a little, flopping back into a reclining position on the sun chair. Well,

I'm here now, so I may as well try to get something out of this awkward encounter. "Did you change the Wi-Fi password?"

"It took you all day to notice?"

"That was incredibly childish of you."

He snorts. "That's pretty funny coming from the woman who had a full-blown tantrum earlier."

"I didn't have a—"

He pries his eyes open with visible difficulty, but just so he can quirk an eyebrow at me.

"Fine. But can I have the new password please? You've had your fun."

He snorts again, as if I've just asked him for the moon.

"I'll bother you less if I have Netflix to entertain myself. Unless you've decided to go home?"

"It *is* incredibly annoying that you're here, but you know what would be worse?"

"What?" I ask.

Our gazes lock, and there's something oddly intense about the way he's staring at me…so much so that I actually think he's going to say something profound until he snaps me back to reality with a sardonic half grin and a drawled "if I passed up the last chance I'll ever have to mess with you."

I break the eye contact, then reach for his beer and take a healthy swig from the bottle. It's warm and flat, but it's alcohol, and right at this moment that's enough.

"You didn't even like beer when we met," Paul

says suddenly. "Remember? You only drank wine, and *organic* wine at that."

I lower the bottle to scowl at him. "And you looked like a stick figure. People change."

"I should probably thank you for introducing me to a healthier lifestyle. It's much easier being single this time around."

I barely hear him. I'm still thinking about how determined he is to stay this weekend and how frustrating and bewildering that is. Our marriage didn't end because he was cruel or mean, it ended because he disconnected from me and retreated into his own world. But this year since I left, he's been harder... *fiercer*. I set the now-empty bottle back onto the table between us. "When did you get so nasty, Paul?"

I don't expect him to respond, so I'm surprised when he sighs, the sound heavy with regret. Glancing at him, I find his eyes have drifted closed again.

"And you, right? I mean, you *aren't* nasty. You were all the good things. But you aren't now. And I was, and you wasn't. Weren't," he mumbles, then he opens one eye, then the other. We make startling, shocking eye contact as he asks, "But weren't you just?"

An unexpected laugh bursts from somewhere deep inside me. Paul squints, then he shakes his head and finally seems to wake up the rest of the way. He sits up clumsily in the chair as he mumbles, "I'm just trying to say that I wasn't always like this. Was I? I feel like this divorce has really made me someone else."

Those words hit like a sucker punch right to my gut.

"This year has changed you," I whisper. "It really *has* made you someone else."

I'm so touched by this moment that I almost reach to console him, until he adds, "Well, if I'm someone else, you are, too, you know. And *New* Isabel is kind of a bitch."

I don't even try to defend myself against that accusation. We both know he's right.

"How is this even going to work? If we both stay here, we're just going to fight," I whisper miserably. "You *have* to leave."

He's still for a long moment, then he rubs his eyes. After a minute, he looks right at me and his gaze is clearing. It seems he's sobering by the second, or possibly, just shaking the last of the sleep from his mind.

"My plans for this weekend include drinking some beer and maybe catching up on some sleep. I'll do as much of that as I can in the master bedroom, but I'm not going to promise you I won't come out, and if that's going to make life awkward for you, you should probably just leave and come back next weekend."

"No chance of that," I say bitterly.

"So we agree, then."

"What exactly did we agree to?"

"I'll stay drunk, and you'll try harder to be nice to me."

I think about his bulked-up frame and the vulnerability in his tone that he doesn't seem to be in any hurry to hide and I'm so confused that *I'm* starting to feel drunk. None of this makes any sense.

Paul Winton is not a man who says things like *be nicer to me.* Paul uses unnecessarily big words and cold tones of voice and he doesn't often have discernable emotions, let alone openly express a desire for someone to be nice to him.

I look down at the beer again. There's an unopened bottle, the bottle I just finished, and five other empties. He's been up here all afternoon. I think about the nights we shared with our friends in Manhattan, parties on Jess's rooftop patio where we'd devour cocktails and laugh at Paul as he sipped her crazy pink creations even as he complained about the sugar content. I also reminisce about dinners at Marcus and Abby's apartment, where Marcus would buy a case of expensive wines and we'd all pretend we knew what a top note was…

And how rarely Paul ever seemed drunk. He always handled alcohol well…and that was before he added so many pounds of muscle this year.

"Why *are* you so drunk? I've seen you drink a lot more and stay fairly lucid, compared to this…"

Paul frowns, again. He ponders this for a moment, wearing that thinking face I know all too well. Suddenly, his expression clears, and I know he's solved the problem.

"I didn't eat today, and I didn't really sleep last night. Probably not the smartest time to drink, but there you have it." His gaze travels up and down my body, and he frowns a little. "But you're the last per-

son who should be judging me right now. Clearly you
know all about forgetting to eat, Bel."

The barb about my body isn't anything new—
this year, I feel like every person in my life thinks
they have a right to comment on how I look. Some
people stress-eat, but when I'm stressed, my appetite disappears. I've always been slight, but at the
moment, I'm looking and feeling a little gaunt. I've
been working on it—making an effort to look after
myself more, to treat my body and soul with a little
more kindness. I'm not self-conscious about the way
I look, and while this is none of Paul's business, I'm
not even offended that he commented.

No, what gets me about that statement is the nickname. *Bel.* No one else has ever called me that—not
even Paul in this last year that's passed. It was like
the moment I left he lost his last shred of affection
for me, and that fond, special nickname he'd granted
me was suddenly revoked. I was no longer Bel—no
longer his wife, no longer his lover. Instead, I became Izzy to him—still a nickname, still familiar—
but somehow so much more distant because that's
what everyone else calls me, too. I'm still not sure
why that hurt so much, but I also know I don't at all
like the sudden revision to the way things once were.

"Don't call me that," I say abruptly.

He looks at me blankly and he's not playing dumb.
He's slipped back into the nickname purely out of
habit. "Call you what?"

I swallow. Hard. "Bel," I say. "My name is Isabel."

"I can't help it, I hate calling you Isabel. And

your friends call you Izzy," he says, then he closes his eyes. "Nuts."

"What's nuts?" I'm resisting the urge to grab him by his shoulders and shake him awake again.

Or maybe that urge is just about grabbing his shoulders.

Bad Isabel. No touching the awful ex-husband, even if his biceps are pretty much the perfect size and shape.

"No...not nuts," he corrects me. "*Nuts*. Nuts are a high-nutrient and high-calorie food. You like macadamias."

Good God. The man is positively delirious.

"I have a personal policy to never take nutrition advice from drunk computer nerds."

"But are you okay?" Paul asks me, and there's a sudden, shocking concern in his voice. It's out of place, just as the remorse was. Paul is not an empathetic person and I'm starting to feel dizzy from these uncharacteristic displays of emotion. I knew he was angry. But remorseful? Concerned? Worried? Upset? These are not words I associate with Paul Winton.

Now, our gazes lock, and my stomach sinks all the way to my toes. There's no denying the misery in his gaze as he adds, "This is bad. All of it is bad, and I hate everything about this...but I can handle it as long as you're okay. Tell me you're okay."

"I'm okay," I whisper, and he gives a satisfied sigh and shuts his eyes again. "Paul," I blurt. "Why are you here?"

"Same as you, I guess," he says, and he opens his eyes again. "I'm licking my wounds and hoping and praying that after next Wednesday they'll finally start to heal. That's why you're here, too, right?"

"That's exactly why I'm here," I whisper.

Just as my tears start to rise, he shrugs and says easily, "See? This arrangement represents an exact symmetry. We should be here together."

I laugh weakly. "That's completely fucked up, Paul."

"Maybe," he concedes, then he adds, "I really am hungry, now that you've got me thinking about food, and Vanessa didn't get the email I didn't send so there's no food in the fridge." Before I can even untangle that, he perks up and says, "We should go out for dinner."

I laugh in surprise, but then I glance at him and he's staring at me expectantly. My jaw drops. "You've got to be kidding me. Two minutes ago you were trying to force me to leave and now you want to go out for *dinner* together?"

"Oh, come on. For old times' sake. We can go to that Japanese place we liked and drink sake and curse the world."

"That sounds like a recipe for disaster."

"Burgers and fries at the marina?"

I groan and stand. "I came here to get away from you, Paul. I didn't even want to think about you this weekend!"

"Get away from me?" he repeats, then he laughs, freely and easily, as if *I've* made the joke. I scowl at him. "Why would you come here to get away from me? For fuck's sake, Bel, this is where we met and decided to live together and got engaged and shared most of our best days together. Say you came here to sulk over me. Say you came here to grieve our marriage. That I could believe. But to avoid thinking about me? Give me a little credit." He shrugs, then he meets my gaze directly.

I'm embarrassed by his observation, but then Paul reaches up and fumbles for my hand.

What is he doing? It's a tender gesture, not at all the kind of thing I've come to expect from Paul Winton. As his skin slides against mine, my heart starts to race, and I have no idea what to make of that. No idea at all. This moment just feels dangerous in every possible way.

"Please, Bel?" he whispers.

Fuck marriage counseling and fuck legal mediation—Paul achieves more with that wide-eyed plea and the touch of his hand than the therapist and our attorneys have in all of the months that have passed. I stare down at him, stricken.

"Paul…"

He brings my hand to his lips, and he clumsily kisses the skin there once…twice…three times. There's no finesse whatsoever in the movement— he's far too drunk for seduction. It's a ridiculous gesture that suggests an affection I know he doesn't even feel for me now.

Still, I haven't really had contact with a human male other than clients at work in ten months now, and the touch of his lips to my hand has an immediate and unexpected impact.

I want him to kiss me more.

I'm conflicted, because I genuinely do not want to be anywhere near the man, but at the same time, apparently, I wouldn't actually mind all that much if he kissed his way along my arm to do that thing he used to do to my neck that somehow was the perfect blend of tickle and tease.

I snatch my hand away and groan. "Fine. Dinner, just so you can sober up and...not injure yourself, I guess. Then we avoid each other for the rest of the weekend, you give me the Wi-Fi password, and then you stay in the bedroom as much as you can so I can use the big TV in the living room." I remember the laptop, then add another caveat. "Also, since I'm doing *you* a favor, you have to promise to forgive anything else I may have, you know, *inadvertently* done to offend or upset you since we arrived. Anything. Deal?"

"Absolutely. That all sounds great," he says, and he swings his legs over the edge of the sun chair and stands. The blanket falls to the ground.

"And you have to wear clothes, Paul."

"Also a very reasonable request," he agrees, but then he sways and throws his arm across my shoulders for support.

I automatically wrap an arm around his waist and steady him, and then find myself in the bewildering situation of being tucked under his arm as if he's hugging me. And *oh my God*, that scent—it's Paul's scent, and this is exactly why my first impulse was to wash the damned throw blanket, because now I'm drowning in memories again. I'm surrounded by musk and deodorant and *him*, and that combination is the perfume of love and lust and the very best years of my life.

I look up at him, and his eyes are sad and distant and guarded but then suddenly he's gearing up to tease me, and I know it because his gaze lightens, and the corner of his lip turns upward just a little. I had actually forgotten that relaxed Paul can be pretty funny. It's been a long time since I saw him let his guard down.

"I mean…yes, Bel, I can wear clothes if you want. If you're sure that's what you want?"

"It's what I want," I croak. "Can you dress yourself?"

"Almost definitely," he says.

I help him inside, then he lifts his arm from my shoulders and walks to the open suitcase on the bed. I head down to my own room and pull on my shoes and a sweater over my tank top, but then decide I really should keep an eye on Paul, in case he trips or something. So I jog up the stairs again, then wait at the door to the master bedroom as he drags briefs on and then fitted jeans and a T-shirt and jacket.

This time last year, Paul would never have worn that outfit—it's new and a little trendy, the kind of outfit a budding tech entrepreneur should wear, not at all his old, lazy style of jeans three sizes too big and T-shirts with holes on the seams. I wonder if his sense of fashion really has changed so much and so quickly. Did he have to buy new clothes to accommodate all of that new muscle?

Or…*oh shit*…

Does he have a girlfriend?

Because now that I'm really looking at him—there are other changes in his appearance, too. He's always worn his dark brown hair short, in a no-nonsense buzz cut, but since I last saw him he's grown it out and the softer style just suits him so much. Paul was always clean-shaven when we were together, but he's sporting a heavy stubble right now. On anyone else, I might have called that same look "designer stubble." Maybe his new girlfriend prefers him with facial hair, and I could almost understand why. That stubble is like an underline, emphasizing the strength of his jaw and that square chin.

Suddenly, I'm certain he's seeing someone. She's smarter than me, and she's like his ex-girlfriends before me—a programmer or an engineer or some other tech-savvy profession so they have that in common—unlike Paul and me. I mean, I remain genuinely confused about what "the cloud" actually is, even though he's tried to explain it to me no less than half a dozen times.

Paul probably texted her to tell her that I'm here, and I'll bet she's not pleased. Maybe she's even going to come out here to be with him. What if he has a girlfriend and what if she arrives and they're fucking in the room above me? What if I have to hear his *orgasm groans*, and I'm not the person causing them?

I'd have to leave the house if that happened. I just could not bear it.

It was my decision to leave him, and I have no right to be jealous. Reminding myself of that doesn't change the fact that I am—not one little bit. I am jealous, and suddenly I'm stung by the very thought that he might have moved on from our marriage already.

"This isn't a good idea," I say suddenly, and Paul looks up at me. He's pulled his shoes on, and now he stands, evidently oblivious to the fact that his fly is still undone. He crosses his arms over his chest and the T-shirt pulls around his biceps.

His shirts *never* used to pull across his biceps. My gaze catches there for a moment too long, and out of the corner of my eye I see that Paul has tilted his head and he's staring at me. I force my eyes onto his, to find his gaze is questioning.

"Why isn't this a good idea?"

"I just…" I don't want to ask if he's seeing anyone. It would be awkward, and I don't want things to be awkward. I'm well acquainted with angry by now, and shit, it seems I can even deal with rolling drunk, but *awkwardness* between Paul and me is an unknown factor.

He's still staring at me, so I blurt, "Are you seeing someone?"

There's a long pause. Paul's gaze doesn't shift from my eyes. Great. He picks today to decide he's comfortable with eye contact after all. For the first time in living memory, it's me who looks away from him.

"Why would you ask that?" he asks eventually.

"Your clothes. You have new clothes…" I swallow the lump in my throat. "Nicer clothes. And the
haircut and the… You just never cared about that
kind of thing before so…"

Paul blinks, then he takes a step toward the door.
I can tell he's pissed and he seems defensive. That
seems a confirmation that he *is* seeing someone, and
I can't help the way my shoulders slump.

*Don't you dare care, Isabel. Stop caring! You
shouldn't care. Why do you care?*

After a fumbled first attempt, Paul scoops his
wallet off the dresser and presses it into his back
pocket. He leaves his cell phone on the dresser, and I
notice that because he always takes it everywhere. He
was always working on it in one form or another—
answering emails in the back of cabs, texting at the
dinner table, reading code or reference guides or design specs as we supposedly watched TV together.

"So I'll stay here?" I throw after him, as he disappears into the stairwell. "Will you be okay?"

"No to both," he snaps, and he fills the doorway
again. My gaze drops to his still gaping fly. He mumbles a curse as he bends to zip it awkwardly, but then
he lifts his gaze to me and he says flatly, "No, you
won't stay here, no, I won't be *okay.* You're coming
with me, so let's go."

"But if you have a new girlfriend…" I start to protest, but I trail off because I don't even know how to
finish that sentence.

He looks away to the floor beside me, and a thick,

heavy silence fills the room. When Paul eventually speaks, his voice is so quiet I have to strain to hear it.

"How *little* you must have thought of our marriage to think I would move on so quickly."

The bitterness in those words cuts across everything else in the room—across the tension and across my stupid, irrational jealousy. It even cuts across my hesitation to go to dinner with him, because now, I actually want to follow him down the stairs to see if he'll talk some more.

When I first started thinking about leaving, I worried that I might hurt Paul, but over time, I consoled myself that I couldn't. I mean, he'd never seemed hurt about anything that happened in his life—Paul is the kind of guy who just always seems balanced. The way he failed to react the night I left seemed to confirm my suspicions.

I told myself that the walls around Paul's heart were so high and so strong that not even the breakdown of our marriage could cut through. Even over the months that have passed since that night, Paul has seemed angry at times, but he's never seemed wounded.

This very moment happens to be the first time in our entire life together I've seen evidence that *hurting Paul Winton* is actually possible.

I really thought I wanted this.

I thought I wanted to lash out and to wound him the way he'd wounded me when he pulled away from me. But forced to face the proof that Paul Winton does indeed have a softer side, I suddenly feel sick.

I'm embarrassed at the way this conversation has gone and the very obvious reality that my jealousy was the thing that pushed it there, and hopeful only that he is drunk enough to forget this tomorrow.

Paul raises his gaze to mine, and he motions vaguely toward the stairwell. "It's just dinner, Isabel. I want to eat with you. I want to sit with you on the pier and hear how you're doing. We meant something to each other, something more than financial settlements and lawyers and litigation and all of the *shit* of this year. Can't we just share a meal without it being complicated?"

"But it is complicated."

"It's as complicated as we let it be," he says, and the slur is clearing and he's making more sense than anything has in the longest time. I'm still hesitating, but he extends his hand toward me and his gaze shifts—no longer hard at all, those beautiful brown eyes are now pleading with me.

It actually matters to him that I join him for dinner. I had convinced myself that it didn't matter to Paul what I did or how I felt, and yet here I am, staring into those intense brown depths and facing the undeniable evidence that if I was ever right about that at all, things really have changed. Holy shit, it's like I've slipped into an alternate universe.

"Are you coming? *Please* do."

I swallow, and I look at his hand. Does he mean to entwine our fingers, to let those hands swing between us as they always did? Because now that I force myself to think about it, he always held my hand. Always. Even at the end, when we used to walk side by side in silence, it was always hand in hand.

I can't let that happen now. It's not appropriate for where we are now. I shouldn't even want it. How could I even want it? I can barely even stand to be in the same house as the man these days…

And yet, I slip into autopilot and walk to him briskly, then I let him take my hand. His fingers slide through mine, and then his hand locks in place. It feels better than good. It feels better than relief. The simple contact is everything, and it's nothing, and I'm too bewildered and exhausted to process any of this.

Paul doesn't smile. He just stares at me for a moment, and then he gently tugs me down the narrow staircase behind him.

"First stop," he announces as we step through the front door, "the liquor store."

"I think you've had enough for tonight," I say weakly, and he shakes his head.

"Not for me," he says grimly. "For you."

CHAPTER SIX

Paul

WHAT THE FUCK am I doing?

Actually, I know what I'm doing. I just don't know *why* I'm doing it.

I'm walking to the burger joint Isabel and I used to frequent when we visited Greenport. This will be our second visit today, the first being ten minutes ago when we climbed out of the cab and stopped in to order. While they cooked our meal, we walked along the street to the liquor store—now I'm carrying a bottle of organic Riesling in my right hand.

My left hand is still threaded tightly through the fingers of my almost-ex-wife.

I should not be holding Isabel's hand. It's a pretty, soft hand—a hand that knows how to work magic—but it's not my hand to hold anymore. I keep telling myself to let it go, casually, of course. She won't mind at all. Frankly, I don't have a clue why she let me take it in the first place.

Isabel's curls are loose around her face and shoulders tonight. She's wearing a sweater over her yoga pants and she looks fucking magnificent—

breathtaking, actually, because when I forget I'm not supposed to look at her and I flick a glance her way, I do forget to breathe. I remember that used to happen when we first met, but it's a novelty to have it happen again now, when my life feels so utterly devoid of novelty. I feel old and stale and cynical about every aspect of the world these days, except, perhaps, these bewilderingly magical moments, when I can look at Isabel and once again feel the magnificent shock of my breath catching in my throat at the sight of her.

"Quit staring at me," she mutters as I go in for one last sneaky glance, and I play it cool and shrug and don't say anything, but I'm not entirely sure I stop myself blushing at having been caught out. I feel like a teenager on my first date, but this isn't a date—I don't even know what this is. Is this a thing? Do almost-ex-spouses sometimes hold hands and have meals?

I've often felt like someone should have been appointed as a mentor to guide me through the divorce and to explain to me how the hell things escalated the way they did and to give me definitions for legal terminology and words for all of the bewildering feelings that have been bouncing around inside me for the past year. Now I picture that wise, older mentor sitting opposite me at a coffee shop, explaining this new development.

Occasionally, just before a divorce becomes final, a husband and wife might find themselves sharing a vacation home for a few nights and if that does hap-

*pen, you're allowed to hold her hand and share a
meal with her. It might feel a bit weird after months
of hostility, but just go with it. What harm can it do?
You used to hold hands all the time, every single day
for years, actually. It's only natural to do it one last
time. You're allowed to enjoy it and you don't have
to think too much about why.*

My imagination suddenly corrects this scene into
something a little more plausible, so now the mentor
is staring at me in horror.

*Uh—no, Paul, that's not a thing. So let go of her
fucking hand before you make things worse. What's
that? Things can't be any worse? Well, let me break
it to you, son—I know it's hard to believe, but there
really are ways you can fuck this up more and holding her hand leads to every single one of them.*

Right at that moment, Isabel releases my hand and
walks to the counter of the burger joint to ever so
politely thank the server and take the paper bag with
our food into her arms. She comes back to my side,
but now her hands are full and that effectively solves
the problem of that messy holding-hands situation.
Now we're just walking side by side, Isabel holding
the parcel of hot food against her chest. I shuffle the
wine out from under my arm to cradle it against my
chest, too, mirroring her posture.

I've learned a thing or two about communication
this year. One surprising discovery I made is that
when someone is listening, they tend to mirror the
speaker's posture. It's amazing what hundreds of
hours of therapy can teach a guy.

"Are you still living in the brownstone?" she asks me suddenly, and now that we're talking, I feel like maybe I'm allowed to look at her again and so I do. She has magnificent blue eyes, and she uses eye contact like a red carpet to welcome conversation with people.

I loved her from the minute our eyes met, and that still doesn't entirely make sense to me. Love at first sight is a ridiculous notion. I always thought the very idea of it to be a romantic fallacy, a trope that existed only in movies and books. But there's no denying that there was something about Isabel that entranced me right from that first second, and it wasn't just her beauty. It was her openness. Her warmth.

Work had been so busy in the months leading up to that weekend, and Jess, Marcus and I had decided to take a long weekend together to relax and regroup. We'd planned to just head away by ourselves, but somehow our little trio expanded until my house here at Greenport was bursting at the seams—my brother Jake had joined us with his then-girlfriend, Marcus invited Abby and she turned up with her then-boyfriend, and then Jess told me she'd invited her new friend Isabel. I don't love crowds, but Marcus and Jess happen to be social butterflies, and that wasn't the first or the last time we had so many people at the vacation house that someone had to take the pullout sofa.

Over the years I learned to go with the flow with Jess and Marcus when it comes to social engagements. I mean, left to my own devices, I probably would never have had much of a social life at all, so it only made sense to let them set the pace.

Everyone else had arrived, except for Jess's mysterious friend. When the doorbell rang that day, I left the other guests out on the deck while I went to answer it. I threw the door open and everything changed.

Hi, I'm Isabel Parker. I'm Jess's Pilates instructor and I have no idea why she invited me this weekend but I've never been to the North Fork before so I came anyway. It's so nice to meet you, I've heard so much about you.

Paul, Paul Winton. And I've heard all about you, too, although Jess somehow forgot to mention that you're the most beautiful woman on earth.

Okay, I didn't say that last bit, but I sure as hell thought it. The truth is, I still think it. Did I ever tell her? Definitely not. It's probably one of the many vitally important things that used to cross my mind on a daily basis but that I somehow never got around to saying aloud. I'm just not good with flowery declarations like that. I'm sure I felt the right sentiment, but translating it into poetic words was a skill I never mastered. Even when I did figure out what I wanted to say and the words would sometimes make it all the way to my tongue, I'd swallow them down before they could escape.

I was never sure that I could nail the delivery. My voice defaults to a flat tone sometimes, and I'm reasonably certain that *you're so fucking gorgeous* doesn't have quite the same impact when a robot says it.

"Paul." Isabel is impatient now, and I try to rewind to her question.

I draw a blank. "Sorry. What did you ask?"

"Are you still living in our brownst—" She breaks off, then tries again. "I mean, are you still living at the place in Chelsea?"

The day we moved into that place I finally felt like I'd made it. Beautiful wife, successful career and now a magnificent family home ready to fill with noisy kids. It's hard to force myself to leave work and head there each day now. It's hard to call it "home" because it's not home anymore. Without Isabel there, it's just a stupidly expensive apartment. I still haven't replaced any of the scant items she took when she left. I almost like the way my gaze sticks on the empty spot on the wall where the art she loved once hung. It's a bizarre form of self-flagellation.

"I'm still there," I say. "And you're…in a place somewhere?"

"I have a little loft. It's small, but it's nice."

"And is your job the same?"

"Mostly, but…" She trails off. The silence feels odd and I'm tempted to fill it with words, but I've been working on that, too, this year. I want to be a better listener, and I'm learning that sometimes "being a better listener" just means letting silence punctuate a conversation. After a minute, Isabel asks a most unexpected question. "Your dad hasn't said anything to you?"

"Dad?" I repeat blankly. "What's Dad got to do with your work?"

Dad's a semiretired mathematics professor. I see him every Sunday night. He hasn't mentioned Isabel to me at all since she left, other than to ask about our progress in mediation from time to time. Now that I think about it, that might be a little odd. Dad and I are actually pretty close, and usually he would pry.

"When Martin was diagnosed with diabetes, he asked me to help him lose a little weight and I started running some personal training sessions for him on my lunch breaks," Isabel says.

"Oh," I say, eyebrows high. "That's kind of you. But no, he didn't mention it." I mean, he did mention diabetes, and I did notice the weight loss, and he did mention how much better his health is now. So it seems like a pretty big omission on his part, not mentioning that *my wife* was responsible for all of that.

"Well, soon he started bringing some friends along from his building," she adds carefully. "First it was just John and Ira, and soon there were some others, including…" She breaks off. "Has Martin really not told you any of this?"

I'm not actually sure what's going on here. It seems like Isabel is hesitant about something, but I can't imagine what that might be. I frown at her. "He hasn't talked about you at all."

"The thing is…soon there were five of your dad's friends, and then ten, and then I started a Thursday group, too, because he had invited so many of his friends that it was becoming unwieldy, so I realized

I had to do something more formal. Well, Nick loved the idea, and so now I'm running a seniors fitness program at the gym. So your dad and his…uh, his health stuff ended up inspiring this whole new role for me and it's going so well."

"It is strange that Dad didn't tell me any of this," I say.

"But the thing is…" She clears her throat. Once, twice, three times. Now I'm certain there's something she's not sure she should tell me.

"The thing is…?" I prompt.

She swallows. "Martin didn't mention… Elspeth?"

"Elspeth?"

Isabel looks away. "Maybe you should ask him about this."

"Just tell me."

"I really don't think it's my place to—"

"Isabel."

"Your dad has a girlfriend, Paul," she blurts. "I think the whole 'help me get fit' thing was a ruse to spend time with her because she was interested in fitness."

"Dad? A girlfriend?" I repeat, then I laugh. "No. Definitely not." When I glance at her, her gaze is steady. "Seriously?"

"Yeah."

"Why wouldn't he…" But then I realize why he wouldn't tell me. If my dad really is in love, he would hardly want to rub that in my face while my whole world was caving in. "Oh."

Dad's been single since Mom died—that means

he's spent twenty years alone. As far as I know, he hasn't dated anyone in all of that time.

"Yeah. They're adorable together. He seems very happy."

He does seem happy. It's just frustrating as fuck that I didn't think to ask why he was suddenly taking better care of himself and laughing more. I'm sure I'm getting better at this interpersonal shit, but it's still so much effort for me. I wonder if there are always going to be aspects to my relationships that I'll miss until someone else points them out.

"That's great for him."

"Yeah."

We walk in silence for a few moments as I digest this news. I'm not sure how long we can stay silent without it becoming awkward, though, so soon, I try to get Isabel talking again.

"And you're enjoying this seniors fitness thing?"

"It's challenging but fulfilling. I work a lot more than I used to, but that's been good for me, I think."

How odd that the year I learn to put hard boundaries around how many hours I work each week, Isabel learns to soften hers.

"I thought you might be planning to move here," I admit, cautiously approaching the subject of the vacation home.

"I don't know what I'm going to do with this place yet. My dad suggested I should lease it out."

That surprises me, and I feel an odd sense of alarm at the very idea of strangers in *our* space. "If you need more money, I'll—"

"I didn't want this place for money, Paul." She glances at me briefly, then avoids my gaze again. "I wanted it for the memories."

"Ah." I nod. "Oh. Okay." I understand that better than she could ever know.

"Anyway." She lifts her chin. "It's all fine. I'm fine, you're fine, we're both going to be fine and after next week everything will be easier because it will all be final. Where should we sit?"

We've arrived at Mitchell Park, home to the marina and Greenport's famous antique carousel and camera obscura. It's quiet here tonight, with only a handful of people roaming here and there. Once summer comes and brings the crowds along with it, this place will be a bustling hub of activity at all hours of the day and night.

"On the grass," I say, because that's where we always sat. We often ate here when we were in Greenport, although tonight I settle at a well-lit spot, right beneath a huge streetlight. Generally, we used to sit in semidarkness, because after a while our hands would get bored and almost automatically, they'd start to explore.

I wonder if Isabel remembers those nights as vividly as I do—the way that the chemistry between us seemed endless and miraculous, like it didn't even obey the laws of physics because it was perpetually recharging itself. Touching her only made me want to touch her more and I was in constant amazement at the infinite cycle of it all.

Just for a moment, I let myself wonder whether

we would be divorcing next week if I had managed to tell her, even just once, how deep the awe I felt for her ran. But I know all too well that thoughts like that are circular. They lead only to more questions that can't be answered…and that leads to still more misery. I refuse to let myself get sucked into a vortex like that tonight.

Isabel stretches her legs out and sets the parcel of food on her lap, then unwinds it to expose the fries and burgers within. I twist the cap of the wine we picked up, and then it occurs to me that of course, we have no glasses. Isabel looks at me, and then she bursts out laughing and reaches for the bottle. I pass it to her, and she lifts it between us and pauses.

"To moving on?" she says softly.

"To moving on," I echo, but then I watch as she lifts the bottle to her mouth and she takes a drink, then passes it right back to me. There's a simple intimacy in sharing the bottle that makes me feel all sorts of things I shouldn't be feeling. There's sadness in Isabel's expression, but not even a hint of anger, and that about sums up my feelings right now, too. It's shocking how much easier it is to be around her tonight than it has been through the settlement mediation.

Shocking, and…well, kind of confusing. Because from the moment I said goodbye to her on the sidewalk outside of our apartment eight months, three weeks and four days ago, we haven't had a single civil conversation until this one.

"Why aren't we fighting?" I ask suddenly. Isabel frowns.

"I don't know." She turns to me, and her eyebrows knit.

"I don't *want* to fight," I clarify. "It's just that—"

"I know. I think it's…" She starts to finish the sentence for me, but then she hesitates. "I think it's because your guard was down when I woke you up and you were…" Her gaze is searching as she stares at me, concentrating fiercely.

I tell myself to let the silence stretch—but when she breaks the gaze to look toward the water, I'm too impatient to wait for her to speak and I prompt, "I was what?"

"You were vulnerable," she murmurs.

I turn toward the water, too, thinking about this for a moment. Vulnerability? Well, that sure as fuck wasn't on purpose—not this time. Isabel has hurt me. My guard should be up.

But I purposefully set out this year to learn how to be more open with people, and every time I force myself to do it, it's worth it. This moment alone has proved to me that when I do pull my guard down, even god-awful situations can change for the better.

"This is kind of surreal," she says suddenly.

"That's for damned sure," I agree.

I want to get her talking—I want to hear about her life now. I used to wake up in the morning and I would know everything about Isabel Winton's life. The whole reason my body clock is stuck waking me up at stupid o'clock is that I always made a point to get up before she left for the day—and Isabel often has to be at work by 5:30 a.m. so she can set up for her early classes. I knew what she had for breakfast and what she wore to the gym and what her plans were for an evening, and I noticed every little thing about her, because she was the center of my world. Maybe I wasn't great at telling her how much she meant to me—but at the deepest level of my existence, I lived and breathed for her.

And overnight, she was gone. One of the strangest things about this year was losing that window into her life. Even when I was most angry with her, I still cared, and I was still curious…and sometimes jealous, because a goddess like Isabel Winton does not stay single for long.

"So, dating anyone?" I say it lightly.

She gives me a rueful look, as if I'm making a pointed joke. "Sorry about that, before. I just… I don't want to cross any boundaries."

"It's okay. I get it," I say. Now that I'm thinking a little straighter, I almost admire her wanting to avoid complicating things for me. It shows she still cares about me, at least a little, at least on some level—although if that's the case, what was behind her little game of let's-fuck-Paul-over-as-much-as-humanly-possible since she left?

But then it strikes me that her assumption that I am dating might be based on a logical conclusion: she probably assumed I was dating someone because *she* is dating someone. For just a second, I'm so jealous it nearly overwhelms me. I clutch the bottle of wine so tightly in my hands that it almost slips from my grasp, and I have to juggle to catch it. "But are you seeing someone?"

She snorts, as if the idea is completely reprehensible. Relief floods me, and then we share an awkward laugh, because what else is there to do?

"Tell me about this new physique," Isabel says suddenly, and she reaches for the wine and helps herself to a hearty swig.

"Ah, just a way to fill the hours outside of work." I probably should also be embarrassed at how much time I've spent naked since I found her in the house, but I can tell she's impressed, and I can't help but take some pleasure in that. "I was trying to structure my life a little better. I've been lifting weights and boxing, and I still run with Marcus... It adds up, I guess."

A standard work week for me last year was ninety or a hundred hours. Now, I use an app on my phone to track my work, and once I hit fifty hours, I stop. Even if I'm midway through a sentence on an email, or mid-conversation with an employee. My team is still adjusting to that change, even though I've promoted Audrey *and* hired a new coder to make up the deficit.

Maybe that's part of the reason why the new version of the software is still such a mess. This new approach to my working life has left a fuck-ton of empty hours outside of work this year, most of which I've filled with working out and reading.

"It does add up," Isabel says.

I grin at her. "Want me to take my clothes off again?"

"No," she says hastily, and she takes another drink of the wine, this time, a longer, more determined gulp—like she's a teenager at an illicit party, not a thirty-four-year-old woman in a serious conversation with another adult. But I can hardly judge her. The world's edges are still a little blurry to me after the day I spent stupidly self-medicating and napping on the balcony. "And now Marcus and Abby are having twins. You'll be a quasi-uncle soon."

"You keep in touch with Abby much?" I ask, attempting to make conversation. I'm like a bloodhound on the scent for information about Isabel whenever she comes up in my conversations with Jess and Marcus, which admittedly hasn't been often, but I know enough to know that Isabel, Abby and Jess still spend a lot of time together.

"Yeah. We're still close." Then she looks right into my eyes as she suddenly asks, "Are you glad I said no? When you wanted to have a kid?"

I haven't even thought about that in years, but I did bring the subject up with her once. It wasn't that I was desperate for a baby, more that it was something we'd talked about when we were dating, and when we moved into the brownstone after our wedding, I wondered if it might be time to start thinking about it. Isabel was totally unenthused about the idea, so I dropped it right away and that was that.

In hindsight, I probably should have asked a few more questions about why she didn't even want to talk about it. Perhaps things had already started to derail for us, all the way back then.

I scrub my hand over my face, suddenly feeling weary. I like to tell myself Isabel blindsided me when she left, but when I really sit down and think about it, it's pretty obvious that any "blindsiding" she may or may not have done happened only because I wasn't paying any fucking attention to her. *That* is entirely on me.

"If you'd been ready for kids when I asked, we'd be negotiating custody arrangements now and if you think that financial settlement was hard to agree on…" I trail off, wary of bringing a topic so contentious into this peaceful conversation.

"Maybe. But at least if we'd had a kid, something good would have come out of our clusterfuck."

I can't help the scowl that forms on my face and in an instant, tension begins coiling tight in my gut. "You can't possibly mean that. Do you really believe that nothing good came out of our marriage? We had good years, Isabel. We had the best years."

She stares out at the water for a moment, then she shrugs and tosses some fries toward a greedy seagull.

"Sure, we had some good times in the beginning," she says. Her voice is hard, and suddenly, so is her posture. "But if those years were really so great, it wouldn't have been so easy for me to leave you, and I wouldn't be so much happier now without you."

She might as well have punched me in the balls. I'm so hurt and shocked for a moment that all I can do is lean back against the streetlight and try to remember to breathe.

I want to rail at her—to call her out on the blatant lie. Maybe she's at peace with her decision to leave, but she'll never convince me it didn't hurt like hell to do it. I can see it in her eyes—in her smile—in the way her *curls* seemed weighed down, for God's sake. Isabel looks every bit as tired and drained by this year as I know I do.

I'm trying to think of a way to respond to her without using the words "cruel" or "fuck," and Isabel is staring out at the ocean, seemingly at ease. But then she turns to me, and I realize she's actually battling tears.

"Why am I so awful now? I kept saying shit like that at mediation, too, and then we were always fighting and…we never fought before, did we? And why would I do it now, when we're suddenly getting along?"

She chokes on a sudden sob, and I don't know what to do. I'm still bracing myself in case her mood swings back to vicious, but even so, I want to reach to comfort her, and that's against the rules now.

"Maybe I just can't let myself think about the good times yet," she whispers now, and the hurt and disappointment on her face hurt me just as much as the god-awful comments that preceded them.

We stare at each other for a minute, and then she looks away to stare at her shoes. "This was a stupid idea."

"Shit, Isabel," I breathe, but my voice breaks midway through her name.

She looks hesitantly toward me. I'm still winded by her cruelty and there's no way I can hide it. I don't even want to hide it, because I would go on the defensive again and that would lead to me being angry and...

It's an endlessly awful cycle.

Anger begets anger. Hatred begets hatred. And the one thing that's worked to break that cycle this year has been me waking up half drunk and forgetting to be defensive. I can't ignore that lesson. This is an odd, tense reunion, but in some strange way, the world seems to have righted itself a little tonight, even though my once-lovely ex-wife apparently has a hidden talent for intense cruelty. I knock the back of my head gently against the cold metal of the streetlight while I try to make sense of it all.

"I'll go—" she says now, and I can see her shifting, as if she's going to stand.

I reach to touch her arm gently. "Don't."

"But—" Her voice is still wobbly, so I exhale, sit up and tentatively slide my arm around her shoulders. I'm tense—mostly because there's a very real chance that she's going to elbow me in the balls. I'm almost surprised when she doesn't. Instead, she relaxes just a little into my embrace.

I squeeze her shoulders, and then I whisper gently into her ear, "Just stay and talk to me. It was just a bad moment, but if we stay here, we can push past it and I know we'll be glad we did."

She squeezes her eyes closed, and I can almost see the battle playing out in her mind. I don't even know why I want her to stay—apparently even a civil conversation with Isabel these days is like playing Russian roulette.

When she pulls away from me, I think she's about to storm off, but instead, she looks right at me and she blurts, "I didn't think I had the power to hurt you, Paul."

I don't know what to say to that. She couldn't be more wrong, but the fact that she's managed to draw that conclusion is probably my own fault for holding her at arm's length when things between us began to strain. I desperately want to avoid her gaze right now, but I *will not* allow myself to retreat.

Instead, I look right at her. "You did. You still do. You always will."

She swallows hard as she looks back to the pier.

CHAPTER SEVEN

Paul

WE FALL INTO silence after that, as if we both want to stay but we're too scared to try to converse. We simply sit side by side, watching the water as the sun sets and the darkness takes hold. We pass the wine back and forth occasionally, but neither one of us is taking more than tentative sips. The food, on the other hand, all but evaporates as we both tuck in like we haven't eaten for months.

I find that I actually like sitting with her; even in silence, even with the emotional distance between us. There's something both familiar and alien about this moment, but it's strangely comforting and I don't want it to end.

However, it's getting late, and while we really should go back to the house to get out of the increasingly cool breeze that's now coming off the water, my mind starts flicking forward to ways to stay. That means I'm well and truly ready with a response when Isabel says suddenly, "It's colder down here than I realized."

I automatically sit up to slip out of my jacket.

"Oh, don't do that… Paul, I wasn't hinting for that—"

"I'm still drunk enough that I can't feel a thing," I lie as I pass her the jacket.

Isabel pulls it around herself and a flush steals over her cheeks. She glances at me, almost shyly, and murmurs her thanks.

"It swims on you."

"But I'm sure it still looks fabulous. Black is definitely my color, right?" she says wryly. *There's* Funny Isabel—I miss Funny Isabel. She's so much more endearing than Bitter Isabel.

"You look good in any color," I say impulsively, but I do mean it.

Isabel blinks, apparently shocked by the compliment, and then she tries to deflect it. "It's the hair," she says, with unconvincing and clearly artificial confidence. She flicks her hair off her shoulders and flashes a duck face in my direction like a fourteen-year-old Instagram star. "I could look good in a burlap sack."

"You could," I whisper, and then I have no idea what comes over me, but with what's left of the bottle of wine caught between my legs, I push myself out of my semi-recline against the streetlight and I cup both sides of her face in my hands.

She's staring up at me, and she's really here—Isabel, my beautiful, magnificent wife. She was the best thing in my life, and then she was *gone*. Somehow, she's right back here and it feels too good to be real. Maybe that's why it's easy for me to speak freely—to tell her exactly what I'm thinking, just like I should have done every time my heart was full during all of those wonderful wasted moments over all of those wonderful years.

"You're *beautiful*, Isabel. You're perfect, actually. Whatever happens after tonight, just promise me you won't ever forget it."

She's startled—her hand is still in midair near her shoulder—but she's holding her breath and her eyes are huge.

I'm not going to kiss her. Holding her hand was stupid—an old habit, nothing more—but kissing her, well, that would be a disaster.

But our faces are getting closer. I don't exactly know how that's happening since I'm telling my body not to move and I'm pretty sure that Isabel shouldn't be moving either, but…our lips are now almost touching.

Don't you dare kiss her, Winton.

She wets her lips, and her breath catches. *The anticipation is delicious for her, too.* The instant I realize this, I'm lost.

I kiss her gently, but as I do, I'm waiting for her to push me away furiously—which she should, and I know I deserve it because this is insane. And at first, she doesn't kiss me back—she is completely still—but she's also relaxed and her lips are soft against mine as they even fall open just a little. I lean into the kiss like I'm sinking into a glorious daydream, reliving the best moments of my life as I pull her closer to me. But this is really happening; I can taste wine and salt on her lips. I can taste *my* Isabel, and oh God,

I've missed her in ways I haven't even let myself acknowledge over all of these months since she left.

And then, something switches, and Isabel is kissing me back—hard, every movement of her mouth against mine a declaration of a longing every bit as intense as my own. Soon her arms are around my neck, pulling me firmly against her. As if I could ever want to escape. My hands contract, I'm impatient to feel more of her skin. If we were back at the house, I'd be tearing her clothes off, but we aren't and so I do use some restraint. She's well sheltered by the oversize jacket, so I lift the bottom of her T-shirt and stroke the taut skin of her stomach and back, leading upward to the clasp on her bra. I unclip it easily, and she releases her breath in a hiss against my mouth.

We both open our eyes at the very same moment. We're on the same page like that; years of living together and making love will do that to a couple. We can read each other's bodies and minds when it comes to sex now—it's the bodily equivalent of finishing one another's sentences. Maybe for some couples, familiarity leads to boredom, but for me, it led to comfort and security and a depth of love I didn't even know I was capable of before her.

"This is such a stupid idea," she whispers, but the depths of her blue eyes are dark with desire and I know that she's no more put off by this realization than I am. That's why I have no hesitation at all in agreeing with her.

"Possibly the worst idea anyone ever had," I whisper back, and I slide my hand from beneath the soft fabric of her T-shirt to run my thumb over her lower lip.

She stares at me, her eyes wide and her pupils dilated. "We should stop this right now and go back. To our own beds."

"We definitely should." I'm still whispering, too scared to speak normally in case I break this spell.

"We're not going to, though, are we?" Isabel asks suddenly. She's daring me to talk her out of this, and I'm apparently foolhardy but I'm not a masochist.

"Well, I do think we should go back to the house." I keep my voice low as I glance over her shoulder. "Especially since there's a family over there trying to eat their dinner and I'm not sure the mother appreciates the show we've just given them."

Bel turns back to the family with a gasp, then looks down at her shirt. It's bunched up just below her breasts, and underneath it, her bra is still over her shoulders but loose because I undid the clasp.

I chuckle and pull the jacket closed, then zip it up. "Better?"

"Not really."

I scan her face, then dip my gaze to the bottle of wine resting in the grass beside us. It's still more than half full. I'm relieved because if we're doing this, it's not going to be some drunken mistake. Maybe it's going to be a sober mistake, but we won't be able to blame the wine.

"So. What are we going to do, Isabel?"

She hesitates a moment, then she leans forward and kisses me again.

"This is just one of those 'for old times' sake' fucks, right?" she whispers against my lips.

"Is that a thing?"

"I think so," she whispers, just as I think, *I hope so*. I climb to my feet and reach down to help her up, and when she's standing, too, I contract my fingers around hers.

"Then let's go."

CHAPTER EIGHT

Isabel

IN THE ORDINARY course of growing up and making my way to adulthood, I made plenty of mistakes. My mom would say I made more than my share of them. I always thought the important thing was to learn from my mistakes so I'd never repeat them.

But now, even as we're traveling back to the house in the back of the cab, I already know I'm going to regret what I'm about to do. That's why I'm trying to talk myself out of it, because when you know you're going to regret something deeply, you should just not do it, right?

But I want to.

Okay. I'll make a mental list of all the reasons why I shouldn't sleep with Paul.

1. He let me walk away without so much as a fight.
2. Maybe he's not in a relationship, but *we* never went more than a few days without sex, so him waiting for ten months as a single man?

Not a chance. Does that matter? It shouldn't,
but I feel like it does.
3. See point 1, and remember that mediation?
He couldn't be bothered fighting for me, but
he had plenty of energy to fight for his stupid
house. Seriously. I hate him so much.
4. See point 2. I hate that (those? *Oh God*) other
woman so much.
5. I really want to.
6. He's looking seriously good at the moment.
7. I haven't run my hands over those muscles
on his shoulders and arms yet, and to do so, I
need to get him naked, and if I do that, we're
going to sleep together anyway, so why fight
the inevitable?
9. Wait, wasn't this a list of reasons *not* to sleep
with Paul? And what happened to point 8?

I'm not drunk—not drunk on wine, anyway. I
threw the bottle in the bin as we left the waterfront
and was surprised to see how little we'd consumed.
Instead, I'm caught in some bizarre dreamlike state
that makes it very difficult to think clearly. It's the
surreal nature of this moment, I think.

I'm not at all equipped to deal with the confusing
reality that it feels good to be here with him right
now, like relief and happiness and coming home and
a reprieve all at once. It's his scent and the warmth of
his hand in mine and the fact that I forgot about this.
I forgot how easy it was before it wasn't easy anymore, and how good it was before it stopped being

good, and I have a feeling in an hour's time I'm going to be thinking *and I forgot how great the sex was*, although right now, I'm rather enjoying my own efforts to remember that even before he reminds me.

We leave the cab and cross the front lawn toward the house...toward privacy, and I know what's going to happen once we close that front door behind us. That's why, with every step I take, I'm more and more aroused.

I try to remind myself that nothing has changed. Sex was never the problem for us, it was everything else, and *everything else* matters. The thought of that is like ice water on my long-neglected libido and I have a moment of startling clarity among the raging hormones just as we step up onto the front porch.

"Paul," I say urgently, and even in the darkness, I see his face fall at my tone.

"So close." He sighs, and he releases my hand.

"We *can't* do this," I say.

"Okay," he says. He turns to face me and offers me a sad smile.

"I..." I reach a hand up to touch his cheek, because I'm wavering again already. He steps away from me, giving a frustrated groan as he goes. I miss him the second the contact is gone, and maybe that's why I can admit the truth to myself for the first time in a long time.

I have missed this man. I've missed him for years— since even before I left him, because he was slipping away from me long before that. And maybe, just for tonight, I want to ease that missing and longing.

Nothing has changed and nothing is fixed, but what was always good was the sex, and I want to enjoy that again. Paul's gaze is still dark with desire. He runs his gaze from my face to my hand—outstretched toward him again, and he shakes his head sharply.

"Don't play games with me, Isabel. Do you want this or not? I promise you that either answer is completely fine. It's just pretty messed up to give me both in the same breath."

It's two steps to catch up to him. When I do, I throw my arms around his neck.

"Fuck it," I say, and then I reach up and I kiss him, deeply.

He breaks our mouths apart to whisper against my lips, "You're sure? You *have* to be sure. If you're not 100 percent sure, let's just go inside and go to our own rooms. I promise you, I'm okay with that."

I raise my eyebrows at him. "Are *you* going to talk me out of this now?"

"Fuck no."

And then he's cupping my head in his hands and kissing me back, and I can't get close enough—I want to shred those stupid trendy clothes right off his stupid hot body and mount him here, exposed on the front porch. But common sense prevails. We're still kissing, but Paul somehow has the key in his hand and he opens the door without letting me go.

"Nice," I whisper, but then I squeal as he lifts me into his arms and kicks the door closed. It's ten steps to the sofa, where Paul carefully sits me down.

"Here?" I squeak, and he nods and lifts his shirt over his head. I reach up to his shoulders, but he brushes my hands away impatiently and moves onto his jeans. He slides his wallet from his back pocket and dumps it onto the floor beside us, and then kicks his jeans away, stripping down smoothly and efficiently. I finally catch on—shrugging out of his jacket and then my sweater and then my tank, tossing my bra into the irrelevant space beyond us.

Paul is naked now, but before I can make the most of this opportunity to enjoy the sight of him, he comes back to me and goes for the zip on my jeans.

"Lift," he commands and I comply, helping him to shrug my jeans and panties down over my legs and ankles. I gasp when my naked skin makes contact with the cold leather and Paul flashes me a wicked grin and takes me back into his arms. Finally, I get to run my hands over those supremely sculptured shoulders, identifying and appreciating each muscle as I go.

Deltoid. Teres major. Supraspinatus. Infraspinatus. Pectorialis.

For a moment or two, I ponder his body almost clinically. He feels so different in my arms from the endless memories I hold of earlier moments like this. He's harder now, solid and strong and powerful, and I feel soft and sheltered in his arms.

Right now, his lips are working magic—magic on my mouth, magic against *that amazing spot* beneath my ear, magic when he shifts his attention lower. His palms line up against my breasts, and he groans

softly, and then bends to plant a soft little kiss between them, a moment of surprisingly gentle affection tucked in among all of the raging lust.

"I've missed these so much."

I let my head fall back and my eyes close as I
focus on the sensation of his mouth as he roams
from one nipple to the other. He nibbles, licks, sucks,
and bites—gently, and then harder, and there's pain;
the kind that offers only shades of dark among the
blinding light of the pleasure, and in doing so height-
ens everything else. When he stands, I fumble to
reach for his erection, but Paul gasps and catches my
wrists, dragging my hands back to set them firmly
against the leather sofa.

"It's been a while, I won't last," he mutters, and
I'm triumphant even though I know that makes me
a bitch. Maybe there hasn't been anyone since I left.
Maybe he was sincere when he said he couldn't move
on so fast.

*Why do you even care, Izzy? You left him. You
have no right to judge and even less of a right to
care.*

Then my mental lecturing vaporizes because he
kneels on the leather, presses my knees apart and
crawls along the sofa between them. Then he's kissing his way up my inner thighs, and I whimper and
collapse back to rest my head on the armrest.

Paul is not in the mood to tease me or draw this
out. He remembers me—he knows the pressure and
the variation I like, and he gets straight to work. His
tongue flicks against my body, very gently at first,

and then with increasing pressure and intensity until I'm spiraling and barreling headlong toward my climax. I'm vaguely conscious that I'm begging, and that I want him inside me. Now. It's not pleasure I've missed—I can give that to myself. It's Paul.

"Enough," I gasp, and I tug harder at his hair, and he rises. He fumbles for his wallet from the floor beside us, and I'm momentarily confused until he withdraws a condom.

Why does Paul have a condom in his wallet?

Paul has a condom in his wallet because we aren't together anymore, and even if he hasn't slept with anyone else yet, inevitably, he will. I can't believe I'd let myself forget the reality of our circumstance.

We are not the people we once were. We're free agents, and who knows what he's been up to while we've been apart? It makes perfect sense that we'd be safe and use protection. I actually admire that Paul has had the presence of mind to think logically like this.

But of course he has. Paul is all about logic.

Yet the fact that we need to use protection startles me. The very sight of that condom is like a momentary bucket of cold water splashed over me. And if he didn't ever so gently slide his hand along my neck and cup my jaw and move to kiss me again with that tenderness I had completely forgotten he was capable of, I might have freaked out altogether. I think seriously about pushing him away, about fleeing to my room…but I realize *I don't want to stop*. I want to feel Paul, at least one more time.

Paul stretches his body out over mine and leans over me, his elbows on either side of my face on the cushion of the sofa. He stares right into my eyes as he pushes into me and I'm startled to find that in the depths of his gaze I don't see a man I dislike or a man I resent or even a man I hate. Instead, I see every little thing that I have lost. That's why I break the eye contact. I stare at the ceiling beyond Paul, and I force myself to focus my thoughts on the sensations in my body instead of the conflicted emotions in my heart and mind.

This is casual fucking, Isabel. You're not making love here, you don't need to gaze longingly at him while you do it.

"What's wrong?" he asks, stilling. Even this shocks me. Since when does Paul read me well enough to correctly interpret my body language?

"Nothing," I lie, and I slide my arms around his neck and bring his face down to mine so I can distract him with a kiss. He's trembling, and there's sweat on his skin and sweat on mine and soon we're moving against each other faster and harder, each desperately seeking release. Paul's stubble is short and soft, but it's scratching my cheek a little, leaving my face feeling raw, and that's somehow fitting. Everything feels raw right now—and I know it will feel even worse later. If the wound of our separation had even started to heal for me, then right now, I am tearing it back open with a callous disregard for my own feelings.

"Isabel," Paul whispers.

"Hmm?" I'm too out of breath to reply properly.

"I'm so sorry, honey, I'm sorry—I can't hold on…"

His face contorts, and when I understand that Mr. Stamina himself is so caught up in this that he's already about to lose control, *that* discovery is just enough to tip me over the edge. The delicious pressure builds deep in my belly, and then it bursts, and I cry out as my orgasm breaks over me. For a beautiful moment in time, I'm not conflicted or sad or confused. It's a singular moment of pure pleasure and joy.

As soon as I come back to earth, I'm conscious of the cold leather of the sofa beneath me, and the way that Paul is sprawled over me but still somehow half kneeling on the floor, too, and the angle is all wrong and he's still shaking and now I realize it's because he must be uncomfortable in such an awkward position. He's panting as if he's run a marathon, and so I close my eyes and I focus on the good sensations that linger—the feeling of him still inside me, the aftershocks that catch us both by surprise, eliciting fresh gasps from each of us when they hit, the pleasant heaviness of his body against mine and the scent that I want to wrap around me like a blanket that I could keep forever.

This was such a stupid idea.

And the worst thing is, I had plenty of opportunities to back out. I kept actively talking myself back into it. I was determined to make this mistake.

When Paul catches his breath, he slides gently from my body with a groan. I stay prone on the sofa as he deals with the condom, but then he rushes back to me and if I didn't know better, I'd suspect that he couldn't bear to be apart. He lifts me high into his arms, and I wrap my hands around his neck and let him carry me. As he walks, I sigh deeply, satisfied, riding the wave of bliss high enough still that I don't even open my eyes to see where he's taking me. He rests me on a mattress, and then climbs in beside me and lifts me so that I'm resting across his chest.

Maybe I'm lying over him on the bed and it's a damn sight more comfortable than the sofa, but mentally, I hit the ground with a thud and a tremor of tension runs from my head to my toes as I recognize that I'm back in the master bedroom.

With Paul.

Naked.

Sated.

Stupid. Stupid. Stupid.

"Don't," Paul whispers into my hair. "Don't think about it. Not yet."

He should be asleep now. That's what he always did—came, rolled away from me, dropped into a deep sleep. We didn't talk at all after sex the last few years…and my God, did I need to. I'm a woman who needs a cuddle and some pillow talk, but the intimate conversations and cuddles Paul and I had shared in our bed across the early years gradually faded away to nothing. By the end, he barely stayed awake long enough to embrace me at all.

I tried to fix that dynamic between us. I tried to shake him awake to hold him, especially toward the end, when he seemed so determined to retreat from me. Sometimes he'd turn the light out after we made love and I'd get right back up and turn it on again, but he'd still roll over and go to sleep.

Nothing worked—and eventually, even as I longed for the way he made me feel while he was inside me, I'd dread the way he made me feel afterward when he rolled away from me to sleep. I was lonely. Coupled, married, partnered—but always alone. By the time I left him, I was avoiding intimacy with him altogether. Meaningless sex was fine and fun when I was single. From my husband? It was fucking insulting.

Sex did not come easily to us at first. I'd never been the kind of woman who climaxed easily, and it took us weeks to find our rhythm when we first started sleeping together. But Paul mastered sex with me like he masters any task he commits to—with an intense, singular focus. Every time we tumbled into bed together, Paul was on a mission to learn my body and how to pleasure me.

I remember the struggle we had to work through once we stumbled upon the discovery that I reached orgasm *much* easier if he stared into my eyes when he was inside me. That level of intimacy was difficult for him, but sex with Paul was never just sex to me. I needed the added closeness of eye contact when we made love, even though I didn't want to need it, because I could see it was difficult for him.

Looking back, those moments of tension almost sum up our entire relationship. I desperately craved an emotional connection, but Paul only tolerated it because I needed him to. I tend to think of him as a man who never compromises, but I'm struck by a sudden realization that when it came to sex, he did more than meet me halfway. It was a challenge for him to let me see him when he was losing himself to pleasure. But he did it. For me.

Why didn't I stop to appreciate that at the time?

"Isabel," he says, and he shifts me a little, then tilts my chin until I'm looking into his eyes again. "Stay with me here. Don't freak out."

Stay with me here. He's wide awake. He's staring at me with visible concern.

Concern.

I'm not alone right now. I'm not even lonely.

And not feeling lonely right now is about the most confusing thing I've felt in my entire life. I'm so bewildered by this, the urge to lash out almost swamps me.

"We shouldn't have done that," I say. My throat is tight and my voice uneven.

"I know."

"That was so fucking stupid," I say.

Paul brushes my hair out of my eyes, and that's when his wedding ring flashes in the moonlight. I squeeze my eyelids closed. I'd actually forgotten all about that in the tension and confusion this afternoon, but what the hell does it even mean? Is he hoping we'll reconcile? If that's the case, why hasn't he tried to reach out to me this year?

Oh my God… am I leading him on right now?

To do so would be unforgivably cruel. And I *hurt* him tonight at the waterfront. It was shocking, and it was shameful, and I simply cannot bear the thought of seeing that kind of pain on his face again. Maybe, just maybe, I don't hate Paul Winton as much as I like to tell myself I do. Or it's just way too hard to hate him when I'm actually looking right at him.

Perhaps it's just easier to hate someone you don't actually have to face, because you can forget about their humanity when you don't have to see the consequences of your actions.

"Yeah, it was probably stupid," Paul murmurs.

"Why are you so calm about this?" I ask, pulling away from him and fixing my now-customary scowl back in place on my face.

He hesitates, then shrugs. "I just figured something out."

He's always two steps ahead of me. That was part of the problem. Light-years behind me emotionally, intellectually my superior in every way.

"What's that?" I ask stiffly.

He pauses before he answers me, but we're still cuddled close, and as I wait for him to speak I listen to the steady rhythm of his breath—he's genuinely at peace, so his inhalations and exhalations are easy and relaxed. Meanwhile, I'm now so tense that I'm positively vibrating in his arms and I'm actually terrified of what he's going to say. Because he's going to say something cold and dismissive, and it's going to shatter me. He always did that—I'd try to open up, to make myself vulnerable to invite him to do the same, and he'd either walk away or dismiss me and shut me down.

"Worrying about this tonight is redundant. We can't undo what we just did, and honestly, I don't even want to. Maybe we have some unfinished business between us. Maybe we were never meant to part on such bad terms. I've changed this year, and I'm sure you have, too. We both came here this weekend because we felt we needed to do something before next Wednesday so we could move on. Maybe tonight is just our way of saying goodbye to each other."

Huh.

That is the least Paul-like diatribe in the history of the world. I expected something spawned from cruel logic, like *it was just sex and it didn't mean anything*, or something rational, like *don't be hysterical, Isabel, if you make a big deal out of this, you'll make it worse*.

I'm so confused. None of this feels like our pattern.

"Come on, Bel," he whispers softly. "At least enjoy the afterglow before you implode your brain overthinking it."

...and, there it is.

I stiffen in his arms, but he tucks me up closer against his body, and his arms contract around me, as if he can counter the tension just by hugging me with more determination. And I desperately want to start an argument with him because I'm angry with myself—but I'm the one getting sleepy, and if anything, I want to retreat more than I want to battle. The urge to lick my wounds and find some space becomes overwhelming—it's certainly more urgent than the urge to fight with him right now.

I tell myself I'll just lie there until he falls asleep, and then I'll make a nondramatic, easy escape.

Right up until sleep takes me, I'm still telling myself that I'll just enjoy the warmth of his arms for one more minute.

Part Two

Saturday

CHAPTER NINE

Isabel

PAUL IS GONE when I wake up and the room is still and silent. I roll over and feel his side of the bed. It's cold, but I know he was here for most of the night because I roused several times and he was always either cuddled up around me or stretched out beside me. One time, when I was lying there trying to convince myself to get up and go back to my own bed, he actually woke up, too. His voice was rough with sleep, but ripe with concern anyway as he mumbled, "Are you okay, Bel?"

I'd have done anything for him to say those words in that soft tone of voice once upon a time. It's strange how easily the question came from him last night. What's changed? Is it me, or is it Paul…or is it both of us?

It's early now, close to dawn, judging by the soft light that's filtering through the gap in the heavy drapes. I try to go back to sleep, but my mind will have none of that—it seems I am destined to ruminate today. Last night was a mistake. It was stupid and foolish and impulsive, and I can't even say I didn't know what I was doing.

The problem is, in the cold light of this morning, the complete lack of regret I'm currently feeling about Paul and I falling into bed together is somehow stranger than the fact that it happened in the first place.

I head downstairs to dress in my workout clothes and step onto the pavement just as the sun hits the horizon. The breeze is cool this morning and it's a little too gusty for comfort. I'm glad I brought my hoodie, although it's inevitably going to wind up around my waist once I get going. I stretch, then walk a little to warm up, and soon fall into the rhythm of my jog.

Here at Greenport, I've always run the same loop from one side of the island to the other, taking a much longer trek than the few short miles I do once a week back home. Time, like sunshine here, seems a less precious commodity and so I always liked to linger on this ritual, sometimes letting it drag all the way through a morning or an afternoon. Often, I'd stop for a coffee and pancakes at Marie's before I made the return trip home. I'm starting to think about doing just that when I remember that Paul and I established this habitual loop together, and that it had been his idea to go for coffee and pancakes after our very first run here together all of those years ago.

I see him just as this hits me. He's just ahead of me on the sidewalk, but running back toward me, no doubt completing the same loop I intended to take. And of course he is. Where else would he be? I'm sure he's just following his regular weekend routine, just as I'm following *my* regular Greenport routine.

I wonder if it's going to be awkward if he stops

to talk to me. But for last night, perhaps he might have just flashed me a scowl as he ran past me. Now, though, I am not sure where we stand—does one encounter make us lovers again? That doesn't feel right. Will we just ignore last night and go back to the way things were, with the two of us unable to even have a polite conversation?

Huh. It turns out, I hate that idea most of all.

Paul stops running when he sees me and slows to a walk. I've only just started running so I have no intention of stopping yet, and I'm not ready to dissect what happened. I decide I'll just smile and nod as we pass one another.

"Morning," Paul says quietly, then he turns and starts jogging alongside me.

"Are you following me?"

"Following you?" he repeats, and then he laughs softly. "I think you'll find *you're* following me, since I was here first."

"Well…" I say, indignant, then words fail me. "Fine. Sorry. It's a habit to do this loop."

"Yep, same for me. So listen—"

"I'm not in the mood for a postmortem." I cut him off, and my tone is a little too sharp.

"Postmortem? I was going to give you a performance review."

I gasp in indignation, and Paul's easy grin does terrible things to my composure. We're jogging at a decent pace now, although not fast enough to leave me out of breath—but he's got me so flustered I'm starting to struggle to get enough air anyway.

"Kidding. No, I have a proposition for you."

"Oh, shit, Paul," I groan. "Haven't you messed enough with my weekend?"

"I think we should have breakfast together. Talk some more."

I stop dead in my tracks, and when Paul stops, too, and turns back to me questioningly, I gape at him. "You've lost your fucking mind."

"Hear me out," he says, and his mild, reasonable tone enrages me. I'm further infuriated by the way he starts jogging again and, after a few steps, turns back to gesture for me to follow him. I do so—but I tell myself I'm doing it because I want to keep running, not because he effectively told me to.

"We're getting divorced," I remind him pointedly. "On Wednesday. People who are getting divorced in a matter of days don't sleep together, and they don't have cozy fucking breakfasts together."

"If we leave things as they are now, we'll never be friends again. But I really think there's enough between us that if we take the time to part properly, we can undo some of the hurt we've caused each other, and maybe then we can actually get on with our lives."

"I'm going to move on just fine," I mutter, and he snorts.

"You're here to mope, and so was I. Even the fact that we both had exactly the same idea for this weekend tells me something."

"I don't even like you!"

"No, you don't like the version of me that you've

seen this past year, and I don't blame you because I hate that guy, too," Paul says, and I bark a surprised laugh. He glances at me. "Well, that's not me, just as the version of you that I've seen this year wasn't you. We've treated each other like shit since you decided you wanted out, but it doesn't have to be that way. That's exactly why we should hang out together this morning."

"Paul…" I'm actually lost for words. I mean, who is this guy, and what has he done with my ex-husband?

"I want to remember and to respect the Isabel I was happy with for years. I want you to remember and respect the Paul you were happy with for years. I want to put the bitterness behind us, and then we can part from our marriage properly."

I can't think about the good times yet. It's almost a traumatic response, the way I've set up a mental block in my mind. I focus so hard on that awful last year because it hurts too much to remember what came before it. Paul's reference to our earlier years enrages me, and I feel that now-familiar anger rising again like a tide. My footsteps on the pavement land heavier, and my hands start to clench into fists.

"I was not *happy*—" I start to say, but Paul abruptly breaks his stride, coming to a dead stop on the sidewalk. I stop running, too, and I also stop speaking mid-sentence because when I turn back to him, he's staring right at me, but he's clearly braced himself. He knows I'm about to hurt him. His words last night echo in my mind—the way his voice was raw with vulnerability and pain and how I was immediately sick with remorse and shame.

You did have the power to hurt me. You still do. You always will.

Now, we stare at each other—and the space between us is positively volcanic.

My rage is fading so quickly I could almost convince myself it was never there. Suddenly, I'm simply relieved that he stopped and cut me off, because the memory of my cruelty last night is still fresh, and I was about to do it all over again. What the fuck is wrong with me? It's like I can't stop myself from being hurtful toward him, but he's actually right—that is not me at all.

I force myself to raise my gaze to look at him again. His eyes are guarded now, his stance still wary.

Without a single word, Paul has reminded me that my words have power. And it's bizarre and unexpected because none of this makes sense from the man I was married to. I know I'm remembering him correctly. He was never the kind of partner who was conscious of the impact his actions would have on my emotions, let alone someone self-aware enough to teach *me* a lesson about empathy. Paul was closed off emotionally, and yet here he is, tearing himself wide open and letting me know that I am still important enough to him to bring him to his knees.

This Paul deserves better from me. If I'm honest with myself, even the old Paul deserved better.

"I'm sorry," I choke out, staring at the pavement

beneath my feet, then I force myself to be vulnerable, too. Because his vulnerability yesterday meant we could have a night of peacefulness together, and I am grateful for that. "Okay. Yes, we had some good times. Great times. It would be amazing if we really could part on good terms. That's what I originally wanted...that's what I expected all along." Still I hesitate, because as appealing as the idea of a persistent state of harmony between us is, I'm not sure such a thing is actually possible. "It's just... Don't you think all of this is just going to make it harder?"

"Do you really think it could be any harder?" he asks me. That intense stare is entirely focused on me and is completely, heartbreakingly open. This was what I wanted all along—just a glimpse of the man behind the cold facade. Never in a million years would I have left Paul if I'd seen that he was still capable of this kind of interaction with me.

And here it is. It's just happened ten months too late.

I look away hastily, and I crack a stupid joke because it's the only way I can think to stop myself from bursting into tears. "Are we still talking about emotions?"

It's Paul's turn for a surprised laugh, but he quickly sobers.

"I'm not even talking about sex. Although, you know, last night was..." He trails off.

I glance back to him again and something flares between us—a spark of remembrance that in this early morning light looks a whole lot like longing.

Paul doesn't need to finish his sentence. Last night was nothing, and it was something and everything, and neither one of us knows what to do with it. Eventually he gives me a helpless shrug of those deliciously bulked-up shoulders and admits, "I don't think it's a good idea for us to repeat it, but it was a pretty spectacular one-off."

At least this part of what Paul is saying makes total sense. We should definitely not jump into bed again. Yet I am completely bewildered by the disappointment that now sits in my gut like a stone. "So, just to be clear—you're proposing we just share another meal. We hang out."

"Yep."

"We don't have sex."

"No."

"We don't…" I hesitate, reluctant to even say the words aloud. My gaze drops to his left hand, and the wedding band he's still wearing. *Jesus.* I'm pretty sure he has no interest in reconciling, but I need to be sure what his intentions are here. We might clear some of the air between us, but there's no way we could ever undo what's happened this year. "…we don't get back together."

Paul grimaces, as if the idea is completely distasteful. I suppose it would be awkward and awful if he were desperately hoping for a reunion, so his reaction to that suggestion should be a relief to me, too.

"Definitely not," he says.

I'm not disappointed. But strangely, I'm not relieved either.

"I just don't understand why you want this, Paul. And I really don't get why that ring is still on your finger."

He offers me a somewhat helpless shrug. I think he's going to admit that he doesn't really understand it either, but then he asks me quietly, "Tell me the truth, Bel. None of this kick-Paul-in-the-balls-while-he's-down bullshit, just some honesty," he murmurs, and I feel my cheeks heat. "When you look back at our marriage, do you think it was a mistake?"

Oh how I loathe that particular question! It's just not something that can be summed up with a yes or a no. Paul scared and entranced me from the first moment I met him.

I'd been hearing about Paul for two years by then. I got the train schedules mixed up the weekend Jess invited me to join her here at Greenport with her partners, and the party was in full swing by the time I arrived. When I first knocked on the door, no one answered. A few, louder knocks, and it opened to reveal Paul.

From the way Jess had described him, I'd pictured someone brilliant, awkward and maybe shy. But he wasn't some shrinking computer geek—he was arrogant and bold, and he held my gaze as though he had a right to it. And despite the lazy styling of the worn swim trunks and oversize T-shirt he was wearing, Paul was still vastly more attractive than I'd anticipated. He shook my hand in the doorway, and while I was still trying to make sense of the shivers that ran through my body at the contact of skin against skin, I managed to stammer out, *Hi, I'm Isabel. I'm Jessica's Pilates instructor.*

Just then, Jess burst into the room. She threw her arm around my shoulders and laughed. *Oh, fucking hell, Izzy. By now you've surely earned the title of my friend, although yes—you do still happen to teach me Pilates sometimes, too.*

Paul invited me in and showed me around the house, then we sat out on the deck with the rest of the gang. Everyone else was talking and drinking and someone ordered pizza. The night wound on and on, until people started disappearing into the bedrooms, but I barely paid a shred of attention because Paul was increasingly absorbing my focus.

By the time the sun rose the next morning, we'd been chatting for eighteen hours and I was already completely infatuated with him. I laughed at his jokes even when I didn't get them, because I wanted desperately to keep his attention. I was lost to his sharp wit, ambition and intelligence—even Paul's arrogance appealed to me because he was brilliant and he knew it. I'd never met anyone like him.

As morning broke, we walked to Marie's for our first ever coffee date. Paul only ever drank bitter black coffee, but that day, I convinced him to get a sickly sweet hazelnut latte, and he tasted it and told me it was like candy and coffee had a baby together, and I told him he was hilarious.

We sat on the grass at Mitchell Park to drink the coffees so we could watch the sunrise. Just as he finished his drink, I launched myself at him for our very first kiss. The sun breached the horizon before us as we kissed and kissed, with the sea breeze in my hair and the fluttering of something miraculous in my heart.

All of that led to this sunrise moment, with things broken and ugly between us. This time instead of the wonder of a new beginning, Paul's presence here with me can, at best, mean getting closure.

"Our relationship was a mistake," I whisper. "And it wasn't."

"You can't really have it both ways, Isabel."

"I can. They were the best years of my life, at least at first. But that's what makes where we wound up so hard."

"We used to bring out the best in each other. Falling in love with you gave me a confidence that I'd never even known was missing, and everything I've done since has been a result of that. And I know that falling in love with me changed you, too. You'd never been so happy. You told me that on our wedding night."

I do remember saying that, but I also remember thinking that he wasn't even listening, because he was giving me that glazed stare at the time. The pattern of emotional distance that eventually destroyed us had started right from the very start. I had been so confident that I could reach him because I was sure that one day, he'd reach for me, too, and we'd meet each other somewhere in the middle.

"I want to be friends with you, Isabel," Paul says now. There's a sad, slightly pleading tone to his voice, and the part of me that once loved him is gripped by the soft way he says my name. "I want to be able to see you around and ask how you're doing and to celebrate with you when the answer is 'fantastic.' I want to email you when great things happen in my life and I want you to be excited for me. I want to go to Jess's stupid rooftop extravaganzas and know that it'll be okay that we're both there." He clears his throat, and then adds very quietly, "Most of all, it really matters to me that those years we spent together were real. And if they were real, we *can't* part on such bad terms. People who love the way we loved each other shouldn't wind up separated by hate."

The wind is blowing right in my face and my eyes are starting to water, but I don't want to stop running because if I do, I'll have to look at him. Everything he's saying makes sense, but every single word feels like a knife to my heart.

"So what does this look like?" I ask him unevenly.

"I'm not talking about us throwing ourselves into a full-on relationship of any kind—it's just sharing breakfast as friends. I mean, if that works, then potentially we could spend time with our other friends in the future as a group without it feeling fucking awful for everyone. Can you at least try to work toward that with me? I know I let you down, and I have to live with that. But I do still care about you, and I want us to find a way to put all of the anger behind us."

At long last, I slow my steps, and then I stop running altogether. Paul slows and stops in time with me. When he turns to me, our eyes lock.

I'd eventually have told him to leave me alone this morning, except for one thing: Paul has just said the magic words. He's given me the one thing I have so desperately needed to hear from him over these past few years.

I've let you down.

I have to live with that.

I do still care about you.

Somehow, out of the pain and confusion of our separation, he's garnered…what? Sensitivity? Humility? I'm not entirely sure what it is, but there's no denying that something in Paul has changed. Last night, I thought it was just alcohol and exhaustion, but he's well rested now and sober as a judge.

This is the new Paul. This is undeniable evidence of real emotional growth.

Later, I'll reflect on that and I know I'll cry about it. There's a lost opportunity for us somewhere in these circumstances. If he was capable of change after I left, then maybe he could have done it while I was still there, and maybe we could have found a way forward together.

For now, all I can do is give him what he's asked for and try to maintain this harmony with him. I know this is going to be uncomfortable, and it's not at all what I planned when I decided to come out here this weekend. But there's a big part of me that's relieved about the chance to interact with Paul more, because I am desperately curious about this modern-day version of him.

"Okay," I say. He raises his eyebrows, as if he can't believe I'm agreeing to this either, and I shrug. "But…no trip down memory lane, right? Just hanging out. Rebuilding a friendship."

"Exactly," he says.

My gaze drops to his left hand, hanging loosely by his side, and I hesitate. "But…seriously, Paul. *What* is with that ring?"

He glances down at his hand, and then he gives me another one of those helpless shrugs. "It didn't feel right to take it off."

"You weren't wearing it at mediation." I remember staring at his finger and thinking how strange it was to see that space bare. "You must have taken it off, at least for a few months."

He hesitates, then he admits, "Bel, I just didn't want you to see that I was still wearing it. I took it off just for those meetings."

"But then you put it back on."

"Yeah."

"Huh," I say, and he glances at my finger.

"Yours is gone," he points out.

I stormed out of that marriage counseling session in a blind rage because from the minute Paul started explaining our situation to the therapist, he dismissed me. He was angry that I'd walked out, and he was adamant that our life together was perfect so if I wasn't happy, I must be impossible to please. I was so angry I couldn't even convince myself to stay

and share my own perspective—I just had to get out
of that room before he diminished me.

But that didn't mean I didn't want to fix things—
I did, and desperately. Even as I tumbled into bed
that night at the hotel, I left my phone on its loudest
setting because I was so sure he'd at least try to contact me and I didn't want to sleep through his call.

After that, I waited for days, and then weeks. I
was constantly checking the screen between clients
or classes, hopeful I'd missed a text or a call or,
Jesus, at that point I'd have happily received an email
or a telegram. A whole month went by before I could
bring myself to accept that Paul wasn't even going
to try to contact me.

In all of the scenarios I envisioned when I decided to leave, radio silence was not something I'd
considered. I spent hours trying to figure out why
he wasn't coming after me. And yes, I know I could
have contacted him.

But something awful happened inside me over
those weeks. Every single day that passed without us
reconnecting, my frustration toward Paul evolved. I
hadn't really doubted that he loved me until I left—
that's why I was so sure he'd come after me. And
when I realized he was just going to let me walk
away, something ugly began to simmer in my chest.

I'd rolled the dice on what was left of the goodwill
between us, and I'd lost. Loneliness, disappointment,
rejection, and sadness all bubbled away until what
was left was a seething, furious resentment.

I spent my thirty-third birthday alone, refusing

Jess and Abby's attempts at cheering me up. Even Nick tried to convince me to go out for cake after work, but that day had become some kind of invisible deadline in my mind. If Paul couldn't even find it in his heart to send me a happy birthday message, I'd be justified in finally giving up on him...in giving up on us.

I took my wedding and engagement ring off at midnight. They're still sitting on top of the jewelry box on my new dresser, out in the open not because I like to look at them, but because I'm half hoping someone will break in and steal them.

That was months ago. I don't even have a tan line on my ring finger now.

I glance back at Paul, and he gives me a lopsided smile.

"You've always been better at embracing change than I am," he says softly. "Maybe you can teach me how to take the ring off. I promise you, I'm not wearing this ring because I think you're coming home, if that's what you're worried about. I don't want to get back together. Last night was fantastic, but it's pretty obvious that there's too much chaos in our past now for us ever to go back. I'm wearing the ring because I can't break the habit, that's all." He grimaces. "Marcus has been calling me Gollum."

I chuckle reluctantly, and Paul's smile returns. I see the sincerity in his gaze, and the last of my concern fades. I return his quiet smile with one of my own.

"Okay—fine." I extend my hand to him. "Truce?"

"Truce," he says, grinning as he shakes my hand. As soon as he releases it, I get into the starter's position, and he raises his eyebrow at me. "I said truce, not 'race.'"

"You're carrying a lot of very heavy muscle there these days, and I'm a lean, efficient running machine. I just want to see if you can keep up."

I set off at a sprint without waiting for his response, because I know he'll catch me and even outrun me, but I also know that if we're really going to spend this morning together, we're going to have to shift the tone of our interactions from raw tenderness back to something like a friendship. And if there's one thing Paul and I used to enjoy, it was a good competition.

When I finally give up ten minutes later and admit he *can* well and truly outrun me, I collapse on a park bench gasping for air as Paul does an effortless victory lap around me. I feel like maybe there's a chance the better versions of ourselves can find something amicable out of the chaos.

CHAPTER TEN

Paul

I'M SITTING AT a café eating breakfast with my wife.

I'm sitting at a café eating breakfast with my wife, and it is beyond surreal.

The truth is, I wasn't at all sure how today was going to play out. I just don't know what to make of last night. I want to chalk the whole encounter up to good old-fashioned sex, but I can't. Good old-fashioned sex might explain what happened on the sofa, but it doesn't explain how much I got out of that chat at the park, and it sure as hell doesn't explain Isabel and me sleeping in each other's arms. If we were just scratching an itch last night, she'd have left the bed after we finished, and I wouldn't have desperately wanted her to stay.

How to define last night feels like some exceedingly complex logical problem that I just can't solve—and what's missing is data. I need more of it…a lot more. I just didn't know exactly what that data looks like, or how to get it. I'd been pondering that very question as I ran until I saw her on the footpath jogging toward me. Then, in a heartbeat, it came to me.

Find common ground.

I mean, there's clearly still something between us—some deeply buried atom of mutual respect. Last night, we uncovered it, and maybe today, all we need to do is stop ourselves from burying it in our garbage all over again.

Could we really form some kind of new friendship, even after all of the pain and heartache? I'm not even sure how to feel about the idea of Isabel being my friend. I'm attracted to her on a level so deep that even when I was utterly livid with her, I was still aware of her... It seems a fair assumption that I'll want her until I die.

But given our circumstances, I know I'd happily put that aside if it meant we could exist harmoniously in the same social circle...and I'd probably chop off my own dick if it meant I didn't have to wake up in the morning and think frustrated, angry thoughts about her. As we raced one another to the café, it occurred to me that what I crave more than anything right now is peace, and that the only way to get it is to reconcile with Isabel in some shape or fashion.

So here we are—at Marie's together for the first time in over a year. Isabel stopped on her way into the café for a long chat with Marie, who seemed very surprised to see me and far less surprised to see Isabel. That makes me suspect that Isabel has been visiting our vacation home in the year since we separated. I'd assumed her bloodlust for that house was entirely about inflicting pain on me, but maybe Isabel really does intend to make good use of the place.

Right now, Isabel and I are seated at a table, two steaming meals in front of us. We made some somewhat awkward small talk about the weather and Marie's new decor while we waited for our food. Now, Isabel is eating her ricotta pancakes, and she's periodically reading a newspaper, except that in between brief stints staring at the paper she keeps glancing at me quizzically, as if I'm doing something odd.

I smile briefly at her the first few times she looks at me, but then she starts to frown, and eventually she says abruptly, "Paul."

"Yes?"

"What are you doing?"

"Eating?" I say, glancing down at my bacon and eggs.

Isabel regards me suspiciously. "Since when do you *just* eat?"

"How else do I get food into my body?" I frown, and she sighs impatiently.

"You don't ever just eat. You always read while you eat—in fact I only picked the stupid newspaper up when we came in because you always read and eat in the morning." Her gaze sharpens, and she crosses her arms over her chest. It seems that Isabel has already become both defensive and irritated. "You pick today of all of the days in your life to stop doing that?"

"Oh," I say, and I look at the newspaper she's holding. I suddenly remember times when she'd

be inexplicably furious with me over breakfast—
including one or two particularly harsh encounters
that evolved into her giving me the silent treatment
right here in this very café. But toward the end
there, it felt like Isabel was vaguely angry with
me all the time and I could never really pin down
exactly what I was doing to upset her. I always assumed those snippy comments over breakfast were
actually about something else, something deeper
or more important. Maybe I was wrong about that.

"I try not to read and eat these days," I admit.

"Why?" she says, and she closes the newspaper,
and she turns a little in her chair so that she's facing me fully. Her gaze settles on mine. I notice it
now—the way she removes all the distractions because she's interested in what I have to say. I never
noticed those things before. Maybe I'd have felt her
attention, but I wouldn't have taken the time to understand exactly how she gave it to me.

"It's rude," I say stiffly, and her eyebrows nearly
disappear into her hairline. She blinks at me, and I
feel compelled to explain, even though the thought
of doing so makes me feel awkward as hell.

Isabel is still staring at me as if I've lost my mind,
and it seems the only way out of this moment is
through it. "I was absorbing information from the
minute I got out of bed until the minute I went back
to bed. If it wasn't the tech pages of the paper, it
was emails, and if it wasn't emails, it was reference
books. I was never really anywhere, because my
mind was always elsewhere. So I broke the habit of

trying to digest data twenty-four hours a day. I don't look at any electronic devices until I get to the office, and I still read the tech news or reference guides or whatever, but only when that's all I'm doing. If I'm eating, I just eat. If I'm spending time with someone, I try to give them all of my attention. It's not a big deal."

"For anyone else it wouldn't be a big deal," Isabel says. Her voice is very small. She looks at me hesitantly, then looks at the table again. "For you, it is a big deal."

We sit in silence for a moment. It's my instinct to end this conversation now. I want to cut it off before I have to reveal any more parts of myself that I'm not proud of. I'm tensing up at the very thought of splitting myself open to her and handing her information that she could effectively weaponize.

But Isabel still looks wary, as if this is some kind of trick. I've made a few lifestyle tweaks because I learned from the failure of our marriage. Some naive part of me wants her to know that. A stupid legacy from the connection we once shared makes me wish she'd be proud of me for the way I understand myself now.

"I figured something out this year," I admit tentatively. Isabel flicks her gaze back to my face. "I can't multitask."

She snorts. "That's ridiculous. Your entire life is multitasking."

"Maybe it looked that way, but that's not how my brain works. In fact, hardly anyone can effectively multitask—the human brain just can't effectively complete more than one high-level function at a time. I only really realized this year just how singular my focus actually is. I can eat and read, but I don't taste the food. I can run and listen to a podcast, but I either tune out of the podcast or I'm not concentrating on the run. I can pack the dishwasher and have a conversation, but I'm not really listening. I don't need to tell you I'm not exactly a people person."

"Right," she says, wincing a little.

"I realized that part of the reason other people bewildered me was that I just wasn't listening in the right way. If I stop everything else and force myself to pay attention to body language and tone and the words people use, I actually hear more of what they are saying. Does that make sense?"

"Oh," Isabel says. She takes a sip of her juice, then lowers the glass. "Yeah, okay. I can see that. So it's kind of a mindfulness thing."

"Exactly. And it's kind of ironic if you think about it."

"It is?"

"I remember you talking to me about mindfulness one day. You read an article about how some businesses were introducing mindfulness practice to increase employee morale and efficiency."

"I remember that article."

"Then you likely also remember the way I rolled my eyes and scoffed at the idea when you told me about it."

"Yeah."

"I probably rushed off to get on with whatever things I was half doing that day. Then you left me, and I wasn't paying attention and I didn't see it coming." I shrug. "Bang. The concept of mindfulness suddenly makes a lot more fucking sense."

She turns her gaze away from me. Her gaze is intense, her brows pulled inward.

"What did I say?"

Isabel hesitates, then she looks back to me. "It used to drive me insane how I never had your full attention, but you never understood why I was upset about it."

"Well, I didn't actually realize how much it bothered you. It's not like you called me out on it," I say easily.

"I spent years trying to call you out on it! Why did you think I mentioned that article to you?"

"Hoping I'd read an article and somehow in doing so also read your mind is a little different than 'calling me out,'" I say with a confused laugh.

Isabel's mouth falls open. Her big blue eyes go wide and her nostrils flare. Oops. I hastily backpedal.

"I just meant—my listening skills are awful. I know they are. You could have hit me over the head with a brick to try to get my attention and it wouldn't have worked half the time. But you have to admit, you never told me what you wanted from me. I always had to guess, and then you'd get pissed at me if I didn't guess correctly."

"Seriously? This 'truce' lasted less than twenty

fucking minutes," Isabel snaps, and she stands. I stand, too, and I catch her hand gently in mine.

"Bel…just hang on—"

"This is exactly why this is a stupid idea," she says. She snatches her hand back and presses it into her temple. "You promised me no trips down memory lane. That was less than half an hour ago."

"I know. I didn't mean to bring up the past, I was just answering your questions. I'm really sorry."

She scowls at me, and I prepare myself, knowing she's going to storm off and that when I reflect on this later, I suspect I'll discover it was my fault. However, right at this minute, I have no idea what I've done to provoke her to a reaction like this. I'm surprised when she sits heavily, but I quickly, cautiously follow suit. I watch her as she picks at the ricotta pancakes on her plate, and then as she opens the newspaper again.

"You're staying?" I check carefully.

She glances up at me, then looks back to the newspaper, but her gaze is clouded. Finally she closes the newspaper again, and pushes it away.

Our eyes meet. There's so much pain in her gaze I have an irrational desire to hunt down whoever hurt her and punch that bastard in the face. Unfortunately, I'm the culprit. It's a bewildering sensation.

"You said sorry," she says.

"Of course I did. I upset you."

"You noticed you upset me and you said sorry," she says. Her voice breaks, and I glance at her, stricken. She blinks rapidly, then says, "We're going to be friends, right?"

"Yeah." That's the goal here, although I do recognize that outcome remains somewhat unlikely.

"That's what friends do, they apologize. And that's how friends forgive each other, they accept the apology."

Would I not have done that before? I pause, scanning my memory, and the images that flick by me do nothing to assuage my sudden guilt.

No, I wouldn't have apologized. I'd have glossed the moment of tension over and I'd have accused her of being oversensitive. And maybe she is a little oversensitive right now, but I can see why. It's hard to be rational about all of this because we're navigating an emotional minefield.

"I really am sorry," I say, then I close my eyes and admit, "Fuck it, Isabel. I'm sorry for pretty much everything at this point."

"Well, I'm staying," she says stiffly. "But you better change the subject before we push things too far."

I scan my mind for a safe subject…something I know she'll engage with.

"Tell me more about this seniors fitness program."

I'm listening to her. I swear I am, especially since we just narrowly avoided an argument about communication and multitasking.

But I also can't help but notice the way the tension drains from her face, and her eyes light up as we talk about her work. She just loves the human body, and she takes immense satisfaction from helping people achieve fitness—I know instinctively that this seniors program is the perfect blend of technical challenge and sheer altruism that brings Isabel to life.

"You should have seen your dad the day he bench-pressed one hundred pounds for the first time." Isabel beams. "He had this look of surprise on his face afterward, as if he still couldn't believe he'd done it. And I swear I floated around on cloud nine for the rest of the day. I was so proud of him."

"So you've got Dad and his buddies doing weights?"

"Progressive resistance training is ideal for seniors. As we age, we lose muscle strength, so that kind of training can help maintain or even rebuild it. Your dad has a great approach to his fitness now—he's constantly looking for the next goal, so weights are great for him because the quantifiable data of his performance keeps him motivated. I have some of the other seniors doing different activities. I'm coaching an under-nineties basketball team, and I run a ballet class for a group of octogenarians on Tuesdays."

"You're teaching ballet?" I say, eyebrows lifting. Isabel was raised on ballet but stopped dancing in her teens. Until now, the closest she'd come to dance was the barre classes she instructs.

"Just that one class, and mostly because the ladies were so excited about the idea of it and I couldn't find anyone else to teach them."

"And are you enjoying it?"

"You know I've always loved to watch dance."

"I remember that."

"Well, everything I love about dance as an art form is palpable in that group of women. They love the idea of telling a story through movement. One of the women told me she'd stopped exercising when she was in her twenties because it started to feel pointless, and it became a chore. That's almost sixty years of inactivity, which is brutal on the human body. But it's never too late. Now, that same woman is doing two sessions a week for the dance class and she's added extra time in the gym to help her balance and strength. This was a woman who was struggling to walk up and down stairs when we started three months ago.

"I think the secret to that class's success is that I understand where those women are coming from. Dance once felt like a chore to me, in the same way that exercise became a chore to them. But now that I'm using those skills to help those women, I'm actually enjoying it again. Purpose brings meaning. These seniors classes have made me fall in love with my work all over again."

"And apparently your classes are a hotbed of romance for the gray-haired set."

Isabel laughs.

"That's just your dad and Elspeth, as far as I know. Although those retirees sure do know how to socialize. I don't think your dad's friends even realize that it's possible to work out and go right home afterward, without going out for lunch or dinner or drinks."

"The way I remember it, you, Abby and Jess seem to have much the same approach."

"Yeah, there's some truth in that accusation," Isabel chuckles.

It's peaceful. It's good. It's easy. This kind of conversation was the absolute best-case scenario I had in mind when I suggested breakfast this morning. Sure, these are surface-level chats—nothing more than small talk, but small talk can be a big deal sometimes. Especially when it's between two people who've dug out space for an ocean of hate between them in the recent past. This kind of lighthearted chat is precisely how we lay down the foundations for a bridge to span the distance between us now.

We finish our meals, and I see Isabel finish her coffee, so I order us another round, as I remember Isabel likes a second cup most mornings. Every now and again, a thought forces its way to the front of my mind.

I'm enjoying this too much.

This conversation is nothing at all, and yet it feels like the most meaningful thing I've done all year, and the more aware I am of that conundrum, the more confused and conflicted I become. Soon, I'm a giant, pulsing ball of conflicting emotions that I'm all too aware of, and I hate every second of it. Pick up the newspaper and zone out? That sounds fucking divine, thank you.

But now I know that kind of dissociation comes at a cost. It cost me my marriage. It cost me the love of my life. It's far too late to undo any of that—but

Isabel is here, and this is a once-in-a-lifetime chance to reach for closure. So I focus on her, and I focus on the casual conversation, and I try to force myself to do something I've never been good at...not with her. Not with anyone, if I'm really honest with myself.

I try to be her friend.

"Ready to head back?" I ask her.

She smiles quietly at me, almost shyly, and she nods, but then she warns me, "I can't run after all of those pancakes."

"Let's just walk then," I say. "It's not like we're in a rush to be anywhere."

"What's happening with your retreat?" she asks.

"Who knows?" I shrug. "I'll call Jess when I get back, but between her and Audrey, it'll be fine."

"You can call now if you want," Isabel says. "I don't mind."

I shake my head. "No, I'm hanging out with you now. Besides," I turn out the pockets of my running shorts. All I have in my pocket is a credit card and the key to the house. "I never run with my phone anymore."

Her brows knit, then she nods and smiles. She looks happy and more than a little surprised. And it takes a lot of effort on my part not to revel in the fact that I can see that she's actually proud of me.

CHAPTER ELEVEN

Isabel

THERE ARE SOME things in life you can fake, but for the most part, I truly believe that people eventually give away their private thoughts in their behavior whether they want to or not.

Right at this moment, I'm sure I'm giving off a genuinely confused air that I couldn't hide if I wanted to. And Paul seems to be displaying a genuine desire to make amends and reconnect.

He seems so different from the man I lived alongside for four years. He's focused. Self-aware. Thoughtful. The man I was married to would rarely have noticed I'd finished my coffee, let alone have thought to ask if I needed a refill.

But I just had his full attention at breakfast, and the force of it was powerful and enticing...and bewildering. We're walking back toward the house and he's talking about his work—but I asked him about it, and honestly? He sounds kind of bored, almost like he'd rather talk about my job again.

"...upgrade and the development team is trying to fix this macOS bug and we're not—"

"Paul," I interrupt him. He glances at me warily. I was always so frustrated about how much he worked, and I have a feeling he's expecting me to leap down his throat now. "I'm getting the impression that you actually want a weekend off work."

He runs his hand through his hair. He looks utterly weary right now. "Yeah. I guess I do."

It takes a minute for me to recognize the feeling that surges inside me as hopefulness. I've never seen Paul look unexcited about his job before, and the possibilities of this unlikely occurrence are almost endless. If he wasn't completely in love with his work, then maybe he could have really loved—

"Don't get me wrong," he says suddenly. "I still love what I do. Me and Marcus and Jess…and the team…we're really just getting started. Jess is working toward us listing on the stock exchange, and if that happens the way we think it will, the sky is the limit. It's just that this weekend was never meant to be about work."

It's impressive that he has finally established a "too much work, need a break" threshold for the first time, but maybe the great love of his life really is Brainway Technologies. And that's okay, because it's *his* life now. I offer him a weak smile.

"Tell me something about you I don't already know," he says suddenly.

"How could there be things about me you don't know?" Is this a trap? This must be a trap. Why would he even ask this?

"How could there not be?" Paul says with a shrug.

"We haven't really spoken in months. I'm sure lots of things have happened in your life that I don't know about. And anyway, were we ever the kind of couple to sit around talking about our deepest thoughts and feelings?"

"I guess not."

"There's got to be a lot of things I don't know about you."

We walk in silence for a few minutes as I think about this. I can give him surface-level answers. I could tell him about my new neighborhood, and Mr. Daskalakis with the food cart just up from my building who makes the best gyros in the city. Or I could tell him about that time I was on the subway heading out to Brooklyn to visit my brother, and a guy in my carriage had cut leg holes in a gym bag so his Great Dane could stand in it, unconvincingly skirting the subway's rule of "no dogs unless they fit in a bag." I could tell him about how his father's friend Ira brings me a bouquet of fresh herbs from his balcony garden every single week to thank me for helping him get active again despite his crippling arthritis.

But I want to tell him something deeper…something private, and I even have some ideas about what that might be. I'm mainly resisting the impulse because I can't tell if my urge to share with him is genuine, or because I want to see him fail to listen, as if that will somehow validate all of the awful things I've thought and said about him this year.

In the end, the desire to share wins out. There is something I've been thinking about lately, and I just haven't quite found the right time to talk to my friends or my brother about it.

"I do feel a bit like I'm failing at life at the moment, and it's not just our divorce that makes me feel that way." *OMG, am I really having this conversation with Paul, of all people?* He looks at me in surprise, and I feel myself flush. "I mean, there's this whole list of things I always thought I'd have done by now."

"Such as?"

"Such as…well, a lot of things actually. I mean, I really thought I'd have at least traveled a bit by the time I turned thirty…and here I am, thirty-four years old and the only time I ever left the US was on our honeymoon."

"We didn't exactly explore Belize on that trip either," Paul points out.

"We had a great time," I say wryly. "But it hardly counts as travel when you barely leave your hotel room for eight days. We could have just holed up in the Plaza Hotel and had pretty much the same experience."

"I'd like to say sorry about that, but that was one of the best weeks of my life so I don't think I can sincerely apologize for it," Paul laughs. "So, where would you go, if you were going to travel?"

"I don't even know. I'm mildly curious about loads of places, but it's the experience of traveling that I feel I missed. I always wanted to do something adventurous and dramatic, you know? But after high school, I went right to college. Then after college,

I went straight to work and then once I had a job, I was just sucked into working life."

"I hear what you're saying," Paul murmurs thoughtfully. "Adult life just kind of started for you, then bam! Suddenly you're in your thirties. Right?"

"Right," I say, but then bark a surprised laugh. "Wait—was that active listening I just saw, Paul Winton?"

He laughs sheepishly. "Maybe. Was it convincing?"

"It was entirely convincing." And more than a little shocking. "How on earth did *you* learn about active listening?"

"Don't change the subject," he scolds. "Do you think you went right to work because you were trying to prove to your mom that going to college was the right decision? You were offered a scholarship to a ballet school after high school, weren't you?"

"Yeah," I confirm weakly. "I turned it down."

"And Veronica disapproved, right?"

"That's the understatement of the century. Mom was livid."

Maybe I had some measure of raw talent for dance, but I lacked something equally important in that sphere—passion for the craft of it. You simply cannot commit to a professional career in ballet if performing fills you with dread and the thought of dozens of hours of practice each week makes you want to break your own ankle. By the time I turned eighteen, I'd endured fourteen years of ballet lessons at Mom's urging, but I couldn't continue to live my life pursuing her dreams.

"I never understood that," Paul says thoughtfully. "I remember we talked about that when we were dating and I couldn't quite figure out why you dancing mattered so much to your mom. I mean, Dad encouraged me to focus on math instead of coding, but I don't think he really cared that I decided to forge my own path."

"Mom only wanted two kids. She wanted a boy and a girl—a perfect pigeon pair."

"So why have seven?" Paul asks me blankly.

"Dad wanted to stop after Zach." I sigh. "But Mom wanted her princess, and I think she was determined to just keep on having babies until she had a girl. She wanted a pretty daughter to dress up in pink dresses, a girl she could take to the salon with her. And maybe most of all, she wanted a daughter who could achieve all of the ballet dreams Mom herself couldn't achieve because her knee gave out when she was seventeen."

"She was trying to live through you."

"And she had no shame about that fact," I mutter. "But that's sometimes how it goes with dance moms. Unfulfilled and unresolved hopes and dreams make excellent fuel for pushy parents."

The day I told her I wasn't going to take the scholarship, Mom told me I'd broken her heart and then she wept for hours. But I expected a reaction like that—I knew before I even sat down with her that day that we'd probably never come back from my decision. I was used to disappointing Mom by then.

"I can't imagine you were a kid who wanted to wear pink dresses and go to the salon," Paul says, cautiously. His gaze drops down over my running clothes, then shoots back guiltily to my face. I'm in tights and a tank today, but not just because I've been running. I wear clothes like this pretty much all of the time because they feel the most natural and comfortable to me.

"No, I didn't want to play makeup and wear fluffy dresses, I wanted to drag my crazy curls up into a ponytail, pull on some sweatpants and head out to climb trees with my brothers in the yard. Enduring several ballet classes a week for all of those years was my way of trying to appease her, but it couldn't go on forever. I think refusing the scholarship was as much an act of rebellion against her as it was me trying to find my own path in life," I admit, then joke, "This might shock you, but I can be pretty stubborn."

Paul and I share a grin that's only a little uncomfortable.

"You're right. I guess as soon as I decided I'd go to college, I was focused on showing Mom I'd made the right decision. So even when my friends graduated and went off working in bars while they backpacked around Europe before they came back to look for internships, I didn't dare follow them because I thought Mom would see that as an admission of failure. So I went right to work and made sure to call home every weekend to rave about how much

I loved every second of my job." I wrap my arms around my waist and look at my feet, suddenly and unexpectedly exposed. "That's pretty stupid, now that I think about it."

"You wanted her to be proud of you, Bel. That's understandable. But it's not too late for you to travel, right?"

"Of course it's not. But I couldn't just take off for a year like that anymore."

"It doesn't have to be a year at a time, does it? There are ways to cram adventure around a career. You know all too well what my work schedule is like, but I found time to go hiking with Jake a few months ago," Paul says.

I give him a skeptical look. "Hiking?"

"It was Jake's idea, obviously." Paul grimaces. I laugh. "We met up in Kentucky and we hiked the Red River Gorge for two weeks. No phone, no laptop, no internet, no electricity."

"No phone?"

"Well, Jake carries a satellite phone for emergencies with his patients." Jake is an oncologist, working out of a clinic at Stanford, so that makes sense. "But I actually left my cell behind when I flew out."

"That must have been quite a shock to your system."

"The first night was. I couldn't wind down, I just kept thinking about what was happening at the office and all of the work I didn't get done before I left. But the second night I started to relax, and I guess I adjusted after that. When it was time to come home,

I didn't want to leave." He pauses, then grins. "Do you remember when Marcus wanted us to go camping a few years back?"

"Yeah." I laugh, too, even as I shake my head. "He thought Abby would be open to the idea if I went."

"And the kicker was…?"

"No showers and no flushing toilets," I finish. Paul was mildly interested at least at first, and I knew I could manage a few days in a tent, but I refused to entertain the idea once I learned there were no restrooms.

"Well, you were onto something with the shower thing," he assures me. "After twelve days of just bathing in streams and hiking ten hours a day, it's fair to say Jake and I were the least popular people on the bus on the way back to the hotel. But it was such a great experience and I want more of that. I love the idea of going off-grid now…maybe even training properly so I can do an endurance hike. Something like the Torres del Paine hikes in Chile, or maybe I'll take a few months' leave from the business and do the Appalachian Trail? I don't know when, but at some point, I just want to take on a big challenge and disconnect from the world for a while. I wouldn't take my cell, or even a camera. I'd just see things and hear things and taste things, you know?"

"I actually love the idea of experiencing a new place and being completely mindful while you do."

"Exactly. Anyway, I'm only telling you that because if I learned anything from that experience, it's that travel has this way of opening your eyes to things you didn't even know you'd enjoy. I hope you do travel, Bel. But don't convince yourself you have to do it in a big block or blow up your career. You could make short trips, and if you can get past the bathroom thing, I actually do think you'd like hiking."

We share a smile, but mine fades rapidly as I realize that we have accidentally just discovered that we still do have things in common, even things we never knew about. This leaves me feeling surprisingly uncomfortable, and so I awkwardly change the subject.

"I have other things I wanted to do, too, besides travel. I have this secret bucket list no one knows about. It's just silly things…like getting a cat. And learning how to knit. Taking a cooking class. And there are things I want to experience but have no control over. I'd like to win something, even just a dumb raffle would do. I'd love to see a flash mob."

"A flash mob?" He looks at me blankly, and I blush.

"It looks like a random thing, but a big group of people get together and do an organized dance in a public place. You can watch them on YouTube."

It occurs to me suddenly that each of our unspoken hopes and dreams says something about us. For Paul, this newfound love of hiking is probably rooted in the reality that he's most comfortable alone. And while I grew to loathe dancing myself, I have always loved to watch it. A well-choreographed group of dancers is like a single organism, each individual dancer a cell working in perfect harmony with the troupe. I'm still fascinated by the way the human body can perform that unique magic, telling a story without a single word. I think that's why the idea of a public performance with no agenda other than to bring joy to a random audience thrills me so much.

"A cat, huh?" Paul says suddenly.

"I know you're allergic to cat hair. That's why I never mentioned it." I smile sadly.

"I don't even remember telling you that."

"Me either, but I know it, so I guess you did."

"You were always so good at paying attention to the little things," he murmurs, and the light flush on my cheeks intensifies.

"But slightly less good at fixing broken Wi-Fi," I muse, deflecting the compliment with another joke. "Well, what's something I don't know about you?"

"I know memory lane didn't work so well for us back at the café," he says after a pause. "But there is something I'd like to tell you about, if you'll allow me a brief reference to the past."

"Well, we've been civil to one another for—" I make an exaggerated display of checking my watch "—almost an hour now, so we're well overdue for an argument. Just make it a good one."

We share a slightly awkward laugh, but when Paul sobers, he points to the laneway that leads to the beach in front of the vacation home. It's a wordless question: we can walk back that way and it's a more scenic trip over the private beach that fronts our whole street, but it takes longer because there are patches of rock we'll need to climb across. I'm in no hurry to wind this conversation up or get back to the house, so I nod in silent agreement, and we start off down the path.

"Remember the night I asked you to marry me?" he asks.

I swallow. Hard. "Asked?" I say lightly.

"I know. It wasn't really a question, was it? More a...suggestion."

We're living together anyway, so I think we should get married.

"No." I pause. "It wasn't really a question."

"I threw up twice that night."

I frown at him. He's looking ahead along the beach, and I suspect he's pretending not to notice my eyes on his face.

"You were sick that day?"

He laughs quietly. "Sick with nerves, maybe. I threw up before I asked you, and then after you said yes and you were calling your family to tell them, I threw up again. I think that second one was from relief, but when I told Jake that story, he told me 'nausea due to relief isn't recognized medical phenomena.'"

"That is not true," I say, and I'm not sure why I sound so defensive. "You weren't even nervous!"

Paul barks a laugh, then gives me a pointed look, and I realize he's serious.

"But..." I begin.

"...but I seemed so calm?" he guesses.

I nod, still frowning.

"You told me once you'd dreamed of getting married in the summer. And it was already spring, so I thought if you did say yes, we could get married right away. Honestly, I just couldn't wait another second. But we'd only been dating for eight months—hell, we'd only been living together for a few weeks. Things seemed great, but I knew it was early, and I had no idea if you would say yes or no, so I tried to play it cool. If you said no, I didn't want you to know how disappointed I'd have been."

"I can't believe you ever thought I might say no," I say blankly. "I mean, it was the worst proposal *ever* and I didn't even care."

"That's the funny thing about life, isn't it?" Paul stops to pick up a rock from the sand, then he skips it out into the water. "I was scared you'd say no and I'd make an idiot of myself by asking, so I put zero effort into it, which probably only increased the chances of you saying no. Sometimes, the very things we do to protect ourselves from failure are the same things which make failure more likely."

"That's insightful, Paul. I'm impressed."

"I've had a lot of time to think this year," he says as he resumes his path along the beach.

"That's pretty obvious. But why did you tell me that?"

"I read a book about relationships a few months ago. The premise was basically that we understand a person by the parts of them we can see. So, most relationships aren't actually between two people, but rather between two masks. But for authentic connection, you need to look behind the masks. The longer you think you've known someone, the harder that is to do, because your preconceived ideas about a person become a part of the mask you see."

He shrugs. "I figured after everything you and I have been through already in the last few years, the only way we're going to re-form a relationship is to change the way we see each other. I can't fix what's happened between us in the past, but I can ask you questions to redefine how I see you, and I can let you peek behind the mask to understand me. What better place to start than by showing you what was really going on for me at one of the most important moments of our shared history?"

His tone barely modulates as he talks, and he's looking out toward the water again, his expression neutral. If someone listened only to his voice and not the words, they might assume he was talking about something exceedingly dry…economics or programming or politics. Paul's speech often defaults to this same flat effect, but it is more than unusual for him to show such insight into something as abstract as forming genuine relationships.

"Profound," I whisper, almost to myself. It's almost like Paul has taken all of that astounding intellectual curiosity and focus, and applied it to learning how to connect with people.

"It's not my material," he assures me with a quiet smile. "Don't give me the credit. I can lend you the book if you like, I've still got it at home."

"I wasn't talking about the analogy. I was talking about the way you applied it to our situation."

"Anyway, enough of all that," Paul says, for the first time looking almost self-conscious. "It's only a matter of time before we stop having deep and meaningful moments and start having furious ones if we don't change the subject. How are your brothers?"

I laugh weakly. "It's weird with all of them now, except Noah."

Paul climbs over a section of rock, then extends his hand to me and helps me do the same. When we're on the gritty sand again, I say quietly, "They worry about me, but when they try to express that, they end up smothering me."

Five of my brothers are scattered in other cities all over the country, so the only one I regularly see in person is the youngest of my brothers, Noah. He lives in Brooklyn with his partner Emma, and the three of us catch up for a meal every few weeks. But since I left Paul, I feel like the rest of my family has kicked into some overdriven support mode.

"Until last year, I hardly ever spoke to them. Remember? Maybe I'd text each brother every now and again or occasionally have a video chat with them to see their various kids, but now, my phone runs hot with some contact from my family every day," I say. "Even Todd, who had never sent me an email in his life before this year, has started regularly emailing me links to self-help sites and articles like 'Should you reconcile with an ex?' and 'Ten ways to get over a breakup' or 'Navigating online dating in your thirties.'"

"Can you forward some of those to me? They sound like really helpful articles," Paul says dryly.

I chuckle. "I mean, what is Todd even doing on those sites? Is he sitting around between earthmoving jobs reading *Cosmopolitan*? And Zach calls me every Tuesday night at 6:00 p.m., so I know he's set a reminder in his phone, and I don't know why he bothers because I teach Tuesday nights at six so he only ever gets my voice mail. Will has visited New York 'for business' six times this year, and each time he stays with me in my teeny tiny loft and we make awkward small talk until he packs his bag and goes home again. Jane recently told me she's getting annoyed with him for leaving her alone with the kids so often. She's convinced he comes for meetings he could have easily done via video conference because he just wants an excuse to check in on me."

"And let me guess, Chad is full of helpful advice?"

"At Christmas, he pulled me aside so he could mansplain nutrition and health to me because apparently I'm too skinny now."

"I'm guessing that went down well."

"He hasn't eaten a vegetable in two decades and the farthest he's walked since he left college is to his car, so no, it didn't go down well," I mutter.

"I'm guessing Owen and Janine would be offering you lots of helpful tips, too."

I laugh softly. "Oh yeah. He got a job at a new church, did you hear?"

"No, I haven't kept abreast of Parker family gossip." Paul winces.

"Owen's pastoring in Iowa now. He calls me every few weeks, even though the calls are brief and consist mostly of him booming questions at me, and he doesn't really give me the time to answer before he leaps off the phone. Whenever I talk to Janine, she makes judgy comments about loyalty and 'fixing what's broken instead of throwing it away.'"

"Ouch."

"Only Noah and Emma actually listen to me. I guess I'm just lucky that the easiest of all of my brothers happens to be the one who lives closest to me."

"And your parents?" Paul asks.

"Dad keeps trying to convince me to move back to Chicago…"

"Will you?"

"Definitely not." I shudder. "Not while Mom lives there."

Paul laughs.

"Instead of property, maybe we should have divvied up family in the divorce," I say. "I'd happily swap a few of my brothers for Jake."

"Your family is a lot," Paul says, with surprising diplomacy.

"I know they all mean well. But Mom in particular just does not understand why I left—" I trail off, realizing that once again, I've flipped the conversation right back to the divorce, and Paul and I sigh simultaneously.

"It's hard to avoid, isn't it?" he remarks.

"It takes real effort," I agree.

"Worth it, though, don't you think?"

I glance at him. It's still early, and the sunlight is still golden, illuminating his face against the backdrop of the sea. There are new lines in his face this year, but they only add a depth of maturity. When he turns to smile at me suddenly, I forcibly extinguish the butterflies in my stomach and make myself return a friendly smile.

"You know what, Paul?" I say faintly. "It really is."

CHAPTER TWELVE

Paul

As I FOLLOW Isabel into the house, the first thing I do is check the time on the clock on the wall over the sofa. It's 9:03 a.m., and I know Jess will be in the office. She doesn't usually come into the office on Saturday, but when there's a retreat scheduled, she makes a point of being there.

Even after working together on our software for twelve years, Jess still doesn't know a variable from an operator. She's no more a programmer than I am a people person. But she comes in anyway and she makes an awful lot of walks to the printer on those weekends, strolling casually past the huge glass wall that separates the development team from the corporate teams.

If she sees my team getting weary, she'll order a round of coffees. When the big screen above our team bull pen shows we're making progress on a tough set of tasks, she'll fly into the room in a flurry of excited pride to lift morale. When it's time for meals, she's handing out the napkins and packing up the trash afterward. If snacks run low, she personally collects the order and makes the trip to the bodega.

Jess is the CEO—but more than that—she's a leader in the truest sense of the word. She's a notorious hard-ass and as ruthless a businessperson as you can imagine. Jessica Cohen also taught me everything I know about leading by example.

Twelve months ago, I'd have been at work for seventy-two hours straight this weekend, sleeping at the armchair in my office, personally supervising every line of code. I'd have fretted like a parent with a sick infant. I'd have felt every failure personally. I'd have felt every success in my soul.

Now?

Things have changed. It's not that I don't care… it's just that I can't quite make myself care *enough,* and I don't actually know what that means. Marcus was right yesterday when he said I wasn't bringing my A-game. I'm not even playing at the JV level at the moment, and that's why the company is in a tough spot. I need to get my shit together, and fast.

But "getting my shit together" is actually what this weekend is all about. And right now, I do need to call Jess, even if I'm not yet calling to check in on the retreat.

"I need to make some calls," I say. Isabel is at the sink, pouring herself a glass of water. She smiles and nods. "The Wi-Fi password is *KatherineMinola.* No space, but both words are capitalized."

"Katherine Minola…?" she repeats, then she scowls.

"As in, Katherine Minola, the shrew from *The Taming of the Shrew*?"

I wince and wonder if I should have waited until she'd put the glass down before I told her that.

"Sorry. It seemed funny at the time. I can change it if you want. Actually, I'll change it to *Edward-Hyde*, from *Dr. Jekyll and Mr. Hyde*, because that seems more fitting now."

Isabel chuckles softly and waves me toward the stairs. "Go make your calls, Dr. Jekyll. I'll catch you later."

I climb the stairs and scoop my phone off the dresser. It's still powered down after my calls yesterday, so I fire it up as I step out onto the balcony off the master bedroom. At the last minute, I pull closed the sliding glass door behind me. I don't think Isabel would eavesdrop, but I'm also not sure she realizes the role Jess played in us both arriving here yesterday. I need to think about whether or not I should tell her.

It's a magnificent day out, and I drop onto the sun chair and close my eyes for a moment, taking it all in. There's a lot going on today, and I'm actually feeling a little overwhelmed. The salt air. The sunshine. Isabel. I can still smell her on my skin from last night. I never want to shower again, because that's the very best kind of sensory overload.

Even if the flash of pleasure I feel just thinking about Isabel's scent on my skin makes me wary.

Today is either a very good day indeed or a deceptively peaceful day that's going to turn to shit at any second. I've been so angry and unhappy this year. I can't even bring myself to enjoy the pleasant aspects of this moment because I'm already thinking about what might come next. That's the kind of fast-forward living I try to avoid at all costs these days.

I slide my phone from my pocket. Jess is number two on my speed dial—right under Isabel, who is still at number one, even though I haven't actually called her in months. I should probably delete her entry. My wedding band glints in the sun beside my hovering finger. Staring down at the phone, my inability to accept the change in my life is mocking me, all at once.

Change is hard for me, even at the best of times, but I'm certainly capable of it. I've more than proven that to myself this year, having adopted this entirely new way of relating to the people in my life.

Embracing change that feels wrong is a whole other story, though. I know Isabel and I are done, but I still can't quite convince myself to cut these last symbols of our relationship from my life. I abandon my plans to delete Isabel's speed dial entry yet again, and instead, stab at the phone to call Jess.

"I was just going to call you! Where the fuck are you? I specifically *reminded* you to be at the retreat!"

She's trying to sound hard-assed, and generally that's her default state, so she's pretty well practiced at it and the sentence should be more convincing than it is. Now that I'm aware of her ruse, the sharp edge to her tone is feeble, and the whole announcement winds up sounding like a somewhat hopeful question.

"I can't believe I let you manipulate me into coming down here. It hadn't even crossed my mind to take some time out this weekend," I say quietly. "I have to admit, Jess—now that I've calmed down, I'm almost impressed."

"I just planted a seed," she says, her tone softening just a little. "The soil must have been pretty fucking fertile for it to have taken."

"And you tricked Isabel into her visit, too?"

She hesitates, and for a moment, I think she's going to play dumb—but then there's a grin in her voice as she says, "*Tricked* is a strong word, Paul."

"What is this, Jess?"

"Just a pathetic attempt to get two people I care deeply about back on speaking terms, so we can all hang out every now and again. You see, Paul, I'm a selfish cow and I really miss the days when I didn't have to get UN negotiators in to formalize a peace agreement between two of my closest friends just to throw a New Year's party," she says flatly, then she adds hopefully, "Is it working?"

I rub my eyes wearily. "We haven't killed each other. At least not yet. We've talked a little bit." We've talked a lot, actually, at least by the standard set by our last year of marriage. That thought startles me, and I pause to ponder it some more.

We really had fallen into a pattern of spending most of our time together in silence—but it wasn't a warm, companionable silence. We just existed side by side, each of us living a different life. I was so focused on work that last year we were together, but what was Isabel focused on during those long months? Why didn't I notice, or think to ask her at the time? Maybe I didn't even realize how far apart we'd drifted. Maybe I'm only just realizing it now.

What is Isabel doing inside right now? I actually want to go back in there and spend some more time with her. And that's curious. Especially given that if you'd asked me yesterday morning whether I wanted to spend a day with Isabel, I'd probably have pulled a muscle from laughing too hard.

"I'll call this project a success, then, since all I was hoping for was for you two to actually communicate," Jess says quietly.

"Is that really all you were hoping for?"

"I mean, you two sorting your shit out and getting back together would be a bonus, too." She snorts. "But it was hard enough to get you two to have a conversation. Anything more would require magic way above my pay grade."

Hearing Jess joke about me and Isabel leaves me feeling a little uneasy. I think about that breakfast and the almost-argument we got into over something so small, and about how the tension between us simmers right there at the surface and it just takes a scratch of the veneer we've painted over it for the pain and anger to bubble out.

No, Isabel and I will never be a couple again. We could never find a way back to where we once were. A friendship is a hard enough ask given the depths we've descended to in the recent past.

"Paul," Jess says suddenly.

"Yeah?"

"Let me just say this, and I'll leave you to deal with this weekend how you see fit. I see you every day, I see her several times a week. Time isn't helping you, and it's sure as shit not helping Izzy. It's been...what? Ten months since she left? Well, you're both still fucking miserable. I know you're thinking that something magical is going to happen next Wednesday when the divorce is finalized and you're finally going to feel better...but think back to your wedding day. Did you feel any different after you signed that certificate? Did you love her any more after the ceremony than you did before it?"

I don't answer that question. I don't need to.

Jess waits just a moment. "All I'm saying, Paul, is that you both seem to think that this milestone is going to magically heal something, and I know you're going to be sorely disappointed."

"I appreciate your concern for me. And for Izzy. But you should probably... I don't know. Mind your own fucking business every now and again."

"I'll take that under advisement," Jess says.

I move to farewell her with a casual "I'll talk to you later," but before I can hang up, she laughs.

"Aren't you even going to ask me how Audrey is handling the retreat?"

"I don't need to ask. You sent me here, so you must have figured out even before I did that the team will be better off without me this weekend."

"Touché." Jess chuckles.

I stand, open the door and step back into the bedroom. The walls immediately feel like they're closing in on me, so I toss the phone onto the nightstand and head back down to the living room. Isabel is sitting on the sofa now, staring thoughtfully into what's left of her glass of water.

"Didn't the password work?" I prompt her.

She glances up and offers me a tentative smile, and the transformation on her face is breathtaking. Her eyes brighten and the tiredness lifts, and that makes me smile, too. For a minute we just stand there. Apparently, neither one of us is sure what to do next.

I want to spend more time with her.

I don't know if I have a right to ask for that, or how to ask for it, or even if it's a good idea to ask for it, or even—

"Remember when we used to rent those bikes?" she blurts.

I look at her in surprise. "That is a fucking fantastic idea," I say.

"It is?" It was her idea, but she doesn't seem convinced. I, on the other hand, have no doubts at all. We used to love biking together—it was one of our favorite things to do as a couple when we were in

Long Island. I'm also more than relieved that I didn't have to come up with an excuse to keep hanging out with her.

"It is," I assure her. "Let's go."

CHAPTER THIRTEEN

Isabel

AT FIRST, BIKE RIDING seems like a genius idea on my behalf. We can do it together, which for some bizarre reason, we both seem to want. But I know we won't talk while we ride, because we never did, and today that's probably for the best. This morning has been relatively civil, in the scheme of things, but I think we're both wary about how long that will last.

We head north, navigating the curves of Route 25 through East Marion. I'm in front for the first few miles, but then, as we pass the village of Orient, Paul silently switches to take the lead. We turn south toward Orient Beach State Park and travel along the narrow peninsula.

I try to force myself to pay attention to the pine-tinged breeze that filters through the nearby maritime forest, and the glistening waters of the Peconic River and Little Bay beside us...and not on Paul's muscular arms and shoulders and ass, which are now right in front of my face and putting up a pretty fierce fight in the battle for my attention.

And suddenly, I can't help but wonder if he was

equally tortured as we made the first leg of this journey. Is that why he moved? Was this position as distracting to him as it is to me?

Not for the first time, I wish that physical attraction was enough, because ours is every bit as potent as it was that very first night all of those years ago. Sure, our sex life went through seasons—patches where we couldn't keep our hands off one another, periods where things were calmer…but right to the very end, I wanted him desperately, and I knew he wanted me.

Maybe that's why, even now and as we ride, I find myself wanting him all over again.

And that's when this bike ride idea of mine stops feeling genius and starts to feel torturous. Because we aren't talking about the past, but I'm sure as fuck thinking about it. I'm thinking about the other times we rented bicycles to take this very route, and how we'd get back to the house, sweaty and exhausted, and we'd strip each other as we tumbled into the shower. Sometimes we'd wash each other off and rush back to the bed, our skin still hot from the exercise and damp from the shower. Other times we wouldn't even make it that far—he'd take me up against the wall of the shower. I also remember us going at it on a hastily assembled carpet of towels on the floor of the en suite more than once.

The tiredness and our familiarity with each other would make things more real somehow—stripping away any pretense that it was just sex—we were giving and receiving love from each other. Our

lovemaking was raw and simple in those moments.
Perhaps that's what made it so beautiful.

"Ice cream," Paul says suddenly, his voice husky.
He pulls to the side of the road and brakes so fast
and hard the tires on his bike squeal, but he comes
to a stop just beside me. Our eyes meet and lock
and I know he's thinking about those very same encounters.

I think we both know it's best that we don't keep
reenacting them, but we can't help reliving them in
our minds, at least not when we keep setting ourselves up in the same patterns of behavior that always led to us getting naked together.

"Ice cream," I repeat weakly.

"Let's cycle back and get ice cream in the village.
Let's do something else instead of going straight
home."

"Before we go back to the house," I correct him,
because I don't want him to call it *home*. We don't
have a home anymore, but *the house* seems less harsh
than saying, *Well, actually, Paul—it's* my *home now,
not ours, and sure as hell not yours*.

Paul looks at me, a flash of confusion in his gaze,
but hot on its heels is understanding and even agreement, because it isn't our home anymore at all, and
of course we shouldn't call it that. He nods curtly,
and then we turn the bikes back. It's not safe or even
courteous, but we ride side by side as we begin the
return journey.

"If only sex were enough, right?" he says suddenly.

I glance at him, and then we both start to laugh. Just like that, the tension shatters.

"When I suggested the bike ride, I forgot what it always led to," I admit.

"Me, too. Or I'd never in a million fucking years have agreed to it." Paul's blue eyes are sparkling with mirth, and I'm startled to realize that maybe I actually like this version of him—this carefree man who's a million miles away from his real life and the career that consumes him entirely in the city.

"You agreed to this because it's the one thing we always did together that involved absolutely no talking," I grin. This is one of those bizarre moments that have transpired today where I can nearly forget we are bitter almost-divorcees. We might have been lifelong friends who laugh together and hang out just for fun.

"There are other things we used to do which involved absolutely no talking," he says with a pointed waggle of his eyebrows.

I burst out laughing all over again. "Even sex involves some talking. When we rented the bikes out here, we'd cycle for hours without a word."

His grin fades, just a little, but then he ponders this for a moment. "Hey," he says, and the faded grin shifts until it's a frown. "You're right."

"Of course I am," I said, then I add lightly, "We'd ride single file for miles and miles in total silence."

"That's not why we liked it."

"Um, it's why *you* liked it. You're definitely happiest in your own head, Paul Winton," I laugh quietly. "This was an activity where you could pretend to spend time with me without actually having to engage with me at all."

"Plus I could stare at your ass for hours, and back then, I knew it would lead to hot shower sex at the end." He sighs.

"And there was that, of course," I agree.

I'm still enjoying myself—still joking around, which is why I almost fall off the bike when Paul says without any humor whatsoever, "I actually thought riding together was quality time for us. This kind of leisure time is one of the few things I was sure I was getting right. It checks all the boxes—you love exercise and the outdoors and Long Island and…it never even occurred to me that when we were busy together like this, we weren't actually connecting at all."

I pull to the side of the road and stop. Paul doesn't react quickly enough to stop with me, instead he has to spin the bike around to face me. His expression is a deep-set frown, and I'm completely bewildered by an instinct to defend him. The smile fades from my face, and I stare back at him, now totally unsure of what to say in response.

"It says a lot, doesn't it? You saw those same hours as me shutting you out. That must have been lonely for you," he says. His eyes widen suddenly, as if this is the first time he's even considered this possibility. "In those last few years we hardly talked at all and I didn't even notice it at the time, not until today when I realized the dynamic was different at breakfast."

He glances away thoughtfully, but then returns his gaze to mine, his eyes blazing with curiosity he asks, "Is that why you left?"

I stare at him in disbelief for a long moment before it occurs to me: Paul is spoiling for an argument here. I just don't understand *why*. Why on earth would he take such a pleasant, easy moment between us and try to implode it like this?

"What do you mean, is that why I left?" I scowl. "You say that like it's a fucking mystery. You know damn well why I left."

Paul just stares right back at me.

I remember Abby's comment on the phone about him being blindsided by the end of our marriage, and for the very first time, I allow myself to entertain the possibility that she might be right about that. It just makes no fucking sense, because I'd been telling and showing him how unhappy I was for months, and I know I explained myself yet again that last night. Even so, an odd adrenaline burst leaves me feeling dizzy and defensive. "But…I told you that night. I said—"

"You probably said a lot of things that night, Isabel," Paul interrupts me, a little stiffly. "That doesn't mean I heard any of them."

I remember that he was staring at me with that glazed look in his eyes, as if I was *boring* him. I suppose, on some level, I should be reveling in the fact that I was right about my suspicion that he hadn't actually been listening to me at all, but I'm not. I'm hurt, and I'm insulted by the casual way he's just confirmed what I feared all along.

He didn't care enough to pay attention, even in the death throes of our marriage. I thought I was leaving him to shock him into action to save us, but he didn't actually love me enough to listen even when I put it all on the line.

I'm seconds away from shouting at him or bursting into tears—maybe both. A strand of my hair has come loose from my helmet and falls over my eye and I push it back impatiently, noting in some dark recess of my mind that my hand is shaking violently. We're standing on a public but thankfully deserted road by the water, and what was a very pleasant, friendly outing less than two minutes ago now has the potential to turn into an all-out brawl between us.

And I want to yell and shout, but this time, I don't. I'm just so tired of being furious with him—so tired of the emotional displays that became the new baseline of our interactions since the mediation. Now, there's not even anything left to fight for, so why would I bother? I *am* sorry for how ugly our separation has become, but when it's all said and done, I owe him nothing. I was happy spending time with him today because he promised we could avoid looking back at our ugly past, but I do not owe him a rehash of the worst night of my life.

"I'm going back to the house," I say abruptly.

"What? We were just talking—"

"Why did you have to do this now?" It seems I can't help but take one last dig, even as I hate myself for wasting my energy. "Couldn't you just let me pretend for one day that we could actually be friends again?"

"Just tell me exactly what I did to upset you just now," Paul says. He rubs the back of his neck, then exhales heavily. "Isabel, I wasn't trying to start an argument. You just pointed out an error of judgment on my part, I was making an attempt to understand how far it went. How could that possibly make you angry?"

"Because I wasted years of my life trying to get through to you about this shit!" I exclaim, and then I hiss, "You didn't care enough to listen then, and now you sit here and act as if I just walked away without a fight!"

"Does it occur to you that maybe we're not hearing each other even now?" Paul shifts on the bike, then straightens himself to his full height. "Or that maybe the problem isn't just that I wasn't listening to you, but that you weren't actually explaining yourself clearly? Yes, I made mistakes, but I'm trying to learn from them. I've spent almost every minute since you left thinking about the man I was and trying to make sure that's the man I actually want to be. You, on the other hand, remain entirely convinced that I'm somehow this ice-cold monster and that justifies you using me as a verbal punching bag whenever we're in the same space. I just don't understand why it hasn't even occurred to you that maybe it took two of us to fuck our marriage up."

My emotions have shifted from weary to furious

so fast, I'm struggling to keep up. I can't listen to this anymore—there is just no point. I adjust my position on my bike and throw him one last, scathing look before I set off at a breakneck pace.

"Fuck you, Paul. Just fuck you."

I hear him call after me again but I ignore him, cycling faster to put some distance between us. He could catch up to me easily, but he won't.

I know all too well now that when I run away upset, Paul doesn't bother chasing after me.

I'M USUALLY A very neat traveler, but then again, I'm not usually rushing to make a train that's due to depart the station on the other side of the island in less than fifteen minutes. My Uber will be here in four minutes, and I'm cutting it close. If I miss this train, I'll either have to pay for a car to take me all the way back to the city, or I'll be waiting until almost 10:00 p.m. tonight for the next one. I don't have time to pack my bag with care the way I usually would.

I don't even have time to stop and think about whether or not I actually want to leave. All I know is that this little attempt at cohabiting with Paul for one last weekend is failing miserably. There were moments this morning where I wondered if he had changed enough that we could be in one another's lives again, but if that interaction on the bike path proved anything, it's that Paul and I can't even be friends these days. There are just too many sore points between us now.

I need to get out of here. *Where* is that sweater

I was wearing last night? Probably somewhere in the living room, because now that I think about it, I stripped it off in a desperate hurry when I was on the sofa in the process of making yet another mistake with Paul.

I jog out of the bedroom to scan for the sweater—but my gaze instead lands on Darby's tulips…and then slides down to Paul's laptop, still sitting right beside the vase. Paul's broken laptop. The one he has definitely not looked at for over twenty-four hours, because I've had his full attention for that entire time. The sweater is on the floor beside the dining room table, so I should run to pick it up, then run back to my room to keep packing, but I don't.

Paul hasn't even noticed I broke his laptop yet. And I have to suspect that he hasn't noticed because other than one two-minute phone call this morning, he has been completely disconnected from his working life for at least twenty-four hours.

Because he's chosen to spend his time with me. Despite the awkwardness. Even though it takes so little for me to react and withdraw. He's more than met me halfway today, and in his typically odd, Paul way, he's actively trying to make some kind of amends.

I stare at that laptop for a minute, then walk back to the guest room to cancel my Uber.

I unpack my bag, turn on the AC, and crawl under the duvet with the TV remote in one hand and my phone in the other. I'll put on some comedy…zone out for a while. First, I check my phone. I've missed a call from Dad this morning, which is unsurprising—he hasn't called for a few days. He's left me a voice mail.

"Hello, love. It's Dad, just calling to see how you're doing. Mom and I love you. Call me back if you want a chat, otherwise I'll try you again later."

My dad is the best. There's another message waiting for me, too, from Abby.

Just checking in, Izzy. Are you okay?

I stare up at the ceiling while I calculate a reply. I've never been particularly good at math, but I figure this kind of math I have at least some small chance of success with, because I'm not actually working with figures. I'm trying to average out the day so I can figure out how to answer that question.

There have been awful moments and angry moments and awkward moments and moments of reconciliation and moments of peace. I don't know if the sum total of all of that is something good or something neutral or something that leaves Paul and me worse off than we were yesterday before we collided again.

Collided is precisely the right word. I feel like I'm recovering from a car accident this afternoon— suffering from emotional whiplash as I try to process where we find ourselves now. I just keep thinking about that laptop and Paul's comments on the bike path.

I just don't understand why it hasn't even oc-

*curred to you that maybe it took two of us to fuck
our marriage up.*

He's actually kind of right. It still seems simple
to me. We were happy, and then he started working
like a maniac and pulled away from me, and now
here we are. What I haven't thought to wonder about
in the longest time is why he pulled away. I could
never have asked the Old Paul about that. That man
wasn't focused or self-aware enough to offer me an
honest response.

But this Paul could. This Paul could also explain
to me exactly what he thought when I walked out
that door and why he didn't try to stop me...why he
didn't come after me. I even have a feeling he *would*
talk honestly and openly about those moments in
our lives.

I'm just not entirely sure that this Isabel is ready
to hear his answer.

I reply to Abby.

I'm still here. So is Paul. I'm okay. Thanks for checking in.

Then I send a message to Dad.

I'm out at Greenport for the weekend. I'll call you
guys next week. Love you, too.

I drop the phone and turn the TV on. I fix the
Wi-Fi password, and Netflix springs to life. But then
I pause, and suddenly the idea of zoning out loses

its appeal. I turn the TV back off and sink into the pillows. Instead, I stare up at the ceiling and wonder if, after all of the fierceness and all of the fighting, I'm actually brave enough to confront the root cause that led to the war.

SEVERAL HOURS PASS before Paul comes home. When he does, I hear him moving around in the living room and at first I brace myself, assuming he's finally going to try to do some work...certain he's about to thump on my door and demand to know what the hell I did to his laptop. When minutes pass and he does not, in fact, thump on my door, I wonder if he's packing up to leave.

I don't know why the thought of that is so upsetting, given I was leaving myself not so long ago. But it is upsetting. There's so much left unfinished between us, and while I'm not yet ready to go back out and face Paul again just yet, I will be disappointed if he does opt to give up on our attempts to rebuild a friendship.

After a while, I hear the screech of the slightly rusty tracks of the sliding door that leads to the deck. Once again, the house falls silent.

All of the rage and frustration inside me gradually settles, until all that remains is a muddled regret. A bewildering desire to reconnect with Paul draws me to rise. I pause at the door, my hand on the doorknob, my heart thumping against the wall of my chest.

I know exactly what I'll see on the other side of that door—I've been here dozens of times. Even so, this time, there's a question hanging over exactly what's going to happen when I step out of this bedroom. That's where my fear lies.

I open the door anyway. It's still and quiet in the living room. My gaze drifts past the table and the ostensibly still-neglected laptop, past the sliding glass doors and to the large deck that sits on the shores of the Long Island Sound. We keep the furniture on the deck packed up to protect it from the weather, but it's all set up now—even the fairy lights around the railing have been hung and are on, giving the space a romantic glow.

The grill lid is open, and I catch a hint of smoke on the air, mingling with the scent of citronella candles. Bugs don't bother Paul much, but my body tends to react badly to mosquito bites, leaving me with itchy welts that take days to fade. On the outdoor table, a bottle of wine is chilling in an ice bucket.

Paul himself is sitting in one of the outdoor chairs. He's facing away from me, but I can see that his legs are propped up on the table, crossed at the ankle. Soft music plays on the Sonos, a quiet, gentle folk soundtrack that I know he would never in a million years have chosen for himself, given his preference for silence over background noise.

He's designed this tableau just for me. In the first few years of our relationship, this was the kind of scene I'd set up for us—all of my favorite things together: eating alfresco on the deck beside the ocean, wine, steaks on the grill…and, once upon a time, him. I have a shocking suspicion that the wine will be sweet and the steaks will be grass fed and the salad will be dressed in my favorite poppy seed dressing, too. Without a single word, Paul has just sent me a series of messages.

I was paying attention to you, Isabel.
I did notice the things you loved.
Join me out here for dinner.
I want to spend time with you again.

"Are you going to join me?" he calls quietly, without shifting on the chair or turning back to face me.

I wrap my arms around my waist and slowly walk to the deck. I don't know what to say, so I slide the screen door open and step outside without a word. I take a seat beside Paul, and he sits up and reaches for the wine. Silently, he pours two glasses, and only when he hands one to me do we make eye contact. Paul looks thoughtful and guarded and sad, somehow all at once.

"This morning, I honestly thought the best way to go about this was to just move toward a friendship without us looking back at where we've come from," he says, straight to the point as always. "I thought we could just let bygones be bygones, you know?"

I take the wineglass from him, but I don't raise it to my lips. Instead, I cradle the glass between my palms, and I stare down into the pale liquid, as if it holds some kind of desperate interest for me.

"But maybe, before we take that last step and become friends again, we need to hash this out. To actually talk it all through, so ghosts stop jumping out at us every time we speak," Paul continues. He turns to me, and I can feel his gaze on my face. "I know you said today you had explained yourself enough but, Isabel, please believe me when I say that I didn't always hear what you wanted me to hear."

Yesterday, maybe I'd have leaped at the suggestion of a postmortem for our marriage, motivated by the righteous indignation that's fueled most of my decisions this year. I'd have sat him down and forced him to hear things from my perspective again—a tirade steeped in bitterness that would have launched at him like a sermon, or a long, rambling diatribe, like the one he inflicted upon me at the therapist's office.

But tonight, I feel almost bruised. There are butterflies in my stomach and my palms feel hot against the cold of the wineglass.

"I know I've been asking just one more thing from you all weekend," he murmurs, "but please, could we talk about where we went wrong? And then, and I promise you this, I won't ever ask you about it again."

"Why would we do this?" I whisper, still staring down at my wine. "Why would we put ourselves through this?"

"The same reason we both came here. The same reason we both stayed. The same reason…last night happened. The same reason you're still here tonight. We both need closure, Isabel."

We fall into silence as I consider this. After a while, Paul stands and sets the steaks on the grill. He's standing to my right, staring down at the steaks as if they need his full attention, just as I'm staring fiercely out over the water as the sun sinks lower in the sky. I try to imagine how this conversation can possibly end in anything other than one of us—almost certainly me—storming off.

"Do you think we can have this conversation without it getting ugly?" I ask him hesitantly.

"I was just thinking about that, too," he says, turning back to me. "Perhaps we just need to set some ground rules."

CHAPTER FOURTEEN

Paul

"LET'S PROMISE EACH other that however hard this is, we'll see it through to the end of the conversation. If we're doing this, let's do it properly and honestly. We tell each other the truth. No matter how painful," I say.

Isabel sits bathed in the golden rays of the dying sunlight—and she's radiant, despite the anxious, uncertain expression she's wearing. It's still and quiet out here this afternoon, other than the soft music playing.

After Isabel stormed off on our bike ride, I spent a lot of time sitting alone by the water, trying to figure out how we find our way out of the emotional maze we find ourselves lost in. The answer gradually became clear. Sometimes when you're lost, the only way out is to retrace your steps.

I knew instinctively that if I burst back into the vacation house, guns blazing to demand Isabel take this trip down memory lane with me, she'd say no. Instead, and for once in my life, I set up an inviting space for her and let my actions speak for me, trying to send an unspoken message: it's far too late to fix what once was, but you still matter to me. I still want you in my life.

Because if there's one thing I'm sure of right now, it's that I don't want this weekend to be the last time I spend time with this woman. Yes, she's stubborn and apparently bad-tempered and *utterly bewildering* sometimes, but despite all of that, I miss her in a way that just hasn't improved even with time. I know it's too late to save our marriage, but I still want to be her friend.

"Okay," Isabel says suddenly, and she sits up a little straighter in the deck chair, as if she's made her decision and she's happy with it. "I agree to that. But I'd like to ask that nothing be off-limits. We promise each other we'll answer any question, even if they make us uncomfortable."

I draw in a sharp intake of breath, then exhale, puffing out my lips. I don't like this rule, but I can't very well ask Isabel to push herself if I'm not willing to do it, too.

"Fine," I say, and I pick up my wineglass so I can return to the chair beside her before we begin, but she doesn't wait.

Instead, she simply blurts, "You pulled away from me. We were so happy over those first few years, but then somewhere along the way, you pulled away. Why did you do that? Was it something I did?"

I look at her in surprise, but it takes a second for my mind to catch up to why that question is so surprising, given I actually do know how to answer it.

No, the question itself doesn't surprise me...the way she delivers it does.

I've never been so conscious of it before, but right at this moment, it occurs to me that Isabel is rarely this direct. And just like that, something in my mind shifts, and it's like the last four years swim into a whole new focus.

Isabel speaks gently. She doesn't always say exactly what she means.

I sink into the chair beside her and take a slow, thoughtful sip of the wine, trying to process this startling realization.

"Well?" she prompts.

"It wasn't intentional," I say slowly. "Remember this morning, I told you about the night I proposed... How nervous I was?"

Her gaze softens. "Yes."

"That was eight months into our relationship, Isabel." I smile sadly. "I was already hiding things from you, even then—not that I have ever lied to you, but there were certainly aspects to my personality I didn't feel I could show you."

"But...why?"

"Mostly because I didn't actually understand myself, I think. At the time, all I knew was that sometimes I felt out of my depth in our relationship. Can I explain why with an example?"

"Of course."

"I remember this one night when we were out with everyone at that bar Jess likes with the crazy hipster cocktails."

"I hate that place. Remember when I ordered a gin and tonic and they served it deconstructed?" Isabel grimaces, then we both laugh softly. I vividly remember the look of sheer horror on her face when the bartender passed her a wooden tray containing glasses of ice, gin and tonic water, alongside a knife and a whole lemon.

"We all hate that place, except Jess, but she's very persuasive." I laugh, but quickly sober. "But no, I'm talking about a different night. You, Abby and I were sitting in a booth, Marcus and Jess were at the bar ordering us all drinks. You told me to go and see if they needed help, so I walked over and asked them, and they said no."

In fact, they seemed bewildered by my offer, which, to be honest, I was, too. And it was crowded at the bar, so it seemed stupid for me to wait with them, so I went straight back to Isabel and Abby at the booth.

"Do you remember the night I'm talking about?" I ask quietly.

She concentrates for a moment, then shakes her head.

"Abby was upset about something that had happened with her ex-boyfriend, but I hadn't noticed that she was especially quiet. You had. You wanted me to give you some privacy, so you could make sure she was okay. But when you asked me to help with drinks, I didn't hear the inference that you needed time alone with her to check in on her. I heard the literal meaning. It was only when I came back to the booth and sat back down and you glared at me and kicked me under the table that I realized I'd missed the point altogether."

"But…" Her brows knit. She turns to stare at me skeptically. "You're the smartest person I know, Paul."

"Sure," I agree. "I'm very, very good at one or two very specific things. I mean, I remember the date that happened and…" I pause, complete the calculation and tell her, "It was five hundred and sixty-five days ago, and about twenty-two hours, although I didn't note the exact time of day, so I can't tell you the minutes. *That* is easy for me. That's how my mind works. It's the same with coding—it's effortless for me to do things that even my smartest coders have to work to understand. But frankly, that's it for me. I'm hardly smart when it comes to some of the things that come naturally to almost everyone else I know."

"So…you're saying you sometimes take speech too literally?" she says, brows knitting.

"There are layers to communication. Sometimes what people say isn't at all what they mean, and a skilled communicator looks at context and body language and tone and even the speed with which a sentence is delivered. You, Isabel Winton, are a master at that shit."

Isabel is watching me closely, and I know that she's reading and understanding all of those things in me, and she doesn't even have to think about doing it.

"You subconsciously pick up on the subtle clues that reveal when a person is upset or excited or angry or confused. But for the most part, unless I'm really making an effort, I just hear words. You see conversations as a spectrum of colors and shades and patterns, and to me, it's completely black-and-white. I'm probably smart enough to bluff pretty well sometimes, but I guess in the close confines of a marriage, that only gets a guy so far. And…you…" I watch her closely as I add, "You can be quite indirect."

Her eyes widen. She pauses for a moment, and then the quietly curious expression she's been wearing shifts, until her gaze narrows, then she turns to face the water again.

"So this is my fault, then?"

I sit up from the sun chair and walk back to the grill. The steaks are sizzling nicely, not really in need of my attention, but I remain beside them, looking away from her. I'm about to split myself open in a way I just haven't done with Isabel before, and it feels risky. It's the only way forward, but even so, I can't make myself watch how she reacts.

"In the second year of our marriage, there was this period at work where things were ridiculously full-on. And I've developed this awful habit of getting involved in every little project my team has on the boil instead of delegating, so I was struggling to keep up, which just made me want to work more. At the time, I told myself you believed in me and believed in the vision of the company every bit as much as I did, so you would understand."

"I probably did understand. At first," she says. Her tone is still tight.

I stare at the steaks some more. "You know I'd had girlfriends before you."

"Yes."

"You also know they were all in the tech industry, too."

"I know."

"In hindsight, what I had with those women was casual sex. I don't think I'd had a real relationship until I met you. I'd never had to balance someone else's needs with my own. When I'm intrigued by a problem, it's all I think about. I don't even stop to eat if I'm really engaged in my work."

"Yeah." She sighs. I glance at her, and find she's drawn her knees up to her chest, and she's staring at her toes. "I do remember that."

"Before I met you, I was just a software developer with a growing startup and so my tendency to hyper focus was a strength, not a weakness. When I hit that first really busy period at the office after we got married, those problems at work consumed my entire mind. And when I emerged from those weeks, something felt off between us."

I glance at her again, and this time, I find she's looking right at me. Her brows are still drawn in, but she looks slightly less defensive.

"I was worried, Paul. You'd barely spoken to me in weeks...and yes, it was because you were consumed by the issues at work, but it scared me."

"It was careless and completely unfair of me to just disengage with you like that. But at the time, I couldn't see it quite so clearly—I felt like what I was doing was important, and I just assumed you'd respect that. I did gradually notice that maybe you weren't as affectionate as you once were or that you weren't smiling at me the same way. I'd ask you what was wrong, and you'd say, 'Nothing,' and I'd take that at face value, especially at first."

Isabel has wrapped her arms around her knees, and her chin rests atop them. She looks angry again.

I try to soften my tone. "Isabel, you must remember the dozens of times we'd have that exact same interaction. *What's wrong? Nothing.* It became a pattern for us. Something was wrong, I asked what it was, you shut me down, and as we repeated that pattern over time, our relationship was becoming yet another social space where I didn't understand the rules of the game."

"So you *are* blaming me. Because you worked hundred-hour weeks long after you had to and that hurt like hell, but it seemed obvious enough that I didn't think I had to say to you, 'Paul, when you work fifteen-hour days, seven days a week for months on end, your partner starts to feel neglected,'" Isabel says bitterly.

"I'm not blaming you," I say, but I'm already struggling to keep my frustration in check and my tone is shortening. I just don't understand why she's so unreasonable sometimes. I'm not talking about emotions here—I'm trying to explain to her a pattern in my thought processes, and a dynamic in our communication. What do I have to do to get through to this woman?

"It sure feels like you are," Isabel mutters.

"If you wanted to learn to code, I could teach you. We'd spend a few weeks learning the basics, then a few months extending your understanding and you're smart enough that a year or two from now, if you immersed yourself in that world, you'd be holding your own with the best of them. But if you and I both quit our jobs and you spent the next few years trying to teach me how to listen and relate to people the way you do, it would still never become natural to me."

Isabel sits up, then shakes her hair back from her face and turns to me. She surveys me for a moment.

"So what you're saying is, even though I was telling you how unhappy I was, you didn't listen to me. You couldn't."

"Maybe if you'd married someone like Marcus or Jake, they'd have realized that you saying 'nothing' or telling me you were 'fine' all of the damned time was a message in itself. But you didn't marry someone like that. You married me, and I had no fucking idea what was going on between us, so I guess I withdrew into my work more and more because I felt in control and capable there, which of course made everything else worse because the more I worked, the more distracted I became…and the less I focused on you, the harder it was for me to read you. The situation started with a small disconnect, but soon compounded itself."

"And your theory is that all of this started because I didn't explicitly sit you down and say, 'Paul, once or twice a week, you should actually have a conversation or a fucking cuddle with your wife,'" Isabel says grimly. She picks at some fluff on her yoga pants, then tosses it into the breeze.

"Let's keep talking while we eat." I run my hands through my hair. The steaks are ready now, so I flip them onto two plates and bring them to the table, where I take the seat opposite her. We silently serve the sides I prepared onto our plates.

"You went to Marie's," Isabel says suddenly. I nod. "This is my favorite poppy seed dressing."

"I know."

"And the steaks…"

"Grass fed, organic. Just the way you like."

"You even picked Riesling again," she whispers unevenly. "I love it. I love all of this. Even if Marcus would be mortified to see you pair such a sweet wine with these juicy steaks."

I laugh softly. "What he doesn't know won't hurt him."

"I really do feel like you're blaming me, Paul. It just doesn't seem fair," she says suddenly.

I try to survey her body language. Isabel's gaze is cast down and her mouth is set in a deep frown, but then there's that hard set of her shoulders and the flare of her nostrils. She looks both defensive and disappointed, and that triggers a memory in me. I've seen her look exactly this way at least once before.

"That last wedding anniversary. What did you *want* me to get you?"

She laughs bitterly, then sips at the wine. "I was really just hoping we'd come out here for the weekend. Things were so strained between us by then. I just wanted to reconnect. Our anniversary was on a Friday and I had the day off…"

"Right. That makes sense." I drop my fork onto the table and rub my forehead wearily. "And I bought you an iPad."

"Yes," she says. She cuts the steak with a little too much force, and the knife screeches across the plate.

"You're still angry about that, right?" I prompt her gently.

"I…" She hesitates. "Maybe."

"I found the iPad in the closet after you left, Isabel," I point out. "It was still in the box."

Isabel raises her gaze to mine. "Okay. I was angry. I was insulted, actually. It seemed like such a lazy, thoughtless gift. I can barely use my phone, and we already had your iPad in the house… Surely you'd noticed that I never showed a lick of interest in it. What on earth made you think I wanted one of my own?"

"In the weeks leading up to the anniversary, you kept telling me you wanted to read more. You told me at one point that you had taken the Friday of our anniversary off so you could relax and read. I even remember that one night you said you'd ferried so many books out here over the last few years, you really needed to actually finish reading some. You must have talked about reading a dozen times over those few weeks. Right?"

She nods, frowning, and I continue quietly, "You also started talking about the weather…you seemed to be constantly wondering what the weather was going to be like on the weekend…whether it would be nice for a bike ride…and you mentioned a few times about how it seemed like it was going to be a great summer."

"I'm always so busy in the city. I always did most of my reading out here," Isabel says defensively. "We only ever rode bikes out here. I was talking about how the weather was *here*. At Greenport."

"I realize that now. As in, three minutes ago when you told me," I say wryly. "But what I heard at the time was *Isabel wants to relax more and she relaxes by reading.* And *Isabel left the books she wants to read at the vacation home and it's a pain for her to bring them back and forth because books are heavy.* And then I was hearing *Isabel really wants more convenient access to weather data.* So I bought you an iPad, and I set up a bunch of e-reader apps on it and bookmarked some bestseller lists, and then even though I had no idea why you were suddenly so fascinated by weather data, I researched and installed a bunch of meteorological apps."

Isabel opens her mouth, then closes it. Her eyebrows knit. "I didn't even turn it on," she admits weakly. She looks at me. "That's actually really sweet."

"On the morning of our anniversary, you opened that gift and I was excited to see your reaction so I was really paying attention, which of course only meant I could see that you were disappointed. So, I said, 'Don't you like it?' And you said...do you remember?"

"I'm guessing I said, 'It's fine,'" she whispers, eyes cast downward again.

"That's exactly what you said. But even so, I knew I'd missed the mark. I just didn't understand where I'd gone wrong. And then two weeks later..."

"...I left." Isabel looks back at her plate.

"You got so angry with me today when I tried to talk about this stuff."

"I was angry because you made it sound like you had no idea why I walked out, Paul."

"I knew things between us weren't what they once were. But please believe me when I tell you that I had no idea that they were entirely broken."

"You don't remember *anything* I said to you the night I left? Or the months before that when I tried to explain to you how unhappy I was? I really, honestly felt like I'd tried everything."

"You never said to me, *Paul, I'm unhappy. Here's what's wrong.*"

She purses her lips. "No. I didn't realize I needed to."

"So what had you tried?"

"How many nights did you come home to find I'd made some huge, elaborate meal that was long cold by the time you walked through the door?" she asks me softly. She's flicking food around her plate now, pushing pieces of steak from one side to the other, but she's finished the salad. "How many times after we made love did I turn the light back on when you turned it off because you were trying to go to sleep? How many times did I 'forget' you said you were going to work on the weekend and organize plans for us?" Her voice breaks, and she pinches the bridge of her nose, visibly struggling to retain her composure. "How many nights did I come to sit in your office on the armchair while you were working?"

"Do you understand now that I didn't deliberately ignore those things? I noticed them, I just took them at face value. When you turned the light on after we made love, I thought you had things you wanted to do before you went to sleep. When you came into my office and sat on the chair behind me when I was working late at night, I thought, Isabel really likes the armchair in here for some reason. I actually thought about moving it out into the living room so you could sit in it when you watched TV. When you made those big, elaborate dinners and left them on the table to go cold, I thought you'd made something you wanted to eat and then just hadn't felt like cleaning up afterward."

"Jesus, Paul." She looks aghast.

I hesitate. "I'm just trying to be honest here. Am I upsetting you?"

"I'm upset for both of us, to be honest." She brushes her curls back from her face, then reaches for her wine. "This is what you meant today when you said we weren't hearing each other."

"Yeah, it was."

"And when I left, I felt like I'd been making every

possible effort to reach you for months, but you really hadn't noticed any that?"

"I didn't even realize you were leaving me until I saw your suitcase. It felt like my world had ended in a single moment." My voice breaks, but I don't look away from her.

Isabel's eyes are shining with tears she's not yet ready to shed.

The bitterness I was determined to suppress tonight leaks out. "If you had just told me you were unhappy, I'd have moved heaven and earth to fix things."

"I told you that night why I was going," she whispers unevenly. "We talked in the foyer before I left. You were staring at me."

"You'd asked me to be home by six, and I was brainstorming with Audrey on a problem and I lost track of time and didn't get home until 7:34 p.m. I was still thinking about work when I stepped in the front door, right up until I saw the suitcase—"

"You said, 'We should talk about this more, Isabel. We should have a meeting.' You didn't even seem surprised."

"I was panicking...in shock. I don't actually remember what I said," I admit heavily. "I'm not surprised I said something stupid. I was just trying to hold on to one last shred of dignity, because it was all I could do to stop myself from falling to my knees and begging you to stay."

"I did feel I'd tried everything. And leaving was like a last-ditch, desperate cry for help. I really thought if I left, you'd realize how unhappy I was, and you'd do something to reconnect with me. When you organized for us to see that couples counselor the next day, I thought that proved I'd done the right thing. I figured we'd go to therapy for a while and sort out what was broken and we'd fix it and I'd come home."

I stare at her in confusion. "You stayed in that room for six minutes. You didn't even explain yourself then! If you were still hoping we'd reconcile at that point, why not give therapy at least a proper shot?"

"You were brutally cold that day, Paul." She rubs her forehead, then gives me a pleading look. "You didn't sound like a man who was devastated. You sounded like an entitled man who was outraged."

"I didn't sleep at all the night you left. I was a mess."

"I felt the same. I guess when we first stepped into that office, I saw that you looked exhausted and I was kind of hopeful that we were about to make a breakthrough. You started to rant and I was getting upset and crying, but you barely looked at me. You were so arrogant and I just…I just couldn't deal with it. I hoped an impartial third party would help us to reconnect, but the truth is, I was humiliated that day. I didn't want a stranger like the therapist to see just how bad our marriage had become."

"I still see her," I admit.

"Who?"

"Alison. The therapist."

"Really? You've been in *therapy*?" Isabel's jaw hangs loose.

I shrug. "Sure. You stormed out of her office that day, I went to follow you, and Alison gave me a reality check. She told me that even in that brief conversation she'd noticed markers that suggested I might..." I break off. Am I ready to talk to her about this?

I look at Isabel, who's frowning, but she doesn't seem upset now. Instead, she seems concerned, and I'm suddenly quite certain that despite the ugliness in our past, I can trust her with this piece of myself.

"Markers?" she prompts me gently.

"Alison asked me if I'd ever been through the process of an autism assessment. She said I showed some classic markers in the way I was interacting with you."

Isabel's eyebrows shoot up, then she tilts her head to the side as she stares at me. It looks a little like a light bulb just went off in her mind, and that's exactly how I felt once Alison's comments sank in that day in her office.

"And...do you think that's the case?" Isabel asks me cautiously.

"I know it is. I eventually had the formal assessment done and my official diagnosis is Autism Spectrum Disorder, Level One. They don't use the term Asperger's syndrome anymore, but once upon a time that's probably what I'd have been diagnosed with."

"Paul...I don't even know what to say. Do I say I'm sorry?" Isabel whispers.

I shake my head. "No, this isn't a bad thing at all. I am who I am, and I'm proud of who I am. I see the world differently than some people, and sometimes that's a real strength—take my work, for example. I do have some challenges, too, but I'm aware of them now. I know, for example, that it's unusually difficult for me to be aware of what other people are thinking sometimes—it's a form of mind blindness. That's never going away, and I have to learn how to interact with the people I care about despite it."

"I just didn't realize..." There are tears in her eyes, and I'm worried that I'm messing this up.

I reach to squeeze her hand. "Please don't feel sorry for me, Izzy. I mean...I already knew I was different. I think you probably knew it, too. Having this diagnosis doesn't change who I am, it just helps me to understand myself. I actually feel relieved because I'd always struggled socially and I could never figure out why."

"But you didn't even tell me about any of this."

"I planned to at first," I admit.

"Well, what happened?" she croaks. Her gaze is dull with hurt, and I suspect mine is the same.

As Isabel and I stare right into each other's eyes, openly displaying our pain, this moment is becoming more intimate than anything we've shared before. Is this what a true partnership is about? Sharing the heights and the depths of your soul with another person? I can't help but wonder what might have been if we'd been able to stare into each other's eyes like this and to speak so freely when we were married.

"You're right when you said I was angry at first. It didn't take me long to cool down, but once I did, I started taking a good, hard look at my life, and soon I was embarrassed at my inadequacy. I didn't yet understand where we'd gone wrong, or what an ASD diagnosis was going to mean for me. For those first few weeks after you left, all I could see were my failures. I saw my relationships with the team at work and with Dad and with Jake and Marcus and Jess and you with fresh eyes, and I did not like what I saw.

"So I kept on seeing Alison and talking it all through, and I started reading and thinking and hell, just searching for ways that I could be a better person…and be a better partner to you. I realized that before I could win you back, I had to learn how to be vulnerable."

She swallows hard, then looks away.

I rub my forehead wearily. "Fuck, Isabel… I knew I needed to be a better *friend* to you, because I quickly figured out that I hadn't fulfilled that role in months. Besides, when you left Alison's office that day, you said you needed space, so I decided I'd give that to you while I worked to sort my own head out. Then the paperwork came from your attorney and once again, you'd blindsided me." I'm tensing, just remembering that day, and I can't help the way my tone shortens. "What was that about? You didn't even think to text me to tell me you wanted a divorce?"

"I wanted to hurt you," she admits. "In all of the scenarios I ran through in my head when I left, not once did I consider the possibility that you'd just let me walk away. Jesus, Paul, I didn't even start looking for a place to live for a month after I left, I just stayed at the same crappy hotel. I slept with my phone in my hand. I'd finish a class or with a client and I'd run to my desk to check my email. It was only when you didn't even contact me for my birthday that I realized we were actually done. To tell you the truth, that's when I got angry. That's when I wanted blood."

"So that's why you hired an attorney? I didn't call on your birthday?" I'm missing something. I know I fucked up, but that seems a serious overreaction.

"If you'd already given up on us, it seemed stupid and embarrassing for me to sit around waiting any longer. I just wanted to move on." Then she adds flatly, "A month of radio silence seemed to be a message in itself, Paul."

"This is what I'm trying to tell you tonight. I didn't go silent on you because I didn't want you back. I went silent on you because you said you needed space, and I was trying to respect that while I figured myself out. My silence wasn't a hint. I don't hint. I…" I struggle for words. "I can code in three languages and interpret design specs and write algorithms and calculate dates in the blink of an eye, but I can *not* hint. Do you see that now?"

Isabel crosses her arms on the table and leans forward, then slowly raises her gaze to mine. "We were barely even speaking the same language."

"That's what I figured out today…tonight."

Her eyes fill with tears, and she bites her lip. "What a fucking mess we made of things, Paul."

"I know."

CHAPTER FIFTEEN

Isabel

WE SIT IN silence for a long time. Paul refills our wineglasses, and we shift back over to the sun chairs, sitting side by side and staring out over the dark expanse of the water.

"That iPad was a final straw for me, you know," I say eventually. "That's why I left just a few weeks later. I saw it as willful ignorance... I thought you didn't want to spend the weekend with me, so you'd made some thoughtless purchase as a token gesture instead. I even imagined you sending Vanessa out to pick something up, or maybe you'd had it in the storeroom at the office and you just grabbed it on your way out the door that day."

"Why didn't you just say that? *Paul, you idiot, you misunderstood me.* And why didn't you just ask me to organize a long weekend out here? I'd have done it."

"Wouldn't that hurt your feelings?" I ask, and I glance at him for the first time since we moved to the sun chairs.

He gives me a blank look. "Because you asked for

what you wanted? Of course not." He pauses, then his eyebrows lift. "Wait, you think that just asking for what you want can hurt people's feelings?" A look of pure horror crosses his expression. "Oh Jesus, Isabel. I must have bruised your soft little heart on a daily basis."

I laugh weakly. "It wasn't that bad, but you can be particularly blunt, Paul. Remember when I asked you if I looked okay in that yellow dress I bought?"

I wasn't sure about how the dress hung—and in an odd moment of self-consciousness about my lack of curves, I was looking for reassurance. Instead, Paul told me that he didn't really understand fashion, but even so, he thought the dress was awful.

"I remember." He closes his eyes. "It's a wonder we stayed together for more than five minutes. You asked me about my new clothes the other day?" I nod, and he laughs gently. "I went to work one day and I'd put on some muscle around my pecs and my button-down kept popping open. Jess told me I looked ridiculous and that I needed to hire a stylist and update my look."

"Now Jess is a woman who can be extremely blunt," I concede. "But she's rare. I think most people communicate the way I do. Most women, especially. I mean, my mom would have an aneurysm if she heard me talk the way Jess talks to people. She'd say it's not ladylike."

"Jess never pulls punches at work. I'm certain that if I'm talking to her and she's thinking something, she just says it. That works for us because I always know what she wants and needs, and I don't ever get offended by feedback." He pauses, then says thoughtfully, "So that's why you express things so… carefully at times. You're worried about hurting people's feelings."

"When we first sat down to talk tonight, I was actually irritated that you would even suggest I'm indirect. But now that we've talked a bit more, I can see what you're saying. To be honest, I was annoyed because you hit a sore spot." I glance at him and purse my lips. "Nick kind of said the same thing to me on Thursday when I was trying to ask for this week off."

I could leave this conversation here. We've covered a lot of ground, untangled a lot of painful misunderstandings. But Paul has been so open and generous with me tonight—sharing parts of himself I'm certain he's rarely shared with anyone else. And that generosity inspires me to open up to him, too.

"It *is* actually really hard for me to just come out and say what I want sometimes," I admit reluctantly.

"But…why?"

"Well, in the case of asking Nick for vacation time, I knew I was asking for something he probably didn't want to give me, and I worried he'd think I was too pushy. Demanding."

"You've worked for Nick for…what…ten years?"

"I know."

"So he knows you're nothing like pushy or demanding. Why did you think one single request would change that?"

"I'm not sure," I sigh.

"Your mom is actually one of the most confusing people I've ever tried to converse with." Paul exhales. "Your brothers and your dad are fine, but your mom? I often didn't have a clue what she's talking about. Remember when they came to visit us and she kept talking about how our house was too big for the two of us?"

"She was hinting that we needed to fill it with children."

"I'm aware." He smiles wryly. "I didn't want to ask, but you accidentally translated the Veronica-speak for me when you were complaining about how unsubtle she was about wanting grandchildren later that night."

I do remember that day. I try to imagine how that felt for Paul, because Mom went on and on and on about the size of our house over dinner. But now that I think about it, that's just Mom. It's how she always communicates.

"My God, Paul," I whisper, suddenly cold. "Mom is so indirect. She never says what she's actually thinking."

Of course I'll still support you, Isabel, even if you do decide to waste your God-given talent and go to some second-rate college in New York. But if you're sure that's what you want to do...

And so many comments about my appearance over the years. Too many to count or even catalog.

Isabel, yoga pants again? They really don't show off those lovely legs of yours.

Which of course, was code for, *go back into your*

room and put on a dress. It still drives my mom crazy to see me in activewear on days when I'm not working. Mom is always so elegant, but she has such a narrow, old-school view on femininity. Her hair is curly like mine, but she chemically straightens it and wears it in a bob so smooth and well controlled, it barely moves when she shakes her head. I haven't seen her without a full face of makeup in years, and she's *always* wearing beautiful dresses and heels.

She just doesn't understand why I don't make more of an effort. Just as, I suppose, I don't understand why she can't just wear sweatpants every now and again.

Izzy darling, ladies don't raise their voice or roughhouse. You want to be a lady, don't you?

The inference, of course, being that because I did sometimes raise my voice and I did often roughhouse with my brothers, I was somehow failing as a female. It seems absurd now that I think about it in such stark terms, but that was the reality of my childhood. And the covert messages continue to this day.

Have you spoken to Paul? I'm sure he'll forgive you for whatever happened between you two if you ask him to take you back.

Code, of course, for *Paul is going to be worth a lot of money one day and no matter what went wrong between you, you should apologize anyway so you don't let that very lucrative fish get away.*

But I can't judge her, because now that Paul has explained his perspective of our breakup to me, I'm painfully aware that I communicate like that, too. I never once said the words to Paul *you're working too much* or *I'm feeling so lonely* or *why don't we talk anymore?* I never asked him to miss a meeting or to spend his weekends at home instead of in his office. I never even told him that the connection we shared was starting to feel feeble on my end, or to ask him if he could feel that, too.

Instead, I locked those words inside and tried to nudge our relationship back to health by hints and gestures that I just assumed he would understand. Even when those attempts failed, I didn't tell him how unhappy I was, and my sadness evolved and grew until it was resentment…and that became this fury I've failed altogether to manage this year.

Sometimes, clarity hurts. And right now, I feel sick with shame and guilt. Yes, he withdrew. He locked himself away in his work. But I'm just as guilty as he is, because he's right. Paul might be a certified genius, and maybe I've only known about his autism diagnosis for five minutes, but I've known all along that he wasn't a great communicator. I *am* a people person—I understood very early on that things between us were souring. Who knows what would have happened if I'd found the courage to actually directly address that distance between us?

"You're awfully quiet over there," he says suddenly.

"You did so much work on yourself this year."

"Yes, I did."

"Why?"

"The same reason I'm having this conversation,

even though it's fucking awful and awkward," he says starkly. "Because it's one thing to be clueless about other people. It's another altogether to lose the single most important person in your universe and fail to understand what went wrong."

"I did not do that this year. I didn't work on myself," I say miserably. "I just felt sorry for myself. I blamed you. In my mind, you went from someone who had passively let me drift away, to someone monstrous who'd actively hurt me. I hated you. I felt sorry for myself, and I *hated* you."

Paul sits up and turns to face me, then reaches across and rests his hand on my knee. It's an innocent gesture—a silent offer of comfort. "We both made mistakes."

"But this is the first time I really understood that this mess wasn't all your fault," I croak.

Paul gives me a sad smile. "My personality doesn't lend itself to emotional intimacy. You're right when you said I'm most comfortable in my own head. In fact, you were the first person I ever met who actually made me want to connect."

"It's hard for me to be direct, and it's hard for you to read nuance," I whisper through tears. "We were doomed from the outset."

"We could have addressed that if we'd seen it. If we'd had the kind of relationship where we could talk to one another about this kind of thing…but I was not at a place where I understood myself well enough for a chat like this, Isabel. Alison spent a lot of the past year trying to help me to understand how to better express my emotions and adjust to change, and through that therapy, I've finally come to see that the way I was living my life was isolating me. Even when things were good between you and me, there was a barrier there. It was only a matter of time before we ran into problems."

Having held myself together since I arrived here yesterday, I'm surprised by the swell of tears, and the fact that I simply can't hold them back. A sob bursts from my throat, and Paul sits up, then shifts to sit beside me on my sun chair. He takes my hands in his, and he squeezes. I feel his gentle gaze on my face, and that only makes it worse.

"Hey," he says softly. "What's this? Tears now?"

"This is guilt. Guilt I deserve, too. It's seriously overdue," I whisper thickly. "I'm sorry, Paul. I promise you, I didn't mean to blindside you when I left. I'm so sorry."

"I know that. Now. And you know what? It's okay, Isabel. I'm okay. You're…" He pauses, then he says a little wryly, "Well, my lawyer could probably mount a decent case against what I'm about to say, but you're a gentle person. Sensitive. You were like that through our whole marriage. I think it's because you're so empathetic. And then all of your frustrations just built up until you couldn't take it anymore, right? That's why you've been so angry this year?"

"For someone who keeps telling me how clueless he is about other people, you've made some very astute observations this weekend."

"I'm only clueless when I'm not focused. And

I hope it shows you how much I want to rebuild a friendship with you that I have been focused today. This is hard for me, but even as a friend—you're worth the effort." He ducks his head to meet my gaze, and as soon as we make eye contact, he gives me a cheeky smile. "Also, now that you've finally let that temper of yours out, I'm kind of scared of you. I'd much rather have you as an ally than an enemy."

I laugh through my tears, then I lean forward to throw my arms around his neck. It's such a fucking mess…such a muddled, awful mess. But as much as it pains me to acknowledge where we find ourselves, this is the reality of relationships. Two people come together, and they bring two different histories and two different personalities, and they try to mash all of that into one shared life. Even when the attraction is intense and the love is strong, sometimes people just can't make it work.

But even as that thought crosses my mind, I wonder if it's really that final. Paul and I made mistakes, but we understand them now. I can't help but think about what might have been if we'd had this kind of chat twelve months ago.

And although I kind of hate myself for even thinking this, what it means for us now that we *have* had this chat. I sit up away from him and glance at him through my lashes as I ask, "Does it feel to you like we could have avoided all of the chaos just by making one or two slightly different decisions at any point along the line?"

"It is what it is." Paul shrugs. "We can't go back

in time, so the best we can really do is to try to respect one another as friends in the future."

He smiles at me, then rises and walks away to disappear into the house.

Meanwhile, I'm trying to make sense of how much that casual dismissal hurt, because it felt very much like a punch to the gut. Regret swamps me, and suddenly, I would give anything to go back in time. I'd just turn that iPad on…or I'd go back to those nights when I was so angry with him but I never actually said why…or I'd stick around in that therapist's office and give reconciliation a real shot…maybe I'd just swallow my pride and be the first one to reach out across the silence those early days after I left.

I'll never get a do-over with Paul, and for the first time since I left, I actually wish that wasn't the case. Especially when he returns to the deck with a box of Kleenex, and he sits beside me again and passes me a handful of tissues.

"See?" he says softly. "Maybe I fucked the husband thing up, but I do think these days, I can be a reasonable friend. And thank you for staying for this conversation. How are you feeling?"

I take a Kleenex and wipe at my eyes and blow my nose. I give him a sad smile. "I nearly left today. I'm really glad I stuck around."

"Good," he says, and he nods, satisfied. "Me, too."

"I'm sorry for all of the ways I hurt you. I kind of wanted to at the time, but I never really meant to. Does that make sense?"

"Completely, and also, not at all," he laughs.

"It doesn't even matter," I choke. Tears well in my eyes again, and I wipe at them impatiently with the Kleenex. "As long as you know that I *am* sorry for how we messed things up, and for everything that's happened since."

"I'm sorry, too."

We share a sad, uncertain smile.

"What now?" he asks.

"I don't know," I admit.

"Should we start stacking the dishwasher?"

I laugh softly. "You cooked. Let me clean."

He helps me anyway, and side by side, we clear the outside table and start to set the dishes into the dishwasher. It's a simple moment of domesticity, but it's a moment like no other—another strange point in one of the heaviest, most emotionally intense days of my life. I feel like the repercussions of the hour Paul and I shared on the deck are going to echo on in my life for decades—because after almost a year of feeling like my entire life was upside down, something has just been set right.

I'm scraping the scraps from my plate into the trash when Paul asks me, "What would you have been doing tonight if you'd successfully bullied me into leaving yesterday?"

I throw a soiled napkin at him. He laughs and catches it easily, then tosses it into the trash beside me.

"I had a whole list of soppy movies lined up on my Netflix queue," I tell him.

"I could watch a movie."

I laugh in surprise. "You really don't have to. What were your plans?"

"I told you yesterday. I was going to drink a lot and try to catch up on sleep," he says. I wince, and he shrugs. "I don't really feel like doing that now, anyway. Entertain me."

"Maybe we can watch something that isn't quite as emotional as the list I had planned."

"Hey, I'm getting over a breakup, too," he teases me. "Go ahead and put on your weep-fest. We can sulk together."

"This is more than surreal. Now it's just fucking weird."

He grins and flicks off the kitchen lights. There's a slight chill to the air now, and Paul pulls the sliding door closed while I run upstairs to retrieve the throw blanket from the balcony.

When we meet back at the sofa, I glance at him one last time. "Are you sure about this?"

"How bad can it be?"

'It can be very bad," I warn him. "Very bad indeed."

"What's the first movie?"

"The Notebook."

"No," he gasps.

"I did warn you."

Paul draws in a deep breath, then exhales. "Okay."

"I'm kidding," I laugh. "I won't make you watch *The Notebook* with me, Paul. You hate love stories. That would be cruel and unusual torture."

"I've already seen it. I'm sure you made me watch it with you one time."

"Yeah, you 'watched' it while you wrote a project plan on your laptop," I tell him. "That's probably the only reason you survived the experience. Let's find something we'll both enjoy."

But Paul shakes his head. "I insist," he says as he takes a seat on the sofa.

I settle right at the opposite end and pull the throw over myself. The blanket does smell like him, but that's far less annoying than I feared it would be yesterday. I pull it up to my shoulders and tuck my legs up alongside myself.

As soon as the title credits start, Paul stands and walks back to the kitchen. I laugh, thinking he's given up on the movie already, but he returns just a moment later with two glasses of wine.

"Oh," I say, surprised. "Thanks."

"I'm going to need medicinal alcohol to get through this," he mutters, and I giggle.

Two hours later, I'm sobbing into a handful of tissues, and Paul is staring at the TV in disbelief.

"Why would you watch that awful movie now? Surely it just makes you feel worse!"

"It's meant to remind me to believe in love," I sob, and he shakes his head.

"That's just masochistic. Jesus. I can't think of a worse movie to watch at this point in our lives!"

"A good cry can be cathartic," I assure him. Paul looks away, but the movement is so subtle I almost miss it. "Did *you* cry this year?"

"I probably came pretty close at a few points, but no. I don't think my tear ducts work anymore. I haven't cried since…" He pauses, then exhales. "Not since my mother died, actually."

"We were always so different," I muse softly. "The woman who cries at Kleenex commercials, the man who doesn't ever cry."

He smiles sadly, and we both turn our attention back to the credits. After a moment or two, he asks, "Should we go to bed?"

"I think I'll watch another movie. You should turn in if you want to, though."

"I'm not tired yet either." He shrugs.

I convince Paul that it's his turn to pick the next movie and he loads an action flick. Less than half an hour passes before my eyes start to feel heavy, but I really don't want to go back to my own room. Instead, I gradually sink into the sofa, resting my eyes for longer and longer periods of time.

I don't want the night to end, and I really don't want to leave Paul and go back to my own, lonely bed. I'm sure he'll go upstairs when he's ready to sleep, and it doesn't really matter if I end up sleeping on this sofa.

Especially now that I'm snuggled up under this throw blanket, and it smells just like Paul. It turns out, I don't mind that at all.

CHAPTER SIXTEEN

Paul

I'M PRETTY SURE that Isabel has fallen asleep. She's curled up against the armrest, and her eyes have fallen closed. The thing is, I'm in a similarly uncomfortable half recline now, and my eyelids are getting heavy, too.

But I can't convince myself to go up to bed, and I'm pretty sure that's because she won't be coming with me.

When Isabel shifts until she's stretched out across the sofa, her feet near my thighs, I decide to give in to the urge to stay. I turn the volume way down but I leave the TV on so that tomorrow, when we wake up, I can pretend all of this wasn't on purpose. Then I shuffle along the sofa and stretch out beside her. I tuck the throw blanket around us both and rest my head on one of the decorative cushions she bought sometime since my last visit.

When I open my eyes one more time to glance down at her, I see that she's shifted her head to face me. Just as my eyelids open, hers slam closed.

Curious.

She's not protesting this turn of events, but it's telling that neither one of us is willing to draw attention to the elephant in the room. Maybe it's unsurprising that we want to sleep together tonight, even if we're not quite willing to admit it aloud.

After all that we shared, it turns out it's just too hard to go to bed alone.

Part Three

Sunday

CHAPTER SEVENTEEN

Paul

I WAKE TO find my face and throat are covered in a blanket of Isabel's unruly curls. She's lying across my chest, her face buried in my neck, one of her arms stretched across my waist.

Miracles of miracles, it's well past dawn—I can't even remember the last time I slept this late. As I run a mental check along my body to see if the night crowded on the sofa has thrown anything out of alignment, I'm surprised to find I don't just feel fine, I feel fucking fantastic.

Yesterday was one of the most exhausting days of my entire life, but this morning I'm shocked by how energized I feel. After all of those months where my world felt alien and chaotic, it's actually incredible to wake to find things feel settled.

I'm still getting divorced on Wednesday. I've still lost my wife. But maybe I can deal with that a whole lot better now that the discord between Isabel and me has been resolved. It still hurts that our marriage ended, and if last night proved anything, it's surely that an open, honest conversation between us at any point during that last year might just have been enough to prevent all of the heartache. But even though that conversation came far too late, it's finally happened, and maybe that chat really did settle something ugly inside me.

This morning, I'm certain in the knowledge that my grief this year wasn't just about losing my marriage, it was also about losing her. Now that there's a way forward where we might just manage to reestablish some kind of friendship connection, I feel…better. Closer to whole than I have for the longest time.

I gently shift the cloud of hair away from my face, and Isabel mumbles something in her sleep and rolls toward the back of the sofa.

I think quickly, and as she moves, I slide out from under her without waking her up. Before I walk away, I pause to stare down at her. Resisting the urge to press an affectionate kiss against her forehead, I instead tuck the blanket back up over her shoulder, then stretch my arms over my head as I walk toward the stairs.

This day feels ripe with possibilities. It's the dawn of a whole new era for me and Isabel—the start of the chapter of our lives where we're just friends, but maybe even *good* friends, because after last night, I genuinely believe that's a possibility. Does Isabel have plans? If she doesn't, will she want to spend the day with me? What would two friends do with a Sunday like this at Greenport?

By the time I emerge from my shower, I can smell coffee on the air. I jog down the stairs, a spring in my step, and find Isabel in the kitchen with two steaming cups on the bench before her. She's holding a carton of half-and-half and looks a bit sheepish.

"Did you run out to the store for me?" I ask her.

She laughs under her breath and shakes her head as she finishes pouring the cream into my cup, then extends it toward me. "I bought it for you on Friday," she informs me.

I raise an eyebrow at her and ask cautiously, "Did you open the carton on Friday, too? If so, should I check it for spit?"

"I think it was just habit, but now that we're friends, I'm glad I could make you a nice cup of coffee." Her eyes dart away from mine, and she asks, "Did you sleep well?"

"I think we both fell asleep halfway through that last movie," I half lie. I'm not overthinking our mutual desire to sleep together. At the time, cuddling up with her just felt natural and right—it doesn't mean I want her back. It doesn't mean she wants me back. It just means we've now walked a pretty intense path together, and it turns out there's a natural intimacy that comes from that.

"Yeah," she says, and she gives me a quiet smile. "The sofa is surprisingly comfortable to sleep on."

"Do you have plans today?"

"No?"

I was about to suggest we try the bikes again, maybe pack a picnic and go for a longer ride, but Isabel and I were always moving. She likes to be active, but it's almost a compulsion for her sometimes, and it's difficult for her to just stop and relax. I guess

I'm the same, although my frenetic activity is usually work, not exercise. But today, all I want to do is to be in the moment with her.

"Can I organize a surprise for you?" I ask her, and she raises her eyebrows at me.

"You've been surprising me all weekend, so I guess that would be fitting," she says, with a carefree laugh.

I can't remember the last time I saw her laugh like that, and I feel an odd twinge in the vicinity of my chest as I recognize that the easygoing version of the Isabel still exists. I shake the sensation off and force myself to smile at her.

"Give me an hour?" I ask.

"How should I dress?"

"Do you have a swimsuit?"

"I think there's one in the closet…"

"And a book?"

"I have many very heavy, unfinished books in this house," she says wryly, but then she quirks an eyebrow. "What exactly are you thinking?"

I wink at her, then take my coffee back toward the stairs, tossing over my shoulder, "See you in an hour."

Jess: Throw me a freaking bone, Paul. Are you two okay out there?

Marcus: Hey there, buddy. Just checking in.

Jake: Have you heard of the John Muir Trail? Was

thinking of hiking it at the start of July. Would take about three weeks. You in?

My phone is still on Do Not Disturb, but the lock screen is full of emails and text messages. I unlock it and quickly clear the email notifications, then bash out some replies to the texts.

Jess, the punishment you face for meddling is that I'm not going to tell you how successful or unsuccessful your meddling has been.

Hi, Marcus. We've talked a lot and sorted some shit out. No need for that shark-infested moat after all, I think we might actually emerge from this weekend on friendly terms again.

Hey, Jake. Let me know the details and dates and I'll check my schedule tomorrow when I'm back in the office. I'll call you during the week, I've had the most amazing weekend.

I spend the next half hour making calls to some local vendors, then I slide the cell into a backpack so I can bring it along. I don't intend to actually use it, but I also don't want to be without it in case anything goes awry during the adventure I have planned for the day.

When I return downstairs, Isabel is stretched out on the sofa again, this time, reading a biography. Her hair is damp and hanging loose over the armrest, already coiling up into the ringlets. She's not wearing any makeup. I can see the strap of her red halter-neck bikini around her neck, but the rest of it is covered by the loose T-shirt and yoga pants she's wearing over top. She looks relaxed, happy and calm and she has never, ever been more beautiful to me.

God, I wish I could tell her.

I have to pause and draw in a breath, and forcibly remind myself that she is just a friend. Friends might hang out and spend the day together, but they don't go around gushing to one another about how beautiful they are. Once upon a time, I'd feel an urge like this and it would be instinct to hold the words in—to let my fear hold me back, worried that I'd fumble the delivery or misread how she'd react.

It's curious how hard it is not to say those words to her right now. It would almost be easier to just let them out.

Now, though, I hold the words in because we have only just defused the tension in our relationship, and I can't risk confusing things all over again.

"Ready?" I ask her.

Isabel looks up over the book and as her gaze skims over my body—from my flip-flops to the cap I've pulled on—she suddenly bursts out laughing. I raise an eyebrow at her, but her laughter bubbles up further, and I glance down my body, wondering what I've done to amuse her so.

"Paul Winton," she says, when she can draw breath. "Two days ago you and I hated one another with a passion, but you were still wearing your wedding ring *and* you told me you couldn't break the habit of wearing it. Today, we're three days from our divorce, getting along better than we have in years, and you've finally taken it off. What gives?"

I look down at my left hand in surprise. Sure enough, I've left the ring upstairs on the basin after my shower. That's not even as surprising as the fact that I have no urge whatsoever to run back upstairs to retrieve it.

"I don't have to cling to it anymore." I stare at my bare finger. "I can let go of what was now, because I understand what went wrong, and I know we can make a way forward as friends again."

Isabel's laughter fades to a sad smile. She stands and crosses the room, then throws her arms around my waist.

"I feel so good today," she murmurs.

Yes. You do. Especially when you're pressed up against me like that.

I plant a gentle, innocent kiss against her hair, then step back, putting some safe distance between our bodies. Will I ever lose the urge to kiss her? Or get past the shock of attraction that hits me when she's in my arms? Will I ever train myself not to notice little details about her—like right now, when all I can think about is that she's wearing perfume today; the citrus one she usually wears for workdays.

"What's on the agenda today, friend?" she asks me with a smile as she rocks back onto her heels.

"We're going to do something we've never done

before, at least not together," I say. She raises her eyebrows at me, and I extend my elbow for her to take it.

"This is intriguing," she says as we head toward the front door. "But you have to give me some more information. I mean, what haven't we done before together? Skydiving? Cross-country skiing? Joining a pie-eating competition?"

"Actually, Isabel, we're going to do something far more radical than all of that."

"Oh, this is exciting! What exactly do you have in store for me?"

"Well, friend…" I smile, as I push open the front door "…today, you and I are going to be still."

CHAPTER EIGHTEEN

Isabel

"Hмм. Your not-so-secret admirer is going to be very disappointed," Marie remarks when I call into her café to pick up the food Paul ordered over the phone. She lifts a picnic basket up onto her counter and gives me an amused look.

I feel myself blush. "Darby and I are just friends. And Paul and I are just friends."

"You used to come here with Paul all of the time. You didn't look like friends back then."

I clear my throat, then assure her, "We're definitely just friends now."

"Just like you and Darby."

"Exactly."

"Yeah, my friends are forever giving me flowers just because and organizing romantic picnics for me," Marie laughs. "Tell me, where are you having this platonic picnic, huh? The Eiffel Tower? A hotel room strewn with rose petals?"

"I don't actually know where we're having the picnic, he's off organizing that now and it's a surprise. But I'm pretty sure it will be somewhere very unromantic, because Paul and I really are just friends now, and even when we were together, he wasn't exactly Mr. Romance."

Just then, the door to the café opens, and Paul steps inside and gives me a broad smile. "Hey, Marie, thanks for this. Ready, Isabel?"

"Sure am," I say lightly, and I scoop the picnic basket off the counter.

"Tell me, Paul," Marie asks. "Where are you two off on this picnic today?"

"I rented a yacht. I thought we'd float around the Basin for a while and relax, maybe go for a swim if the sun comes out later," Paul says easily, and I stumble a little. He catches my elbow and gives me a concerned look. "Are you okay?"

"I'm fine." I shoot a glance back at Marie to see she's laughing smugly.

"You two enjoy yourselves," she calls after us.

"A yacht?" I repeat once we're out in the street. "Seriously?"

"It's a modest yacht." Paul shrugs. "Technically a sailboat, I think."

"Do you even know how to drive a boat?" I ask incredulously.

He shakes his head. "Of course I don't."

"Great. I know we're getting along better now, but I don't think we're quite ready for a *Castaway* type situation just yet."

"Isabel, you wound me," Paul says, playfully clutching his chest. "It would definitely be more of a *Gilligan's Island* type situation. I'm just not sure if I'd be Gilligan himself, or the Professor." I laugh, and he winks at me. "Fret not, Ginger. The yacht comes with its very own Skipper."

CHAPTER NINETEEN

Paul

"THIS IS ABSOLUTE HEAVEN," Isabel says as she stretches like a cat on the sundeck of the sailboat. It's now early afternoon, and we're lying side by side in much the same positions we've been in all day—stretched out on sun chairs on the deck of a Beneteau 50 as it floats on the glimmering waters of the Sterling Basin. We're only a few dozen feet from the shoreline now, at an isolated anchorage. There's a captain at the helm of the boat, but she's inside in the cabin, and she's pretty much remained invisible for most of the day.

Now, it feels a lot like Isabel and I are the only people left in the universe. Other than the sound of the waves lapping on the hull and the gentle breeze as it slips past the boat, the world feels silent and its bliss. Isabel and I have been reading for hours, shifting only to help ourselves from the picnic Marie packed for us.

I'm engrossed in a twisty psychological thriller, and Isabel is still reading that biography. Every now and again, we break from our reading to chat. The book I'm reading is too dark for Isabel's tastes, but I've explained the premise, and she's developed a theory about the ending. She thinks it was the ex-girlfriend, but I suspect that's too obvious—I think the murderer was the mother-in-law. I actually read the book Isabel is devouring over there earlier this year, so we've had a few chats about that, too.

We did a lot of things during the years we were together, but never before have we shared a day like this. We just weren't the kind of couple to laze about, but now I'm starting to suspect that was yet another thing I've been missing out on.

"Going for a swim soon?" I ask her, and Isabel lowers her book and wrinkles her nose at me.

"It's too cold," she points out.

"That never stopped you before," I laugh softly, thinking of all the times she'd dive into the water from the beach in front of our house and I'd stand back on the deck and shake my head at her. "How many freezing cold spring days did you jump into the water back at the house and try to convince me I should join you because it was *invigorating?*"

"I'm old and scared now." She grimaces.

I roll my eyes and set my book aside. "Age is an attitude."

"Easy for you to say," she laughs. "You're two years younger than me."

"So thirty-four is the age where all of the fun stops? Good to know, I'd best pack a lot of it into the next two years."

Isabel grins and sets her book aside, then walks

gingerly to climb down the ladder that leads to the swim platform. I follow her, kicking off my flip-flops and pulling my T-shirt over my head, because I expect she's going to leap right in and I figure, since I goaded her into this, I should at least join her.

Instead, she keeps her clothing over the top of her bikini and sits on the edge of the platform to dangle her feet in the water. I stand beside her, taking in the view and breathing in the salt air on the breeze. The cool breeze. She has a point. It probably is far too cold to swim today.

"Maybe we're both old and boring. Is the water as cold as it looks?" I ask her, but when I glance down at Isabel, she's giving me an odd look.

She stands, and I think she's about to turn and go back up to our sun chairs, but instead, she says with a grin, "Sorry."

"What for—"

I don't even manage to finish the question before she gives me a surprisingly fierce push toward the edge of the swim platform. I shriek, and at the last second, manage to reach out and catch her hand. We both tumble into the clear blue depths, but I keep her hand in mine the whole time—mostly so I can make sure she emerges safely. Unfortunately, that means that when we breach the surface of the water, breathless, we're nose to nose.

There are tiny droplets of water on her skin and on her eyelashes, and she's laughing even as she splutters, and she's just so fucking beautiful. I don't even think as I steady myself with one hand against the swim platform. I just give in to the impulse to pull her close.

Our bodies align naturally, our hips and chests drawn together. I can feel the tight buds of her nipples through two layers of her clothing, just as I'm sure she can feel my body responding, even though the heat from her body is surely the only thing keeping my dick from shriveling up in this freezing fucking water.

We're moving closer together when she pauses, and lifts her hand to gently, tenderly touch my cheek near my eye. And then she pauses like that, staring at me for so long that I'm starting to get confused.

"Is there a jellyfish stuck to my face?" I whisper.

Isabel seems to snap out of her reverie. She smiles back now, and she lifts her legs to wrap around my hips. I steady her by resting my free hand on her hip, but that just means I'm now holding her against my rapidly hardening dick. It's all I can do to stop myself rutting against her like an animal.

"I'm pretty sure you'd know if there was a jellyfish on your face." She traces the stubble on my cheek, then slowly drags her finger back up to my eyes.

"What is it, then?" I prompt her.

"You're smiling all the way to your eyes, Paul," she whispers.

"I'm happy today," I whisper back, and she leans forward as if she means to brush her lips against mine. I just cannot wait to taste her—

Friends do not make out.

We've already ascertained that there's just too much water under the bridge for us to go back, which means we need to move forward in this new direction, and the new Isabel and new Paul do not and cannot kiss.

Even though now *she's* all but humping me through our clothes.

Oh, hell. It would be so easy to give into this pull between us. I could kiss her—she wants me to kiss her. But where would that lead us? Where could it possibly lead us, other than to another round of disaster?

I break the moment because someone has to, and it's clear from Isabel's ever-darkening eyes that she's not going to be the one to see sense this time. I gently disentangle our limbs and turn to duck my head under the water again, trying to cool my raging libido down. I know it won't take long, because all of my exposed skin is covered in goose bumps— the unpleasant kind.

I immediately decide that the best way to get over that little moment of insanity is to brush right past it, so I put a little distance between us and I turn around to say with fake outrage, "Pushing me in was a dirty trick."

Isabel is treading water, a thoughtful look on her face. "We're not going to talk about that near-kiss?" she says, after a pause.

"Do you think we need to?" I ask uncertainly.

For just a fleeting moment, I think I see hurt in

her gaze, but it disappears quickly and she gives me a smile.

"I guess not. I just wanted to show you how direct I can be," she says, and then she splashes me. "You realize I have no dry outfit to change into. That means I'm going to have to lie up there in this teeny tiny bikini while my clothes dry off, and we're just friends so you can't look, and it's all your fault I'm drenched."

Isabel shifts so that she's floating on her back, staring up at the sky above her, a thoughtful expression on her face. Her hair floats all around her, and she looks like an irresistible water nymph, or maybe a mermaid sent to lure me to my destruction. In any case, it is completely unfair that I have to see her like this when I'm trying to shove her back into the box in my mind marked Just Friends, and I'm cursing myself for pulling her into the water with me.

"You pushed me in!" I say, splashing her.

She squeals and sits up to splash me again. "You called me old and boring!"

"I called us both old and boring!"

Soon, we're splashing water back and forth, laughing like children, but it's not long before my teeth are chattering, and Isabel's lips are blue.

"The least you can do is get out and get me a towel," I remark, then I waggle my eyebrows at her. "I promise I won't look at your bikini."

She splashes me again, and I laugh and pull myself up onto the swim platform. That cool breeze is much closer to an arctic blast now that I'm soaking wet, and I'm shaking like a leaf by the time I find two fluffy oversize towels in a blanket box on the sundeck. I wrap one around myself as I walk back down toward the swim platform, but when I reach the ladder, I find Isabel has already pulled herself up onto it. She's standing, staring out toward the shoreline, and she has indeed stripped down to that fucking bikini.

It takes a feat of miraculous strength for me to hand her the towel without looking down at her, and I'm both a little disappointed and proud of my own self-control when I manage to do so successfully, because a split second later her magnificent body is hidden by the towel.

"This was a great idea, you know," she says. "This whole day. This whole weekend, overall."

"You can probably thank Jess for the weekend," I say, and Isabel raises her eyebrows at me.

"Jess?"

"At what point did you decide to take this trip?"

"Wednesday night."

"At your Wednesday night girls dinner?"

"Yeah, Jess said…" Her eyebrows knit, then her eyes widen. "Wait, Jess tricked us into coming out here?"

"She gave me this weird lecture on Thursday about how I shouldn't miss the retreat to come out here 'one last time,'" I laugh. "I hadn't even considered the possibility until she annoyed me by telling me not to do it. She's kind of brilliant, even if she is completely evil. When I called her yesterday, she admitted she was hoping we'd find a way to be friends."

"Did you tell her that her nefarious plan had worked?"

"Nah." I shrug. "I'll let her sweat until I get back to the office tomorrow. Manipulative wench she is."

We both laugh at that, and Isabel turns to face me, leaning against the railing behind her.

"Can I ask you something, Paul?"

"Anything."

"You probably should hear the question before you agree to answer it," she laughs.

"After everything we've discussed this weekend, do you think there's anything I wouldn't tell you?"

"Why did you buy the vacation house?"

I flinch as if she hit me. "Oh."

We stand in silence for a long time, each shivering inside our fluffy towel, staring out at the water of the bay. At first, I'm just trying to figure out how to explain this without making Isabel herself feel shitty, but as the minutes pass, I struggle to resist the urge to avoid the conversation altogether.

"Let's go back upstairs where there's some shelter?" I suggest.

I see the disappointment flash across Isabel's face, and I turn away and climb first up the ladder to the sun deck. But I'm agonizingly conscious of my own hypocrisy—and confused at how fast I've fallen back into the old habit of withholding the vulnerable parts of myself, so when we're once again stretched out on the sun deck, I try to explain.

"This isn't about us. About you and me," I start to say, intending to finish with, *it's just too hard to talk about and I don't want to ruin this great day we're having.*

But then I glance at her, and her gaze is so warm and kind, I'm suddenly struck by the realization that I could have told her why Greenport was so special to me, even years ago. Isabel would have understood. It seems that there's a cost and a benefit to sharing the deepest parts of ourselves. The cost is exposure, the benefit is intimacy, and although our marriage is over, I want to be close to Isabel. I want her to understand, and I know I can trust her.

After a weekend of sharing more and more of ourselves, we've now crashed headlong into a part of my life I haven't really been able to talk to anyone about for years…and I actually want to share it with her.

"You know I don't really like to talk about my childhood," I say.

Isabel's eyebrows knit, but she nods. I can't remember what I have and haven't told her over the years, but I know it's not a lot. "I was a peculiar kid, I guess. I didn't make friends easily…and then once I started skipping grades at school, sometimes I didn't make friends at all. I didn't really care, because I was always more interested in learning than I was in playing. And for the most part, that was completely fine because my family was my refuge. Jake and I were always close for brothers with a six-year age gap, and Dad is just like me so he's always just *got-*

ten me, and Mom…" I close my eyes for a minute, and my mother's face comes to mind.

I remember her, as I always do, just as she was that last weekend before her diagnosis: standing on the pier at Greenport, the wind blowing her hair, her face alight with happiness.

Isabel shifts on her chair, and when I glance at her, I find she's sitting cross-legged. She's turned to face me, and there's no judgment in her expression, only a quiet curiosity. "What was she like?" she asks gently.

"Mom would have loved you, and you would have loved Mom. She was a people person," I laugh softly. "She was nothing like Dad. You know Dad is so smart but…"

"…just brilliant enough to be awkward as hell sometimes."

"Exactly," I say, but then I wince. "Like me, right?"

"No, Martin is even more awkward than you are," Isabel assures me with a soft laugh. "At least you know how to flirt. Your poor dad was like a sledge-hammer when he had a crush on Elspeth. It was painful to watch."

"It's reassuring to know I have more game than my seventy-two-year-old father," I say sardonically.

"So…your mom?" Isabel prompts, and I roll onto my side to face her.

"Well, I guess by the time I was in middle school, life was really busy for us. Mom and Dad were both teaching full time at Columbia, and Jake was in high school studying to take SATs, so between their schedules and me taking on every extra-credit assignment I could, things were uncomfortably chaotic.

"One night, maybe when I was ten, I came home from school and Mom was upset. She said we were all too busy, and we weren't spending enough time together. Honestly, I don't think me, Dad or Jake had any idea what she was going on about—but after that day, she announced we were going to have a weekend away together every month. No work, no study, just us—she decided we would all rearrange our schedules so we could have a weekend completely free. Dad and Jake groaned at first, but we all loved Mom and this really seemed to mean a lot to her, so for a year or so, that's what we did."

"Did you come here? To our place at Greenport for those weekends?" Isabel asks, her voice very small.

I hastily shake my head. "No, we went all over the country. Mom's parents died when I was young, but they'd been wealthy, so she and Dad had never been short on money. Even so, Mom was kind of a minimalist, before that was really a thing. We didn't have an extravagant lifestyle or possessions, but when it came to experiences, Mom was always happy to go all-out. I think we visited ten states that year on those trips," I explain, but then I can feel my throat growing tight because I know what's coming next.

"They were all good weekends, but one summer, we were supposed to fly down to Florida to visit an eco resort she'd read about. There was a hurricane out over the Atlantic, but at the last minute, it changed direction toward Orlando and our flight was canceled. Jake wanted to go home to study, but I was just so disappointed. I remember Mom giving me a hug and then announcing she needed to make some calls, and she left us with Dad while she marched to a pay phone. Ten minutes later we were on our way to Penn Station and we wound up here at Greenport. We stayed at this B&B that used to be on Main Road—it's long gone now, but it was a simple little place. I don't know if that weekend really was as perfect as I remember it, but in my mind, it was just fucking golden."

"Oh, Paul," Isabel whispers. She closes her eyes and swallows, then brings the towel to dab at the corner of her eye. "Jesus."

"On Monday we went back to the city, and on Tuesday she found the lump."

"I'm just so sorry."

"In hindsight, maybe she knew something was wrong. I have to wonder if that's what those trips were about that last year. I mean, Mom was a med science professor, you know? There's a good chance she was well in tune with how the human body works. Maybe she felt something in her body, or she'd seen some sign even before the lump emerged. But anyway…once she was diagnosed, she was straight into high-dose chemo and she was *so* sick, so fast. It took two years for cancer to take her, but we never traveled again."

Isabel has fallen silent. She's periodically dabbing at her eyes with the towel, and I move to sit beside her, then give her a slightly awkward side hug.

"I promise you, Isabel. I didn't tell you that to make you feel shitty."

"I know. But I can't possibly take your house now," she chokes.

"It wasn't like Mom ever saw that particular house. My trust fund matured when I was twenty-one and I was going to funnel the money into Brainway, but Dad talked me out of it. I'd already put everything I had into the business and he was concerned if things went south, I'd regret not using Mom's money for something more sentimental."

"So the house *is* sentimental."

"Of course it is," I say, and when her face falls again, I nudge her with my elbow. "But it wasn't back then. It became sentimental when I met you there, and when we had so many important moments there. But honestly, when I bought that house, I was just a dumb, impulsive, twenty-one-year-old with a social life for the first time in his entire life. I wasn't intending on making it a memorial to my mom, I was picturing long weekends out here with pretty girls and Jess and Marcus and all of the dozens of people who became my friends just through them. I found the house online one night and the next day made an offer sight unseen.

"But that was naive and somewhat optimistic given we were trying to grow a business at the same time, and I didn't use it nearly enough before you came along."

Isabel still looks miserable. She's sitting beside me, shoulders slumped, eyes downcast.

"Bel...just in case it's still not clear—yes, I feel close to Mom's memory at Greenport sometimes, but I didn't give you the village itself. I'll still come out here every now and again. Maybe you'll list the house on Airbnb and I'll rent it from you."

"Don't even joke about that," she whispers. "I just keep thinking if I'd understood there was a connection to your mom, I'd never have been such a bitch about the house when we were in mediation."

"You didn't understand because I didn't tell you. I'm not even sure I consciously made the connection myself until this year. And Christ, if I really needed to keep that particular house, I'd never have given in. I'd have let you take me to court so a judge could laugh your ass out of the hearing."

I'm trying to make a joke, but Isabel doesn't laugh. Instead, she rests her head on my shoulder. "Why did you change your mind and give me the house, Paul?"

"You looked so miserable that day. You'd looked miserable the entire time, but when you realized you'd lost, you just looked...devastated. I couldn't bear the thought of dragging things out any longer."

"I honestly thought we'd gotten all of the emotional stuff out of the way yesterday. This is almost worse. Why didn't you just tell me this all along? If I knew about any of that, I would never have even asked for the house."

"One of the positives that's come out of all of

our upheaval is the work I had to do on myself. The payoff is I understand myself better, and that means I can explain myself to you. Before this year, I couldn't—I was just existing…kind of cut off from my own emotions. That's a lonely way to live, even for a guy who was never really alone."

"I still feel utterly sick at the thought of taking the house from you now."

"If you're really so determined to feel guilty, why don't you focus on making me watch *The Notebook* last night? I'm still kind of traumatized by that, to be honest."

Isabel laughs weakly, then shifts on the chair so that she's facing me.

"Do you think we'd still be together if we could talk like this back then?" she asks. Her gaze is very serious, and I give her a sad smile.

"If we were still together, I would never have learned to talk like this. You said yesterday you left because you were hoping to shock me into taking stock of my life, and I guess that worked, even if it didn't work the way you intended. If you had just stayed and let me continue in my bubble, nothing would have changed."

"I just can't help but wonder what might have been, Paul."

"In programming, we might call this conversation a circular reference, because it just leads us to keep circling back around in a loop forever," I say teasingly.

"How do I fix the circular reference?" she says with a reluctant smile.

"You review the code. You figure out why it keeps looping back over itself, and you change it."

"Like us two rehashing all of this history this weekend, then moving forward as friends?"

"Exactly."

CHAPTER TWENTY

Isabel

A STORM BLOWS over as we're heading back to Greenport late in the afternoon. Rain is starting to pour when we farewell the captain and step off at the marina.

"I was going to suggest we walk home," Paul shouts as we sprint for cover. "But maybe we should just grab dinner somewhere close and wait for the storm to pass?"

"Sure," I shout back.

"What about the bar across the road?"

"Deal!"

We run side by side toward the bar and manage to make it without winding up completely drenched. As we step up onto the porch, Paul asks, "You've been so quiet this afternoon. Are you sure you're okay?"

"I'm fine." I try to flash him a genuine smile. This isn't a passive-aggressive *I'm fine* because I'm angry. I'm telling the truth, because I am fine—but I'm also extremely confused and not at all ready to talk about it.

I wanted Paul to kiss me in the water today, and I was deeply disappointed when he didn't.

I desperately wanted Paul to explain to me the real story behind the vacation house, and now that he has, I feel awful, guilty and uncertain.

And most of all, it's Sunday night, and I remember Paul saying he was here until tomorrow. I should be pleased that he's leaving. I should be pleased only that our little experiment this weekend has resulted in us clearing the air and becoming friends again, but instead, the knot in my gut has returned.

It's a different kind of knot now.

I do not want to say goodbye.

Paul holds the door open for me, and I step inside to find the bar is surprisingly busy. Just as I recognize the trivia setup, I also remember Darby's invitation on Friday.

"I forgot they do trivia here on Sunday nights," Paul says, scanning the room. "It's so busy... Oh, wait. There's a booth free over there." The hostess approaches us, and Paul flashes her a smile. "Two for dinner, please. Do you mind if we take that booth?"

"Sure," the hostess says, handing us some menus.

"Hey there, Izzy! Didn't think you were going to make it tonight."

My stomach drops in slow motion as I turn to face the source of that very familiar voice.

"Hey, Darby," I say, as brightly as I can. I'm aware of Paul stepping back to stand beside me, and so I wave vaguely between the two men. "Darby, meet my…this is my…friend Paul. Paul, this is Darby, also my…friend…from the gym here."

I glance hastily at Paul's face to find that the happy, slightly tired smile he was wearing when we stepped inside has faded, and now he's adopted a completely neutral expression. He extends his hand and shakes Darby's.

"Hi," Paul says.

"Great to meet you, Paul," Darby says, his smile easy. His gaze flicks back to me, then to Paul again, then he says warmly, "Welcome to the team."

Paul shoots me a confused look, and I hasten to clarify. "Paul and I are actually here for dinner, Darby," I say apologetically. "I totally forgot about trivia, I'm sorry."

"Ah, sorry. I just texted you a while ago to remind you, so I figured you were here because of that. But no problem at all, guys. Enjoy your meal. The burrito bowls are good tonight." He winks at the hostess. "Just make sure you ask for extra guac—Bob is working the kitchen and he's stingy with his avocado."

"Darby," the hostess chastises him. "If we loaded up the guac on every burrito bowl the way you like it, we'd go out of business real fast."

Darby laughs, waves at Paul and me, then heads back to his friends. Paul and I stand in stiff, awkward silence, both watching his retreating back.

"That Darby is such a character," the hostess laughs, shaking her head. "Have you ever seen someone so friendly and well connected? I swear he knows the whole town, even during the peak season he's making friends with the tourists."

"He sure does seem friendly," Paul says, not a hint of animosity in his voice.

When the hostess starts to lead us toward the table, I catch Paul's arm. "He's just a friend—"

Paul interrupts me carefully, "You really don't have to explain and I definitely don't want you to feel like you have to lie to me." He points at the booth, then waves vaguely at the crowd. "We really need to get that booth before it goes or we'll have to wait for someone to leave."

I follow the hostess and Paul and slide into the booth. The hostess takes our drink orders, and as soon as she leaves, Paul says, "For what it's worth, he seems like a nice guy. I mean, even the hostess seems to recommend him." He gives me what appears to be a genuine smile. "And friends meet each other's dates, right? This is just one of the things we have to adjust to if we're going to stay in each other's lives now."

"I'm not dating Darby," I say defensively. If the way he avoided my kiss wasn't clear enough today, this moment confirms it. Paul is definitely, completely over me.

I'm sitting here all but drowning in regret that we're really, truly over, and Paul is completely at ease with the idea of watching me date someone else.

"But you've thought about dating him," Paul says, after a pause.

"What makes you think that?" I ask him.

"I told you, Isabel. I *am* capable of picking up subtext when I'm paying attention. So...what's the story?"

"There's nothing going on. Really. But we've had coffee a few times," I say, my voice very small.

But he wasn't you. And even when I was angry with you, I still felt loyal to you. Because maybe I was always still in love with you, and maybe after the last twenty-four hours, I know that I could love you more than ever.

Paul reaches across and he rests his hand over mine, then squeezes. When I raise my gaze to his, he gives me a slightly stilted smile.

"This is weird as fuck for me, too, but it's okay."

We've been silent on and off all day, but it's never felt like this—thick with an awareness of how things between us have changed and can never, ever be the same.

Even if we want them to.

When the waitress finally returns with our drinks, Paul raises his beer toward me. I lift my Moscato, and we knock the glasses together gently.

"To friendship. To moving on, together but apart," Paul says. He smiles at me, and his gaze is bright, as if he's already passed that stiff moment of awkwardness just now, and he's back to being completely comfortable with everything that's going on between us.

I echo the words as brightly as I can, but I'm distracted as hell.

Paul and I have finally made peace with one another, and now I just can't think of anything worse than moving on with my life and leaving him behind.

Paul devours a double serving of crab cakes. I pick at my burrito bowl, but my appetite has disappeared again. He then cajoles me into splitting the tropical fruit sundae with him like we used to. I take a few bites but sit back to let him finish it off. He savors every mouthful, completely focused on the task of eating and enjoying the food.

I like watching him when he's present like this.

I like this new and improved Paul. I like him maybe even more than I liked the old version of Paul at the beginning, and that was a *lot*.

I don't like the sudden shift in my thoughts. I don't like how my gaze follows the movement of the spoon from the bowl to his lips. I don't like how strong his forearms suddenly look, or how much I'm enjoying the fact that we're together right now and things aren't just peaceful; after that amazing day on the boat, the mood is actually fond between us again. I don't like how desperate I am to stay in this moment or how miserable the thought of watching him leave tomorrow is making me feel.

"Did you taste the pineapple? It's so sweet…" he says suddenly, and he raises a spoonful of dessert to me. I definitely do not like how desperate I feel to share the intimacy of putting my mouth on a spoon that's just left his lips. I eat the pineapple but barely taste the fruit because all I can taste is him.

I want to kiss him. I want to taste the fucking fruit

salad right out of his mouth and then slide my way down his body and taste the rest of him.

"Have some more?" he suggests, pushing the bowl toward me.

"It's great, I'm just full."

"You seem… You're upset about something, aren't you?" His eyebrows knit as he stares at me, then lift in surprise. He's trying to figure me out, and it's hard for him, but he's making an effort.

And when it all boils down, that's all I ever wanted.

It hits me with a burst of painful clarity. I never wanted Paul to become a people person. I just wanted him to *try* to connect with me, on his terms, in his way. And I understand now that even in the past when he did try to support me, when he did try to connect with me, I didn't always see it.

But I can see it now.

"I'm fine," I lie weakly.

Paul pauses for a moment, then he turns his attention back to the dessert. He eats in silence for a moment, finishing off the last few mouthfuls, then he pushes the bowl aside and raises his gaze to mine. There's a strange little pause before he speaks, and I watch his neck as he swallows.

"You know, Isabel, I thought I might head back to the house."

The announcement is so sudden and abrupt that I'm shocked enough to sink back into my seat. "Okay, I guess we're done, so—"

"Ah." He clears his throat. "Ah, no. I meant…

I might head back. Alone. We've had such a great day, maybe…you know…maybe it's time for some time apart now."

His gaze flicks past me, and I frown as I follow it. *Darby.*

Paul is looking at Darby. Then he looks back to me, and his expression is completely blank.

"Paul," I protest. "Please. You really don't have—"

He gives me a somewhat forced smile and he's already rising. I'm panicking, because this is kind of like watching a train wreck happen, right before my eyes. It turns out the second last thing in the world I want is for Paul to leave me here, and the very last thing I want is for Paul to push me toward another man.

"Paul, please don't go," I say, but he seems quite determined. I see him wave at Darby, calling him over—*dear God, no, Paul*—then he flashes me a weak smile.

"See you later." Finally he looks a little uncomfortable as he adds, "Or, you know. Or not. That's… you know. That's fine, too."

I feel my face flush and I close my eyes in horror as he walks away. I draw in a deep breath, collecting myself, and as I open my eyes, I see Darby taking his place.

"So," Darby says with a wry smile. "Is that your ex-husband, or the guy you'd like to be your *next* husband? I was watching you two together and I couldn't quite figure it out."

"Ex-husband," I croak. It's not really a lie—in

less than seventy-two hours, that term will finally be accurate.

"Now I understand why you're not up for dinner with me," Darby says, flashing me a charming smile. "Not quite over him yet?"

"I was sure I was," I admit, but then I'm rambling, and I can't seem to stop myself. "I mean, it's been awful…not amicable at all these last few months and I thought I really hated the man but…we ended up here together accidentally this weekend and we talked. I mean, we really talked, and somewhere along the line we'd stopped doing that and…now I'm just so confused. I didn't think I had a shred of warm feeling left toward him, but this weekend has made me question everything."

Darby surveys me curiously. "If you had to sum it up in one word, what was broken enough between you that you decided to divorce?"

I ponder this for just a moment, then I admit heavily, "All of this time I thought he was the problem, but I can see now that we both messed up. We just weren't communicating well. Or at all, really."

"And tell me about your communication this weekend?"

"It's… Well, the thing is that we understand the problem now, and we understand each other better than we ever did. That has made it so much easier to relate to each other."

Darby gives me a proud therapist smile, as if I've just had a breakthrough.

I frown at him. "But things were *so broken*,

Darby! You probably can't even imagine how bad it was. It seems simple right now but believe me when I tell you I was miserable when I left. How do you even put that much pain behind you?"

"When pain is caused by behavior, and that behavior genuinely changes, it's a simple matter of forgiveness. After that, moving on together isn't as hard as you might think, because one rule is absolute in life and relationships—you never have to let the past define your future. Not ever."

You review the code. You figure out why it keeps looping back over itself, then you change it.

"I don't know what I want, let alone what Paul wants." I rub my forehead.

"Forgive me for being presumptuous, Izzy…but I think that maybe you do know exactly what you want. Perhaps you're just afraid to admit it to yourself."

"He didn't seem to want me to follow him just now, and I can't tell if that's because he was trying to be altruistic and he thought I wanted to be here with you, or he didn't want to spend any more time with me today."

"What a perplexing mystery. If only there were some way you could find out the answer to that question," Darby says wryly.

I swallow the lump in my throat, then glance toward the door. It's still raining out there, so Paul's probably already in a car on his way home. I wonder what he's thinking. I'm also painfully aware now that there's only one way I'm going to find out.

"I have a feeling you're an excellent therapist, Darby," I say, glancing back to the man in the booth with me.

"I'm a good friend, too," Darby laughs. "Can I buy you a drink, or are you just going to head home?"

"I'll have another drink." I sigh. "I'm going to need liquid courage before I attempt this conversation."

CHAPTER TWENTY-ONE

Paul

I'M SURE I'M doing the right thing. I'm certain I've read that whole interaction with Bel right.

She was quiet. She was staring at the table. She seemed distracted. It sounds like they've been spending time together, so she must like him. And she'd already made plans with him for tonight, long before we agreed to spend today together.

In short, something was on Bel's mind, and the obvious conclusion seems to be that the guy she liked was in the bar with us and she wanted to be with him, not with me.

It makes sense. We've already confirmed that we're just going to be friends. If Isabel is really ready to move on, then as a good friend, I should encourage her to do so.

And I should be feeling pleased. In one single weekend I've managed to move from burning anger toward her to genuine goodwill.

The problem is that as I push through the door and step out into the street, instead of feeling pleased, I feel like I want to smash something. In fact, there is so much unbridled energy pumping through my veins, I'm positively vibrating with it, and it's all I can do to stop myself from turning around, storming back across the restaurant, picking up that smug bastard and throwing him through a window.

Residual jealousy. This doesn't mean anything. Just keep a calm head and get used to the idea of Bel being with someone else, because she's probably feeling better about things, too, now that she's found some closure and moving on with her life will almost certainly mean dating other men.

An image pops into my mind uninvited. I see Isabel on our wedding day, with the late evening sun filtering through her wild halo of ringlets as she floated down the aisle toward me. Only the image in my mind takes an awful turn, and I see that guy standing there, waiting for her at the end of the aisle instead of me.

It turns out that after a lifetime of living in my head, a mental image like that is more than enough to make me run on pure feeling for just a moment. I spin on my heel and turn back toward the bar but manage to stop myself again at the door. I take several slow, calming breaths, then spin again and walk away.

Heavy rainclouds are still hanging over the village and it's sprinkling on and off. I was going to catch a cab, but now I'll walk. I need to do something to burn off all of these loud emotions.

The problem is that every step feels heavier than the last, and while intellectually I am sure I have made the right decision in encouraging Isabel to stay with her...*friend*, my heart is racing and my gut is churning.

I'm so focused on my inner turmoil that I don't notice the sound coming from within my backpack at first. When I finally realize it's my phone ringing, I curse and drop the backpack to the ground so I can fish around inside to withdraw the device.

I notice the time before I notice Dad's name on the screen. It's 7:35 p.m., Sunday night. I'm thirty-five minutes late for my regular dinner with him because I completely forgot to tell him I'm out of town.

"Dad," I say as I pick up the call. I'm now pacing on the sidewalk, unable to convince my legs to begin the journey toward the house—or more specifically, away from Isabel.

"Son! You're late. Everything okay?"

"I'm so sorry. I forgot to tell you I went to Greenport for the weekend." Added now to the turmoil in my chest is guilt. Dad will have cooked a meal for me. What will he do with the excess food?

"Greenport, huh?" Dad says thoughtfully. "One last time before the house goes to Izzy?"

I barely even hear him. Now I'm imagining Dad inviting his girlfriend to sit at the table to eat the food he's prepared for me.

"You have a girlfriend," I say, and I hear Dad's sharp intake of breath.

"*How* do you know that?"

"Isabel is here. We got to talking and she mentioned it. Why didn't you tell me?"

"Wait...you and Izzy talked?"

It says a lot about how hard our separation has been on the people Isabel and I care about that they all seem to react with shock when I mention we're in the same place at the same time.

"It's a long story, Dad. And don't change the subject. Why wouldn't you tell me you'd met someone? And why tell Isabel but not me?"

"Well, in my defense, I didn't mean to tell Izzy either," Dad says. "I guess she told you I've been working out with her a bit."

"Yeah."

"Elspeth was training with me at the gym, and Izzy asked me if there was something more going on than just a friendship. I have no idea how she knew, but I couldn't really lie to her."

"Why didn't you want to tell us?" I ask stiffly. "Didn't you realize we'd both be happy for you?"

"Son..." Dad sighs heavily. "When I fell in love with your mother, it was like I'd been struck by the very best kind of lightning—like something exceedingly unlikely had happened. I'd met someone who was brilliant and beautiful and kind and giving. How many people do you know who meet criteria like that? And then *she* fell in love with *me?* I'm far too right-brain to believe in 'the one,' but I do believe in statistics, so I was reasonably certain that the odds of someone like me meeting a woman who fit me as well as your mom did were astronomically small, and then the odds of her loving back? It was miraculous."

Dad trails off for a moment. "I saw you fall in love with Izzy. I knew you had that same out-of-body experience—watching a miracle unfold before your eyes, feeling the truth of it all in your very bones. So at the worst moment in your life, when you were watching all of that end, how was I supposed to tell you that lightning had struck me again? I knew you would never begrudge me from moving on from your mom, but I just couldn't bear to tell you that while you were losing the love of your life, I was finding the second love of mine."

"I appreciate you trying to protect me," I say. "But I would have been happy for you. Yes, this year has been shit for me, but Dad...you were alone for twenty years. I would always have celebrated that with you. I want you to be happy."

"I want you to be happy, too," Dad says, his voice suddenly rough, then he adds, "And that's exactly why I want to backtrack for just a minute. Explain to me how the hell you and Izzy went from sworn enemies to vacation buddies in less than a week."

"We didn't come out here together." I stare back at the bar. "We just wound up at the house at the same time and we got to talking."

"And..."

"And what?"

"And did you resolve anything?"

"We've spent the whole weekend together, and all we've done is resolve things. Maybe we resolved everything that was left unsaid." And had sex. But there are some things a father just does not need to know about his son.

"So, what does this mean?"

"It means we're friends now."

"Just friends?"

I swallow hard. "Just friends, yeah."

"Is that what you want?"

"I don't even know," I admit. "But it doesn't matter what I want. Anything else is impossible."

"Paul, you are far too intelligent to use a lazy term like *impossible* to describe an event which is, in fact, possible," Dad scolds. "Let me ask you something, son. What are the odds of shuffling a deck of cards properly and dealing any particular order of cards?"

"Any particular order of cards?"

"Sure."

I pause, begin the calculation and quickly come to a surprising conclusion. "Exceedingly unlikely, I'd say. Close to impossible."

"That's correct. In fact, there are roughly as many variations on how a deck of cards might be ordered as there are atoms in the entire universe. In fact, every single time a deck of cards has ever been shuffled or will ever be shuffled, it's probable that an entirely new and exceedingly unlikely order results. So sometimes, my son, achieving the impossible really is just a question of actually dealing the cards in your hand."

"Dad. You would never use that analogy in one of your lectures."

"Correct. It's an extremely fluffy application of

statistical probability, and one that can only be used by a man in love."

"So now that the secret is out, do I actually get to meet this Elspeth when I come back to the city?"

"I'll make sure she's here when you come for dinner next week," Dad says, then he adds, "And by all means, feel free to bring Izzy along, too. Go get her, son."

"It's not nearly that simple."

"I just used math to show you that it is that simple," Dad chuckles.

"You just used math to show me that when you're in love, you forget how probability works."

"Love you, son. Good luck."

I glance back at the bar one last time as I drop the phone into my pocket and then try to turn to leave.

But I can't.

I just can't.

This jealousy I feel is not some hangover from when we were together. It's fresh and it's new, and it's urgent. On Friday, it wouldn't have occurred to me that Isabel and I could even be friends again someday, but over the course of this weekend, I started to want even more than that.

It didn't happen Friday night when we had sex. It happened yesterday morning when we sat down to breakfast and we chatted about our lives and we connected on an emotional level. Sex with Isabel is amazing, but it always has been. What's been missing, at least for the last year of our marriage, was a solid foundation of friendship.

And we have just spent forty-eight hours proving that we really could build that better than it ever was before we broke.

I take a step toward the door, but my heart is racing now, and I'm conscious that I'm about to take the greatest risk of my life. I've never really risked rejection from Isabel before. She kissed me the first time. She was the first to say, *I love you.* Every time I took our relationship to the next level, I did so in the safest way I could come up with.

Not once have I ever put myself out there for her. *That's part of why you lost her, asshole.*

I've changed and grown this year. I've proven to myself, and maybe even to Bel this weekend, that I can be someone better than I used to be.

I push the door open and stride back into the bar.

She's sitting at the booth with the guy, nursing what's clearly a fresh glass of wine as they share a quiet chat. I can see that their gazes are locked, but I can't read her expression at all and I don't have the time to stand here and stare at her until I figure out what she's thinking, and that means I'm walking in completely blind.

My palms are sweaty like I'm a thirteen-year-old kid about to ask a girl out for the first time. I've had girlfriends, lovers and a wife, which is what makes it very fucking weird that in some strange way, I *am* about to ask a girl out for the first time.

This is a risk. But even if the odds of the cards shuffling out in my favor are astronomically small, Isabel Rose Winton is worth taking the chance.

I stride to the booth and she looks up at me. Her eyes are wide, her brows are knitting. Her mouth falls open, and she shoots a look at the other guy.

What does that look mean? Is it *I'm sorry about this*? Is it *save me, my crazy ex-husband is about to make an idiot of himself*?

The only thing worse than how exposed I feel in this moment is the regret I know I would feel if I didn't at least try to convince her to try again. I won't get this exactly right—I won't have the most persuasive words or the most charming delivery. But I let her slip out of my life once before while I waited for the perfect time, and there's no fucking way I'll ever do that again.

"I know we said we'd be friends," I say. "Maybe a good friend would leave you to spend time with this guy and I know a good friend would support you in moving on. But fuck it, Isabel, I can't be a good friend to you, not like this. I'll always want more than friendship with you. I want to take everything good that's come out of this fucking awful year and use it to build a better future with you—"

Isabel stands, and time freezes as I stare at her and try to understand *this* expression. Her eyes are wide. Her mouth is hanging open. Her cheeks are flushed. Her pupils are dilated. Her breaths are coming faster and faster and then—

She smiles, and it is everything.

I'm vaguely aware of Darby mumbling a farewell and leaving the booth, but I pay no attention, because right then, Isabel throws her arms around my neck and she kisses me hard.

It turns out that tonight, I'm once again the luckiest guy in the fucking universe.

I cup her face in my hands and I kiss her back and I try to communicate with her—to use my kiss to tell her everything that I'm not eloquent enough to say on the fly.

She breaks away from me all too soon and when I open my eyes, her face is wet with tears. When I reach up to cup her face in my palm, my hand is shaking.

"It's still really complicated," she whispers thickly.

"We'll figure it out."

"We hurt each other so badly."

"We can learn from our mistakes."

"What does this even look like?"

"I don't have any of the answers, Isabel. All I really know for sure is that you are my sun and my moon, and that there's nothing I won't do for another chance at proving that to you."

A broad, relieved smile breaks over her face, and she exhales, long and slow.

I wonder if that feels like the first breath she's taken in a year, or maybe more.

I can't wait to get her alone so I can ask her.

The air is heavy with moisture after the storm and in the distance, I see more lightning on the horizon, so I suspect there's more instability coming. That isn't why Isabel and I all but run from the cab to the front door. Unlike Friday night, we're not rushing to make an impulsive mistake now—our steps are sure and our shared purpose is clear.

I open the front door and Isabel slips inside after me. I hang my keys on the hook, and Isabel waits, close to me but not touching. When I turn back to her, we just stare at one another, a question hanging in the air between us.

"What's the next step?" I ask her. "It's probably too late to stop the divorce. I don't even know if I want to—" I break off when she frowns "—let me explain, Bel. I just mean…that era of our lives is over. Whatever happens between us now is new…a new depth of intimacy. New trust. A fresh start."

Her smile returns. It feels like the first rays of the morning sun breaking on my face after the longest night of my life. She launches herself at me and her arms are around my neck and her lips are against mine.

I catch her shoulders in my hands and say hastily, "Wait—should we sit down first? Talk some more?"

"I can't believe I'm saying this," Isabel laughs. "But you've shared so much of yourself with me this weekend. All I want to do right now is get very, very naked with you, as soon as humanly possible. There'll be time to talk later."

"I can get on board with that plan." I grin, and then she's kissing me and we're walking blindly to the stairs, crashing into walls and stumbling as we go. At the staircase, Isabel throws a flirty wink over her shoulder and sprints up ahead of me, two steps at a time. I chase her up, and when I reach the master bedroom—our bedroom—I find her waiting for me, standing by the bed.

I leave the light off as I step slowly toward her. I'm savoring the way she looks in the semidarkness of the bedroom, trying to imprint this to memory. The drapes are open, and over the water beyond the house, lightning flickers, illuminating her silhouette. When we're face-to-face, she starts to unzip her hoodie, but I catch her hands in mine.

"We have all the time in the world now, Bel," I whisper. "Let's take this slow. I want to savor every single second with you this time around."

I'm not actually sure why that's sexy, but apparently it is, because Isabel gives a helpless little moan and then her mouth is on mine and she's tugging impatiently to drag my shorts down.

"We do have all the time in the world," she mutters. "We'll do it slowly next time."

I laugh, and break apart from her to strip, and she's laughing, too, as she kicks her outer clothing away. Now, she's standing before me in the red bikini. Before she can remove it, I trail one finger slowly from her collarbone to the skin above the cups of the bikini top.

"I kept my eyes to myself today when you were standing on that swim platform in this bikini," I tell her. "It was the hardest fucking thing I've ever done, but I did it."

"What a gentleman. And now you get your reward."

She reaches up behind her neck and tugs the bow to the halter top. It comes undone in one smooth movement, and the cups fall forward, leaving her breasts free. I drink her in, watching as her nipples pull tighter under the attention of my gaze, watching as her chest rises and falls as her breathing comes faster.

Isabel slides her hands slowly down her body, tucks her thumbs under the sides of the briefs and pushes them down her legs to kick them away. When she stands, I bend to kiss her, and she wraps her arms around my neck and then falls back onto the bed, dragging me with her. Soft, teasing kisses quickly become urgent and clumsy.

I sit up away from her on the bed, leaving her lying stretched out before me, all so that I can stare down at her in the moonlight. I run my hand over her skin, from the tips of her breasts, across her stomach, back up to her neck. I run the pads of my fingers over her mouth, and then drag them down slowly again, to toy at the hair at the junction of her legs.

Isabel hisses in a breath and sinks into the bed, letting her legs fall open. I'm fixated on a task again. This time, it's touching her in all of the ways she likes best, stroking and rubbing her until she's so wet, she's writhing around on the bed like she's in a fever.

"Paul," she gasps after a while.

"Hmm?" I say innocently.

She growls at me, sits up and pushes me down onto my back, then straddles me and kisses me. I can feel her, wet and hot against my erection. The anticipation of sliding home has turned my brain to absolute mush when she breaks away from me and asks, "Should I run downstairs and get your wallet?"

I look at her blankly. "My wallet? Now?"

"I'm asking if we need a condom, Paul," she blurts, flushing. She avoids my gaze. "It's totally up to you. I haven't been with anyone else, and I still have my IUD."

"Oh," I say. "Sorry. Right. No, I haven't been with anyone else either."

"I'm relieved I don't have to be jealous, and I'm even more relieved I don't have sprint downstairs to get that condom."

"Isabel," I whisper, laughing softly. "I couldn't even bring myself to take my wedding ring off. Plus, I lasted like twenty seconds on Friday night. Did you really think I'd been with anyone else since you left?"

"Don't be so hard on yourself." She gives me a grin, then bends to kiss me again. "That was the best twenty seconds of my year."

And then we're kissing again, and I can't stop touching her—my hands roam up and down her back, along the taut lines of her hips and ass, up to touch her hair and to cup her breasts. When she shifts and takes me into her body, I feel a swell of emotion. It builds and builds as she begins to rock against me, until it's a tsunami of feeling—more than physical pleasure, more than just relief and happiness. There's a throb in my chest and a prickle in my eyes and as

I stare up at her while she moves against me, my vision suddenly blurs.

Isabel pauses and touches my cheek gently, just the way she did in the water earlier today. This time, when she lifts her finger away, she holds it up to show me the drop of moisture she's collected. "You're crying," she whispers.

"I guess I am."

"You don't cry."

"Don't doubt how I feel for you," I whisper back. "Even if I don't tell you often enough in the future, please don't ever doubt it. There's nothing more important in my life than this."

Then she's kissing me again, and soon I'm not sure which tears are mine and which are hers. That's the real magic of this moment: we're in it together. I match her thrust for thrust and feeling for feeling and if this is what partnership is supposed to feel like, I had it all so very wrong the first time around. There's new depth here, new dimensions to explore with her. I'm not sure I'll ever figure out the words to express to her how I feel, but I know I'll happily spend the rest of my life trying. I wrap my arms around Isabel's back, holding her tight against me, somehow still not close enough even though I'm literally inside her.

"I'll never get enough of you," I say against her lips. "Never."

She whimpers in response, and her nails dig into my arms as she suddenly tenses, then comes with a groan. That's it for me, too—she pulses around me and I'm coming and coming, my release leaving me limp and dumb. Isabel collapses over me, and I keep my arms around her and hold her hard up against me.

"I love you," I whisper. I don't know if there's some social convention here—does the clock reset? Do we date again first, and is there a right time to say *I love you* to someone you never really stopped loving in the first place?

All I know is that love is what I feel, and that this time, I'll say what I feel. If Bel isn't ready to say it back, I'll wait.

"I love you, too," Isabel murmurs. "This might be hard to believe, but I don't think I actually ever stopped."

"Maybe the reason we fought each other so hard is that we didn't really know how to fight *for* each other."

"I don't think I'll ever get tired of hearing you say things like that."

For the third night in a row, I fall asleep with Isabel in my arms. This time, I slip into sleep with a smile on my face, because I know I'm going to be doing this very same thing every night for the rest of my life.

Part Four

Monday

CHAPTER TWENTY-TWO

Isabel

I WAKE UP SLOWLY, clinging to sleep as long as I can, mostly because I'm fearful that last night was some delicious dream. In the end, I give in to the pull of consciousness only because I recognize the warm, solid body beneath me is very much real and very much Paul.

I finally open my eyes but quickly shift so that I can look up at him. He's still asleep, the lengths of his eyelashes resting against his cheek. His stubble is so heavy now, it's almost a full beard. I hope he doesn't shave it off because I like it a lot.

"Are you watching me sleep?" he says, opening his eye just a crack. His voice is rough with sleep, but there's an amused lilt to it.

"Hey," I whisper.

"Hey," he whispers back, and then he smiles. "Sleep well?"

"So well."

"Me, too," he says, then he reaches down to brush his lips against mine and excuses himself to use the bathroom. I stretch out across the bed, a contented smile lingering on my lips as I wait for him.

"What time is it?" he calls from the bathroom. I glance down at my watch.

"It's 8:00 a.m." I run my hands over my breasts, feeling my body coming to life at the thought of continuing last night's makeup-sex marathon. "Come back to bed."

"Shit," he says, "The car will be here soon."

At first, I assume he's cursing because the car is coming and he's forgotten to cancel it. I hear him cleaning his teeth, then there's the clink of bottles colliding, and then a zip sounds, and Paul saunters back into the bedroom with his toiletry case under his arm.

"What are you doing?" I assumed we'd talk this morning—to make a plan for the future, to figure out how to make a way forward together again, because there's still so much left unsaid. I'm numb as I sit up in bed.

Paul diverts from his path to brush a kiss against my lips, but then continues his way to the closet. "Packing," he says easily.

"Paul…" I whisper.

He glances at me, but his path doesn't falter.

When he pulls the closet open and withdraws his bag, I clear my throat. "I just… It's just… You're really going back today? Now?"

"I have to," he says. "I'm sure Audrey and Jess handled the retreat, but they'll be waiting on me for decisions. There'll be things that only I can do that will need to be done today." He looks back at me again and frowns. "You get that, right?"

"Oh, I get it," I say. I can't help the bitterness that seeps into my tone. Even after everything we've been through, it seems that the business is still more important than *we* are to Paul. And the worst thing is, he did tell me on Saturday morning that he still loved his job. As much work as Paul has done on himself and as much as he missed me and missed us, his priorities haven't actually changed.

"Why don't you come back early with me?" he says, still cheerful. "We could—"

"No, Paul. I won't be changing my plans to fit in with your schedule," I snap. The warm glow I reveled in all morning as I watched him sleep has vanished. I'm overwhelmed by a rush of dark emotions, and I can't decide if I should climb beneath the duvet and pull it over my head, or if I need to run downstairs and lock myself in the guest room before I burst into tears.

In the recesses of my mind, there's a warning bell sounding: *maybe I'm overreacting here.* But Paul's decision to leave this morning collides with the sorest of my sore spots, and I can't stop and temper my own behavior because the hurt is instantly fresh and raw again.

I can't believe he's walking away from me right now. I let myself believe that things had really changed.

"Hey, listen to me," Paul says, stepping away from his bag to approach me at the bed. He crouches in front of me and tries to meet my gaze. "Just because I have to go back today doesn't mean that *this* isn't important to me. It is. But there are people counting on me in the city. I can't let them down."

"No, you're doing the right thing," I whisper.

He nods, satisfied by this, and he stands, but then hesitates in front of me—apparently reading something in my expression that gives him pause. Meanwhile, my grief is rising all over again. I'm vaguely aware that this time it's going to be even worse, because I had this glorious and awful glimpse of how things might have been.

Paul's still staring at me, increasingly confused, and so I throw the duvet back so I can climb out of bed. "This was a bad idea."

Paul blinks at me. "Isabel, what the fuck are you talking about? Two minutes ago you were so happy—"

"We've been kidding ourselves, caught up in isolation out here. But there's a real world back there in the city, and nothing has really changed." I interrupt him harshly.

"Everything has changed," Paul says flatly, and all I can think is, *My God, I hope he doesn't fight for me this time.* It was hard enough to walk away from him last time, but this time? After the way I stupidly let hope blossom inside me last night? This time, walking away might just kill me, especially if I have to convince Paul not to follow me.

"You're still you. I'm still me. We are fundamentally incompatible, Paul."

"Then what the hell were the last twelve hours about?" he says stiffly.

I feel a twist of guilt in my gut, but it's soothed when I remind myself that *he* is making the decisions that break us. Not me.

"I was wrong," I croak.

Paul's neutral expression shifts, and suddenly he's staring at me with suspicion. "Was this whole weekend just another way to kick me while I was down?"

"No!" This conversation is going nowhere, and I'm going to cry any second now. I reach into the en suite for a towel and wrap it around myself, then head toward the door.

He catches my elbow, and he ducks so that I can't avoid his gaze. "Isabel. Talk to me. What is this?"

"Inevitable," I whisper. I close my eyes and swallow hard. "This was inevitable. I'm sorry, Paul."

There's a long, painful moment of silence. When I open my eyes, Paul is staring at me, tightness in the set of his mouth.

"You're serious."

"I am," I say quietly, then I raise my chin and for the second time in a year, I force myself to turn my back and walk away from him.

CHAPTER TWENTY-THREE

Paul

I LET HER storm off downstairs. We'll talk more—we'll have to, but the clock is ticking now. My driver will be here any minute, and my whole team will be waiting for me back in the city.

It was one thing to take off for the weekend, knowing that Jess and Audrey would hold up the fort. It would be another to fail to not show up today, when the results from the retreat will be in, and decisions will need to be made about the release. My team will be counting on me, and maybe even more important, so will Jess and Marcus—two of my best friends, people who have built their entire careers around mine.

I simply have to go back.

When I bring my things downstairs, I find Isabel out on the deck, sitting on the sun chair, facing the ocean. I pull the sliding door open and step out to approach her.

"We need to talk—"

"Don't do this, Paul," she interrupts me, her tone curt. "Please, just go."

"I can't just go." She flicks me a glance, but then goes back to staring at the ocean. "I love you. And you love me."

"Maybe so. Maybe love isn't enough, Paul. One good weekend together doesn't undo the years of pain that came before it."

"We've both changed," I remind her.

She pauses, and she runs a hand through her hair, studiously avoiding my gaze now. "Paul, we've been in a bubble this weekend and it's been easy to kid ourselves. But there really are very good reasons why we are getting divorced. You need to go, and we need to say goodbye." She raises her gaze to mine, and this time, she holds my gaze without hesitation.

I stare at her, waiting for her to crumble. But even when I know that stare has stretched to the point that it's uncomfortable, all I can see in Isabel's face is stubborn determination and resolve.

She means it. She's actually doing this again.

"Just tell me once and for all, so that when I look back at this moment, I don't second-guess myself like I did last time," I say flatly. "Was there anything I could have done to make you happy? To make you try again?"

"No," Isabel says. "I know you've done a lot of thinking…a lot of reflection and a lot of work on yourself. I'll always care about you and I'm proud of you. I really am. That's kind of why this is so confusing…because we feel so different on the surface. But deep down? People can't change, Paul. Not really. There is nothing you would have done today to make me try again."

I nod curtly, and then I close the door and stalk out to the car.

"Morning, Mr. Winton," the driver says.

I nod at him, climb into the back seat and lean my head against the headrest, then close my eyes.

It occurs to me that I haven't looked at my email in three days, at the worst possible time. If I were a smarter man, I'd check my messages so that I was prepared for whatever shitstorm waits for me at the office. But I can't even motivate myself to pretend to care about work right now. As I feel the shock start to wear off, all I can think about is how wrong it feels to walk away from her and how every single cell in my body seems to be clamoring for me to have the driver turn the car around so I can go back.

I'm pissed off—I'm always mildly pissed off these days, at least I was until this weekend, but this is worse. This anger feels a lot less like the rage that's kept me going this past nine months, and a lot more like grief and disappointment. Maybe that's why I'm more than halfway back to the city before I even realize that I don't have my laptop—it's still charging on the table in the house where I left it Friday morning.

There is nothing you would have done today to make me try again.

I replay those moments on the deck over and over again in my mind as the car winds its way back to Manhattan, and gradually, something about the moment slowly begins to feel wrong. Off. Was it something about the way she held herself or the tone she used?

I don't know, but as I reflect on that moment, I become increasingly sure that I'm missing something. She was telling me something deeper than the words she used. I try to dissect it over the last hour of the drive, as the city traffic becomes thicker and thicker. By the time I reach the building in the financial district that houses Brainway Technologies, the hidden message I can feel but can't yet hear has consumed my entire mind.

I don't even want to go upstairs to my office. I want to lock myself away in a sensory deprivation tank so that I can find enough peace and quiet to analyze that last argument with Isabel until I really understand it.

Maybe I'll do that later. But first, I do have to face the music at the office.

I thank the driver and step out of the car, staring up at the building as if I'm a tourist, new to this jungle of skyscrapers. We share this building with dozens of other businesses, but even so, we've come a very long way from the one-bedroom apartment Jess, Marcus and I started out in.

I know every little thing about our software and our company. I know that Marcus's team agonized over changing the font and the colors of this logo a few years ago, even though the change was simply to make the text slightly brighter and remove the serifs from the letters. I know that we now have 201 employees, which is a seventy-four percent increase over the last five years. I know—to the cent—what our turnover and our profit margin were last year. I know that as of last Friday morning, we had 204 outstanding bugs and defects on the coming version of the browser, and 119 feature requests. I know, by heart, the recent results from each of the performance indicators measured in our last round of QA testing. I know which lines of code I wrote myself in the early days. I still see them sometimes, and those strings of letters and numbers feel like old friends. I know our application better than I know myself. Any single thing it's capable of, I know how to achieve.

There are sometimes still challenges in my work, but there's rarely any mystery in the day-to-day detail of it. Unlike my personal life, which always has and probably always will be full of both. I know a lot of things about Isabel, too, but knowing things about her doesn't mean I understand her. My intellect has meant success beyond my wildest dreams at work, but I'm out of my depth when it comes to my wife and I always have been.

There is nothing you would have done today to make me try again.

I step into the elevator with a bunch of strangers and at long last, I reach into my pocket for the phone I've not looked at since I called Dad last night. There's a bunch of emails from my employees this morning, and a single text from Isabel, sent just after I left the vacation home three hours ago.

Goodbye, Paul. For what it's worth, I really am sorry.

I'm numb as I walk to my office, nodding silently at staff but shaking my head immediately whenever anyone looks as though they might approach me. Vanessa stands when she sees me, her mouth open as if she's going to launch a flood of problems or requests at me, but takes one look at my face, closes her mouth and sits back down.

I close my office door and call for a spare laptop from the systems team. I wait in silence for the laptop, then when it arrives, instead of logging in, I set my phone right on top of it and stare at the blank screen. After a deep breath, I wake the screen to show Isabel's message again.

Goodbye, Paul. For what it's worth, I really am sorry.

Her words play through my mind on a loop, and I keep replaying that moment at the deck over and over because I know she was trying to tell me something and I just can't grasp it.

There is nothing you would have done today to make me try again.

There is nothing *you would have* done *to make me try again.*

There *is nothing you would have done to make me try again.*

There is nothing *you* would have done.

My door flies open and Audrey bursts in without preamble. My senior developer is a mess. Her purple hair is in haphazard pigtails, she's got mascara all over her cheeks, and I don't usually pay too much attention to these things, but even so—she was wearing a Garfield shirt when I left Thursday, which she's still wearing, except now it's splattered with food stains.

"I can't believe you left me alone with that mess." She scowls.

I hide a smile and motion toward the chair opposite my desk. "How did you do?"

"How did I do? How did I *do*? Are you kidding me right now, Paul Winton? Did you seriously not even look at the project management system all weekend? I figured you were bluffing!" The scowl morphs, and now she's staring at me in puzzlement. "You've changed, Paul."

I think back to the last retreat. Thirty-one fewer bugs. Forty-one fewer feature requests. And the look and feel of the browser weren't changing at all—this time it is; we're modernizing the interface completely. Last year's was a much smaller release and we had so much less riding on it.

And yet I lived and breathed that retreat. I planned it obsessively. This time I didn't even make it into the office.

I do still care this time... I'm just not fixated on the details in the same way, and maybe that's not a bad thing. I've set a strategy in place and I've got a team here that really represents the best of the best. They don't actually need me to babysit them, and even more than that, in babysitting them for all of these years, I've both held them back and neglected too many other areas of my life.

"I really have changed, haven't I?" I wake the phone again and read Isabel's message one more time.

Goodbye, Paul. For what it's worth, I really am sorry.

Then I replay her final words to me.

There is nothing you would have done today to make me try again.

That's when I finally hear my wife's message, in all of its bewildering, complicated beauty. She didn't say *could*. She said *would*.

If she'd said *could,* that would mean one thing. Because *could* relates to ability, specifically my ability to convince her to give our marriage another try. But *would* relates to will, and my willingness to convince her.

Isabel Winton in all of her magnificent complication has underestimated me, and she's underestimated my determination to build a life with her again.

I look around my office and take it all in. The awards we've won, the milestones we've celebrated, the profit and the achievement and growth and the *pride* of it all. It's hollow without her. Maybe I knew that all along, because I certainly wanted to build something great for her. Maybe I missed that realization until this weekend because I was still trying to do too much at once, even after all of my hard-won self-development this year.

"…that bug on the macOS still isn't resolved and Jess really wanted the feature request for—"

"Audrey?"

Audrey's babble falters, and her face falls. "Paul, I really, *really* need you to switch back onto work-mode-Paul now," she says weakly.

"I will," I promise her, then I smile. Actually, given how my cheeks stretch, I'm pretty sure I beam at her, because I'm so fucking happy I'm sure it's radiating out from my soul. "You just hop up out of that chair, leave the office and shut the door behind you and give me ten minutes to fix the rest of my life, and then I'll help you sort it all out, okay?"

As soon as Audrey closes the door, I scoop my phone up and call my *wife*. It goes to voice mail, and I hesitate for only a second.

"Isabel Winton. You were so fucking wrong this morning, so, so fucking wrong. There is nothing—nothing—I wouldn't do if it would convince you to try again. You just tell me what you need from me. Let's talk. Let's talk and talk and talk like this weekend over and over again, until we run out of breath and days and hours on this earth. Please, oh please, Bel, please let's try again?"

I stop, take a deep breath and then feel blood rush to my face as I realize I've just left that message on her voice mail. Maybe Isabel was wrong about my father having more game than me. "Call me back as soon as you can, please, Bel."

Then I stand and pace the office for a bit. But the wall to my office is glass, and that means I can't miss the fact that Audrey is standing right outside my office, and she's also pacing. I run my hands through my hair impatiently and throw the door open. "Okay, okay! Let's get this shit sorted."

"Jess really doesn't want to push the release back," Audrey blurts. "She and Marcus met on the weekend, and Marcus is worried that we're going to freak out the corporate clients if we don't have a reliable release schedule."

I turn toward the hall to Jess's office, but Audrey has already started walking back toward the bull pen where our team works.

"Where are you going?" she groans, impatient and frustrated.

"Let's go see Jess," I call back, still walking away from her.

"But you haven't even reviewed the job log! You don't know what—"

"I don't need to!" I call after her.

"But—"

"Audrey, if *you* couldn't get it done, it can't be done."

CHAPTER TWENTY-FOUR

Isabel

THE FIRST THING on my to-do list today was apparently to break my own heart. I got that done in record time, which brought me to my next pressing task.

Crying. Hysterically.

I cried as I texted Paul a final goodbye. I cried as I walked back to my sun chair. I cried when I realized that the box of Kleenex he fetched for me Saturday night was still sitting on the deck beside the chair, and I cried even harder when I picked that box up and remembered how it felt when Paul comforted me. I cried until my throat was parched and my nose was red. I cried until my vision was blurry. I cried until I almost ran out of self-pity, and I do seem to have more than my share of that emotion in general, so that took quite a while.

When I was at last in the nest of used Kleenex I was planning to build when I decided to come to Greenport last week, and my tear ducts seemed to have run out of moisture, I reluctantly dragged myself back into the house for some water and, perhaps equally as vital after the crying jag, some strong coffee. The sight of the carton of half-and-half in the fridge set off a fresh round of weeping, but I managed to make my coffee and pour my water in between sobs.

It was only as I was walking to sit at the dining room table that I saw that fucking laptop, still sitting under Darby's tulips.

Now I'm sitting at the table, nursing the coffee, staring at the laptop and at last, doing a spot of dry-eyed thinking.

On Friday, this stupid little computer seemed to be a symbol of everything that had gone wrong between Paul and me. It represented all of those hours where his business was his priority, and I felt forgotten…ignored…unimportant.

Today, the sight of this broken laptop has entirely lost its sting. It's just an object again, and a pretty sad one at that. This computer is just a tool the man I love has used to build a career he's proud of. It's just a tool the man I love *forgot* or *ignored* this morning, maybe because he was genuinely upset that I was abruptly ending things with him for the second time in a year.

I made a mistake this weekend, but I didn't make it this morning. I made my mistake last night, when Paul and I kissed each other in that bar, and I felt like everything between us was fixed in an instant. Relationships don't get broken or fixed in a single minute, especially when they're as complex as the one Paul and I share.

No, relationships get broken or fixed because of

the pattern of the decisions we make. Decisions to feel sorry for ourselves instead of changing our circumstances. Decisions to refrain from sharing our truths, openly and honestly. Decisions to hide in our work.

Or…

Decisions to forgive. Decisions to talk. Decisions to share ourselves. Decisions to change. Decisions to ask for what we fucking need, and decisions to trust in each other to meet those needs.

That's why now, I need to make the first of a new series of decisions. This time, I'm making the decision to swallow my pride and apologize. The decision to take responsibility for where I went wrong. The decision to belatedly share with Paul exactly what I needed from him this morning and why and even why I didn't feel like I could say those words directly.

And maybe most important, I'm making the decision to be the first one to extend the olive branch, but I'm making that particular decision for me. I'll be the first to reach out this time around, because I don't want to find myself sitting stagnant and sulking about how things turned out in another ten months.

CHAPTER TWENTY-FIVE

Paul

"OUR VIP CUSTOMERS are counting on this release. If we're really going to delay it, we need to find some way to put a positive spin on it," Marcus says slowly.

We're all seated around Jess's desk—me and Audrey, who is stuffing Twizzlers into her mouth so fast I'm scared she's going to choke herself, and Jess and Marcus. Marcus looks tired and a little anxious. Jess is tapping her bloodred talons on her desk in a fashion that can only be described as menacing.

I feel terrible to have let my team down, but I feel positively sick that I've let Jess and Marcus down. I simply couldn't have built this company alone. None of what I've achieved in the past thirteen years would have been possible without their faith in me, and I can't remember another time when I didn't meet or even exceed their expectations. I've been distracted, and I've dropped the ball.

"Paul?" Jess asks. "Any ideas?"

"You know why I was such a miserable failure of a development manager this year?" I say thoughtfully. Even I can't miss the nervous look Jess and Marcus exchange, so I address my comments to Audrey, who stuffs yet another Twizzler in her mouth and shakes her head. "Distraction, Audrey. It's pretty much impossible for most people to multitask. The more they try to do, the less they achieve. What I was missing was clarity, and clarity only comes with focus."

I scan my gaze around the little circle of my colleagues and find that everyone is staring at me blankly. But the idea is picking up steam now, and so I stand and walk to the whiteboard on Jess's wall to scribble out the beginnings of a design spec. After a few minutes, Audrey catches on and shoots to her feet.

"Of course! I *love* this," she exclaims.

"I'm sure I will, too," Jess says abruptly. "If someone could just explain it to me."

"We live in the age of distraction, Jessica." I continue to scrawl on the whiteboard. "And the internet is one of the biggest causes of our malaise. Like it or not, our browser is part of the problem, so let's do something none of our competitors have done. Let's give our users a solution."

"Bucking the trend of doing more, faster," Marcus says slowly, and then he stands, too, approaching the whiteboard, no doubt so he can come closer to read my god-awful handwriting. "I like where you're going with this."

"There are third-party apps that offer the ability to lock out certain websites," Audrey explains to Jess. "Hell, I use one myself, but it's clunky. And there are ways to limit corporate traffic—web filtering, proxy servers, group policy. But all of those components meant one more thing to set up, one more thing to administer for the IT team. We'd make our functionality organic. Simple. User-friendly. And integrated. But best of all, the administrator could set company-wide or role-based limits, but if they don't go far enough, the end user could set up their own rules. I mean, say you're allowed to use Facebook at work, but you've gotten into the habit of looking at it unthinkingly. Or say you've developed a habit of lurking on Twitter as a way to procrastinate when you're stuck on an arduous task. Well, with just a few mouse clicks, you could tell Brainwave that during office hours, it needs to block that request or redirect it back to your company website."

"We could even give users the ability to limit themselves to one tab during certain windows of the week," Marcus adds, with growing enthusiasm. He thumps me on the back. "Paul, this kind of brilliance is why we put up with you. How difficult will this be to build?"

"It's easy," Audrey and I say simultaneously. I glance at her, and she's texting on her phone.

"I'll get the UI team on it right now," she says, without looking up. "The key is making this super intuitive, so we'll figure out the workflow and run some mockups by you all later today or tomorrow."

"Jess?" Marcus prompts. "What do you think?"

"I love it," she announces. "We're swimming upstream. But everyone else is complaining about how downstream is too fucking busy and distracting, so this gives us a positive point of difference. You're sure this is easy, Paul?"

"Audrey could code this in her sleep," I assure her. "We'll get it spec'ed up, put a few developers on it and have the rest of the team focus on the outstanding issues. We can sell this as a whizbang new feature, but it'll take no time at all, it just gives us cover to catch up properly with what our customers are actually expecting. How soon can we be ready for testing, Audrey?"

"I…" She flushes, flicking her gaze from the screen of her phone, back to me, Jess and Marcus. "I really don't know… It's…"

"You've got this, Audrey," I say quietly. "Take a look at the project management app there on your phone and tell me how soon the team can be finished."

She looks down, scrolls around for a few minutes, then raises her gaze confidently to me.

"The original release date was next month. We got a lot done this weekend, but we rushed, and I'm expecting a lot of rework. If this additional functionality means the pressure is off, I'd like to propose you push the go-live back by a whole month so we can do a thorough job."

"Make it happen," Jess says, then she claps. "Great work, everyone."

"I'll get my team onto comms, announcing this new, cutting-edge productivity feature that's 'almost ready' so we're going to delay the major release by a few weeks to include it," Marcus announces, already heading for the door. I hear the snap of Audrey's phone camera as she captures my notes from the whiteboard, and then she's also walking out the door, already emailing our team.

"Paul," Jess calls as I move to follow them. I glance back at her. "Welcome back."

"Thanks."

"That was some of your best work, you know."

I glance at the whiteboard and shrug. "Not really. It's hardly technically complex—"

"I meant with Audrey," she interrupts me, and I blink at her. "I didn't sign on to work with you all of those years ago because you were a great coder. I signed on to work with you because you were a visionary, but you can't be a visionary *and* the guy who personally oversees every tiny decision that needs to be made at the application level. You need to set strategy and lead, but to lead, you have to be able to connect…encourage…delegate." She leans back in her chair, then gives me a satisfied nod. "You're getting there, Paul."

I nod curtly. "Thanks." I rap on the doorframe as I step through it.

"Are you ever going to tell me what happened out there?" Jess calls.

"Maybe on your lunch break," I say, shooting her a look through her glass wall. "Remember what I just said about multitasking and productivity? Don't you have work to do?"

Her laughter follows me down the hall as I head back to my office.

AUDREY AND I hunker down in my office with the senior development staff to come up with a plan to address the outstanding work tasks from the weekend, as well as the new functionality we now need to design and incorporate. I keep my phone on the desk, but I know it's on, and I know it will sound when Isabel replies or calls me.

Except that she doesn't.

Several hours pass, and I'm engrossed in work, which is probably for the best because every now and again I have a fleeting awareness that sooner or later, that silence is going to sting like a bitch.

But then my office door flies open, and I glance up to tell whoever has rudely interrupted us that we're busy, and the words die on my lips because it's not Jess or some rude junior programmer but Isabel and she's flustered and she's in my doorway and she doesn't seem at all fazed by the fact that eight of my team members are staring up at her in bewilderment.

She's also holding my laptop.

Our eyes meet and lock. Isabel looks like she's about to burst into tears, and I stand so fast my chair flies back and collides with a bookshelf.

"Out. Everyone out," I say. My voice breaks, and everyone stares at me for a second, so I raise my hand and point to the door, which breaks the stunned moment of silence.

Audrey panics and leads the stampede for the door, and Isabel shifts into the hallway to make room for the horde of programmers, but by the time they've cleared the room, she's charging in and she's at my desk.

"You brought my laptop," I say unthinkingly, apparently deciding to open the conversation with stating the fucking obvious. In my defense, my heart is racing so hard I'm actually feeling light-headed.

"I also drowned it," she says, but before I can figure out what that means, she adds, "You didn't look at it all weekend, did you?"

"Of course I didn't." I frown.

"I accidentally spilled water on it on Friday afternoon. I thought you'd be furious and I was nervous to tell you and then I forgot to tell you because I got so caught up in what was happening between us. But you didn't even notice."

"This weekend wasn't ever about work," I say softly. "I just took the laptop with me because I had to send some emails in the car on my way out there."

Isabel inhales, then exhales, and then she places the laptop on the couch under the window and pushes her hands into her hair. She takes a step toward me, then stops and our eyes lock again.

"I *needed* you to stay this morning," Isabel blurts. Her eyes are red and puffy, and her cheeks are flushed. "I wanted you just once to choose me over Brainway. I know you love your work, but I do need to know that when it counts, I'm going to be your priority. I completely overreacted this morning, and I'm sorry about that. This is going to be a sore point for me for a long time, and we're going to need

to communicate to overcome it. But if you still want
to be with me, I promise you, Paul. I'll work on it. I
want to work on it with you."

I step to her, entwine her hand with mine and tug
her to the doorway.

"Where are we—" she starts to say, but I glance
back at her and shake my head.

"I want to show you something before we talk."

I lead the way to Jess's office and find her assistant Gina chatting animatedly on the phone, but I'm
in a hurry, so I reach down and press the disconnect
button. Gina scowls at me, and I ask her, "Where
is Jessica?"

"She's in the small boardroom with Marcus working on the comms for the updated release schedule—"

"Thanks," I say, and I pull Isabel down another
hallway. When we reach the boardroom, I push the
doors open and Jess and Marcus look up at us in
surprise. I watch Jess's face visibly brighten as she
sees that I'm holding Isabel's hand, and I don't need
a guide to body language to recognize that emotion
as triumph. It doesn't last long, though, because I
greet her with a cheery, "Hi, guys. I'm leaving. You
need to buy me out."

Jess and Marcus gape at me. There's a long, stiff
moment of silence.

"Ah…what the actual fuck, Paul?" The unflap-
pable Jessica Cohen is, evidentially, flapped.

"Or don't." I shrug. "You can have my shares.

Split them, I guess. Do whatever you want, I quit. I don't even give a fuck. Do whatever you have to do."

I turn back toward the door, gently guiding Isabel along behind me, but she plants her feet into the carpet and refuses to budge.

"Paul!" Isabel chokes. "No, you didn't understand me. You don't have to do—"

"I know I don't have to, but I will. I'll walk away from this place altogether. We can start afresh—go live in a fucking cardboard box in a forest somewhere if that's what you want. Honestly, Isabel, I mean it. I'll do this, if that's what you want."

"I know you love your work. I wasn't hinting at this. I really wasn't."

"But that's kind of the point, honey," I say, very gently. "I don't know what you're hinting at. I never did. But there's nothing I wouldn't do for you—nothing." I release her hand, but only so I can cup her face in my palms so that she has no choice but to stare right into my eyes as I whisper, "I would get the fucking moon for you, if you wanted it." Her eyes are shining, and then she's fighting a smile as I add, "You know I'm smart. I'd find a way."

"You're only smart at, like, three things," she whispers. I laugh.

"Now you're getting it. Maybe we were made for each other—but our flaws do not line up, and they never did. A guy who can't read subtext and a girl who can't ask for what she needs are doomed to fail unless they are determined to make it work. And I promise you, if you give me another chance, I will put everything I have into this thing between us."

Isabel's gaze keeps flicking over my shoulder, and now she leans close to me and she whispers urgently,

"Yes, we'll work on it. Together. But, Paul, seriously. You don't have to leave Brainway, and you need to tell Jess you're staying, because I think she's stopped breathing."

"Okay, you heard the woman. Apparently, I'm staying." I glance over my shoulder just in time to see Jess relax and Marcus wink at me.

"We'll give you some privacy," he says, and he pushes back his chair as if to stand.

"Like fuck we will," Jess snorts, and she leans back in her chair. "It took a lot of effort for me to engineer this reunion. Witnessing it is my karmic reward."

Marcus raises his eyebrows at her, and when she remains stubbornly seated, he pushes her office chair out the door. She squeals in protest, and Isabel laughs freely. I think that might just be the most beautiful sound I've ever heard.

"How do we stop this stupid pattern we keep getting stuck in?" Isabel asks me, as I wrap my arms around her.

"I think we take it slow. We heal. We fight and we make up. And we talk. A lot."

"Maybe we need ground rules again, like we decided on Saturday night. There's nothing we won't talk about, we tell one another the truth and the whole truth, and there's nothing off-limits between us."

"I love that idea. And then…when you're ready?"

Her gaze softens on mine. "Then I'll come home," she whispers, and I grin.

"Then you'll come home."

Epilogue

Three months later

Paul

"PAUL, WAKE UP."

It's very early Friday morning, and I am deeply asleep until my lovely ex-wife violently shakes me awake.

"What's wrong?" I ask, sitting bolt upright as adrenaline floods my body.

Isabel is dressed for her early morning barre class, and she's sitting on the edge of her bed. *Her* bed, because we stayed at her shoebox apartment at SoHo last night, and *sitting* because she has to sit on the bed to talk to me—there's not enough room between the bed and the wall for her to stand.

"I need to tell you something," she says, and then she draws a sharp breath. "I want to come home. I'm ready to move back home. I mean, we're spending every night together anyway and it's silly for us to keep two places—" She breaks off, then draws in another breath. "But the main reason I want to come home is that I love you, I miss living with you, and I'm ready to come home. That's it."

I blink at her. Then I rub the sleep from my eyes and study her—I see the anxiety in her expression as she waits for my reaction and the determination in her gaze, as if I'm going to try to convince her that's a bad idea.

Clearly, she's forgotten I'm a genius. I know an excellent idea when I hear one. I grin and then pull her down onto my chest for a kiss.

"Yes." Kiss. "Please, Bel." More kisses. "Come home." Many more kisses. "I'm so proud of you."

"I'm so proud of us," Isabel says, relief brightening her gaze. "These last few months have been amazing, Paul. Honestly, I couldn't be happier."

We'll see about that. I just smile and nuzzle her nose with mine. "Me, too, Isabel. God, me, too."

It hasn't all been smooth sailing since Bel and I got back together. It's taken real work to rebuild our relationship in a way that will last, including hours of therapy with Alison that's been frustrating and difficult for both of us at times.

But Isabel is worth it. And we are worth it. Sometimes our progress has felt glacially slow, but I realized just how far we've come last week when Alison pointed out that we'd had three sessions with her where she'd barely said a word. That was the day Isabel and I decided it was time for us to step back from couples therapy and to trust in the strength of our relationship again.

That's when I started planning for Isabel to move back into my life permanently. We're divorced now, but still madly in love, and that means I get to propose again—something I'm well and truly ready to do.

But I'm not upset that she's suggested we move in together now. It just shows that I don't need to wonder if we're on the same page these days, because she actually tells me when something is on her mind.

"I really have to get going." She reluctantly sits up, pulling away from my embrace.

"I might see you later," I say tenderly. She brushes her lips against mine.

"Tonight?"

"Sure," I say noncommittally, because I have a feeling it will be a little sooner than that.

Isabel

JESS WANTS TO go shopping for baby clothes to surprise Abby and Marcus. This makes little to no sense, as Abby is with us, and is neither in the mood for shopping nor walking through this busy mall Jess wanted to visit. And as for me, I'm still floating along on cloud nine after the discussion I had with Paul before work this morning. Truthfully, I'd much rather be home packing, but Jess was adamant, and an adamant Jess is a very difficult person to refuse. Even for Abby, who's been holed up in her apartment complaining about the heat for the last few weeks.

"But why today?" Abby asks, or rather moans as she waddles along between Jess and me. She's now twenty-seven weeks pregnant with twins and, although radiant, starting to feel the strain on her body. "I just don't understand why it has to be this afternoon. Can't we just go get ice-cream sundaes and shop online while we eat them?"

"That's not a bad idea," Jess says thoughtfully as she scans the busy mall around us. She seems to find what she's looking for, because she suddenly changes direction. "Okay, I think there's an ice-cream store down this way—"

"Wait," I interrupt her. "You dragged us both out on this crazy hot afternoon because you had to go shopping, and before we even visit a single store, you decide you can do it online after all?"

"What can I say?" Jess shrugs, looping arms through mine and Abby's and pulling us gently forward. "I'm a fickle, fickle woman."

Music starts playing from somewhere to our left, and although I ignore it at first, Jess stops walking, and our elbows are linked, so I don't have much choice but to stop, too. We turn toward the sound, and I see a lone woman dancing in the crowd. A few bars later, a second woman joins her, and then two men begin to perform the careful choreography, too.

"Oh my God, you guys! It's a flash mob!" Abby exclaims.

The group is facing away from us at first, but as it swells in size and the song winds on, it slowly shifts until the troupe of dancers is performing like they are on a stage, and Abby, Jess and I are right in the front row of the audience. I'm completely taken by the performance. It's clearly a professional troupe, because each and every dancer moves with the kind of grace and fluidity that only comes from years of disciplined study. I only wish my Thursday afternoon octogenarian ballet dancers were here to see this, because it really is a sight to behold.

"I always wanted to see a flash mob," I murmur absentmindedly to Abby.

She grins at me as she nods. "This is amazing. It looks like they're performing *for* us. We're in exactly the right spot for the best view!"

"Yeah," I agree, but that gives me pause. "We really are..." I glance at Jess. "Did you know this was happening?"

Jess gives me a very convincing *what are you on about?* look, so I relax and go back to enjoying the performance. The song reaches a crescendo, and the dancers part to make way for...

Paul.

My ex-husband-now-boyfriend is not exactly a natural dancer, but he is an exceptionally disciplined man. I know immediately that a lot of work has gone into learning this routine, because while he's not quite keeping up with the rest of the mob, he is dancing as if he's been doing it for years.

"How did he find time for this?" I ask Jess, without breaking my gaze away from Paul. He's only a part of the flash mob for the last segment of the song, but he lands every step in perfect time, a model of intense focus and concentration.

Jess wraps her arm around my waist and rests her head on my shoulder. "You know how he's going to take on that strategy role, so he could cut back his schedule?"

"Yes?"

"He promoted Audrey to development manager and cut back his working week as soon as you guys got back together. He's been preparing for this ever since."

My throat feels tight. To think that once upon a time, I doubted that I was a priority in this man's life. To think that not so long ago, he struggled to express how important I was to him. And now here he is, working for months in secrecy to surprise me... wearing his heart on his sleeve in public like this...

I'd like to say I can't believe how lucky I am—but luck doesn't get you where Paul and I are now. No, we've built a solid foundation together over the last few months through consistent effort and sometimes, plain old hard work. Paul has more than proven that our relationship is his highest priority since we came back from that long weekend at Greenport, and that was even before he joined a flash mob just to surprise me.

Now, I scan the crowd, and discover that my octogenarians *are* on the other side, along with my under-nineties basketball team, pretty much everyone from Martin's building, and Nick, and not far from him, even Emma and Noah are watching with blinding grins on their faces. As for Martin, he's standing next to Elspeth, holding up an iPad. I don't think he realizes there are two cameras, because he's holding the tablet with the screen facing away from him. That means I can see that he's FaceTimed Paul's brother Jake in, and it also means that Martin can't see that Jake is rubbing his forehead wearily— because Martin has his finger over the lens. It appears that Martin, much like his son, is only a genius when it comes to a very specific set of tasks.

I burst out laughing, just as I hear Abby gasp, "Did you know this was happening, Marcus?"

"Yep," Marcus laughs from behind us.

"How could you keep this a secret from me!" Abby exclaims.

"Well, Abs, Paul wanted to keep it a surprise for Izzy, so we all agreed it was best to let Jess handle the subterfuge," Marcus laughs again.

"I can't believe he did this for me," I whisper.

"You know how much I hate true love and all of that shit," Jess says softly.

"So you say." Abby snorts. "You seem to go to a lot of trouble to foster it."

"I'm a fourth-generation meddler, Abby. It's what I do." Jess shrugs, but then she hugs me again. "I'm not really sure there's anything Paul wouldn't do for you, Isabel. It's enough to warm the cockles of my ice-cold heart."

As the final bars of the song play, the dance troupe fades back into the crowd, until Paul is the only person in the space they've left behind. As the song finishes and when silence falls at last, Paul simply walks up to me and places a single kiss on my cheek.

"I love you," he says softly.

"Marry me," I blurt.

Beside me, Abby squeals with joy and Jess bursts out laughing. I glance at Jess, then back to Paul, suddenly flustered in case I've stolen his thunder. "Sorry. Shit. Wait. Were you about to—"

"No," he laughs, "I actually wasn't."

"Oh."

"Don't get me wrong." He takes me into his arms. "I'm totally up for marrying you again. I was going to ask you later tonight when we were alone, so we could talk it through and be sure it's what we both want. There really was no hidden agenda for this flash mob thing." He shrugs as if it was nothing. "I just wanted to be a part of making one of your dreams come true."

A somewhat undignified sob bursts from my throat, and I throw my arms around his neck and kiss him. There's a relieved cheer from the crowd around us, who seemed a bit confused by the anti-climactic ending.

Beside us, Abby is now in floods of tears. Martin and Elspeth have joined us, and I'm vaguely aware that Jess is trying to convince them she's not crying. Apparently, she's just got some dust in her eye "from this filthy mall." But that's all vague noise around us, and I only have eyes for Paul.

"So, I get to marry you again?" he asks me, linking his arms around my waist.

"This will be the last time, so we better do it right."

"Our anniversary is next month. Maybe we should get married on the same day so I don't forget the date."

"As if that would ever happen," I laugh gently, then I kiss him again because I can't seem to stop.

"I can't wait to spend the rest of my life with you, Isabel," Paul says, suddenly sobering.

"I feel exactly the same way."

Two people come together when they fall in love—they try to smash together different histories and personalities and experiences to create one shared life. If I've learned anything in the last few years, it's that falling in love can be easy, but staying in love takes work. It's hard and it's messy sometimes; there are no shortcuts in building a life together.

Lucky for me, I have the perfect partner in this project we call life. He's great at math, getting better all the time at communicating, and 100 percent *mine*.

* * * * *

*If you fell hard for Isabel & Paul, turn the page
for a preview of Jessica & Jake's story,*

Undone

*another in Kelly Rimmer's bestselling
Start Up in the City series
from HQN Books.*

CHAPTER ONE

Jessica

MY FRIEND ISABEL has big blue eyes and natural curls in a startling shade of ash blond. She's recently turned thirty-five, but she looks much younger even on rare occasions like this one, when she's wearing a full face of makeup. I think her antiaging secret is her wholesome lifestyle, which is obviously an extreme measure and not one I'd ever be willing to try myself. I'm thirty-five too, but when I'm not wearing makeup, I look like an aged, freckled version of Pippi Longstocking, if Pippi partied way too much in her twenties.

It's fair to say that Isabel and I are the unlikeliest of friends. She's sweet, I'm sharp. She's kind and gentle and softhearted, I'm…well, I'm just not. We've had a lot of great times together, but we also have very different approaches to life, and every now and again I wonder why she puts up with me at all. What I don't wonder about is why I've kept her around. Izzy is the lite version of humanity—all of the goodness, few calories. She is easy to love and, for the most part, quite uncomplicated when it comes to her friends—a rare trait, and one I value highly.

I'd be lost without her. Completely, hopelessly lost.

Right now, maybe for the first time ever, I wish that Isabel wasn't an exceptional human being. In fact, I'm wishing that last year when she abruptly decided to divorce my business partner Paul, I'd have done what I usually do when people around me do something stupid—and told her exactly what I was thinking. If I'd been harsh enough, she'd probably have cut me out of her life. Yes, I'd have been lost and miserable and sad and I'd have missed her forever, but then again, even feeling miserable and lost and sad would have been preferable to what I'm feeling right now.

Izzy and Paul sorted their shit out—only, this happened just a little too late to stop the divorce, and now they want to get remarried. So here we all are, at their brownstone in Chelsea for the rehearsal dinner before their second wedding takes place tomorrow. There are fairy lights and candles and big vases of fragrant white roses on the long table that centers their dining room. There's soft orchestral music playing on the speakers. Isabel and Paul are both radiant. It's all so joyous and romantic that it makes me a little ill.

Don't get me wrong: I'm utterly delighted that they sorted their shit out and they're both happy again. It's just that all of this haste and love and joy and renewal means that instead of ordering my first wine for the night in a bar somewhere and scanning the room for a companion, I'm sitting here swilling champagne like it's water and watching the door as if it's about to burst open to reveal some kind of Jess-Cohen-kryptonite.

Which it kind of is.

Because Paul's brother Jake is due to arrive any second now, fresh off a flight from the West Coast, where he now lives.

"What's up with you?" The voice belongs to Marcus, my other business partner, who's sitting to my right. He speaks quietly—keeping his voice low, no doubt so as not to upset the other members of the wedding party. Paul and Isabel are opposite me, and Abby, Marcus's fiancée, is in the restroom. She's very pregnant with twins. As far as I can tell, being very pregnant with twins means you spend half your time looking exhausted and terrified, and the other half peeing.

"What's up with you?" I snap at him unthinkingly, and he slowly raises an eyebrow.

"Ho-ly shit," he whistles.

"What?"

"Jessica Cohen—are you upset about something?" The incredulity in his tone suggests that the very idea of this is impossible. I'm kind of pleased that I've managed to fool him into thinking I really am some kind of superwoman, and also immediately depressed that one of my best friends has no idea I have any emotional depth at all.

"Mind your own damn business, Marcus."

His expression grows serious, and he leans even closer to whisper, "Is everything okay?"

"Everything's fine."

"Things are clearly not fine," Marcus says, frowning. He glances down at my hands, and I realize I'm tapping the table. I stop, but as soon as I do, my knee starts to bounce.

"Seriously, Marcus, leave it," I whisper it back to him, but the words come out as a half growl, half hiss, and he winces.

"Okay, okay," he says, raising his hands in surrender. Just then, the doorbell rings and my heart is suddenly beating so hard and so fast I feel a little faint. I have butterflies in my tummy, and in my back. That's *not* normal. Maybe I need medical attention.

Isabel squeals and stands.

"That'll be Jake!"

And off she goes to answer the door, while I try to figure out just how upset Isabel and Paul would be if I tell them I can't stay for their rehearsal dinner. But what would be a big enough excuse to justify such a dick move? I can't say it's a date, that would make me a bitch. What else is there? Why didn't I come up with an excuse earlier?

Aaaand…now it's too late.

My stomach drops. I stop bouncing my knee, but now my hands start to shake, so I fold them together and hide them on my lap.

Jake Winton strides into the room wearing jeans and a very simple gray T-shirt that stretches over the bulky muscles of his arms and his chest. Goddammit, I *hate* how good he looks. Unlike his brother, Jake is very broad and very tall—far too large for my tastes, really. I like a man I can look eye to eye in my heels, and Jake is six foot six.

I'm good, but even I couldn't manage thirteen-inch heels. Jake is just a veritable giant in every way. Yes, including that one. Men spend a lot of time worrying about size, but frankly, I'd take a skilled guy with a sensibly sized appendage over a horse like Jake any day. I want a man who can get in there, get the job done, then walk away—leaving me able to walk away too…as opposed to limping away. Maybe it's just me, but I like to enjoy a guy's company and not need an epidural if I want to go to spin class the next day.

Not that I was complaining all that much when Jake and I were together. Probably because he *was* a skilled guy. In fact, I do remember relishing that sometimes-morning-after tenderness because it reminded me of the hours I'd spent with him. I was so lust-addled at the time that I actually thought that was a good thing.

But sex is better without complications like that—delicious memories, emotions, huge dicks. So yes, in hindsight, his is definitely too big. And he's definitely too tall and broad. And too compassionate. And too… *Argh…* These days he's just too West Coast. He looks so relaxed, and I can't miss the light tan on his skin and the way that his muddy-blond hair has brightened up several tones. Then again, Jake always loved surfing and hiking. Even when he lived here in Manhattan he was forever planning trips away to commune with nature or some shit.

When his job gets too much, he heads to the outdoors to decompress.

Yes, Jake Winton was and is all wrong for me, in pretty much every way.

I look away, and I plan to continue looking away—but my eyes are drawn back to him and I find myself staring again immediately. I've just missed him so much, and it's been two and a half years since I saw him—apparently that separation has left me weak and hungry. I note the smattering of gray at his temples and just for a moment I wonder if I put it there. Then I do the calculation and realize he'd be thirty-nine now, so I guess a hint of silver makes sense. Also, I'm really not into salt-and-pepper guys, so that's excellent.

Except that it suits him. He is a doctor, after all… A specialist at that, and there's something about the hint of gray that makes him look even more distinguished. And the horn-rimmed glasses? They're new too. He used to make fun of my reading glasses in that flirty, melt-my-panties way of his. He always said they made me look like a sexy librarian.

Seriously, who has sexy librarian fantasies?

Me.

Right now.

I'm fantasizing about a very broad, very tall, very sexy male librarian who's actually a doctor with a huge dick and horn-rimmed frames on his brand-new glasses.

"…glad to be here. Marcus, congratulations on the engagement and the twins and— Oh! Hey there,

Abby! Wow, you look amazing. When are you due?"
Jake's going around the table greeting everyone, and
by the time I check back into the conversation, he's
already up to me. His gaze lands on me, and after a
split second of panic I force my brightest smile. "And
Jessica," he says, then he returns my smile with a
very tight smile of his own.

There's barely disguised antagonism in his gaze,
and it seems I've made a critical error here. I knew I
was at real risk of throwing myself at him like some
kind of lust-sick idiot tonight, but I figured *he'd* be
on his best behavior. I mean, come on—Jake's the
nicest guy I've ever met. It really didn't occur to me
that he'd *ever* look at me like…this.

It seems that in all of my wasted hours over the
last few weeks worrying about seeing Jake again, I
have neglected to consider one very important thing:
I'm the villain here. It was my idea to hide our relationship from our friends. My idea to end things.
My idea to "give one another some space" after we
broke up.

It was *his* idea to pack up and move to California
to get away from me, and I probably should have
given a little more thought to the level of hurt that
might have been behind that decision. I just told myself the job offer at Stanford must have been too
good to be true, and that he was probably ready for
a change after living his whole life in New York. It
was easier to believe my own lies than it was to really interrogate what might actually have been going
on for him.

"Hello," he says now.

"Hi, Jake," I say. My gaze lands on the almost-empty bottle of champagne in the middle of the table. "We need some more bubbles!" My voice is a little too light and a little too high. I glance toward the kitchen, where Marcus's brother-in-law and a pair of apprentice chefs are preparing our meal as part of Marcus and Abby's wedding gift to Paul and Izzy. "I'll just—"

"Sit down, Jess," Isabel says, laughing. She waves at me, playfully dismissive as she rises. "I'll get it. You guys can all catch up before we talk through the plan for tomorrow."

"I need to walk a bit," Abby says, and she stands with some difficulty. Didn't she just get back from the bathroom? I move to rise, but Marcus is right beside her, and before I'm even on my feet, his arm is around her waist and he's leading her away from the table.

"Let me come, Abs," he says softly. "Want to go outside for some fresh air? How's the heartburn?"

"All good." She flashes a smile that looks just a little too bright. "Fresh air sounds great."

That leaves me, Jake and Paul. I mentally beg Paul to stay, but because the universe hates me, he stands immediately.

"Sorry," he says, then he gives us a cheeky grin, "I've been waiting all night for Isabel to get distracted. I've organized a surprise for the honeymoon and I just need to check in on it."

They're going to New Zealand for their honeymoon. I'm pretty sure the "surprise" is a trip to a rugby match, because Isabel is sports-mad. In any case, Paul leaves the room, and…now I'm alone with his brother.

I down the last of my champagne in one gulp, then glance hesitantly at Jake. He's staring at me, his gaze hard, and I try to force myself to be polite and to make an attempt at small talk.

"How have you been? It's been too long," I say. It's possibly the stupidest possible thing I could *ever* have said to Jake Winton. Jesus. I don't know even why I said it. It's just what people say, isn't it? My voice is all wobbly. Where's my supposedly endless confidence when I need it? Where are those "balls of steel" lovers and business rivals have accused me of having? Oh, God. I want the earth to open up and swallow me whole.

Jake sits. He leans back in his chair and surveys me for a moment, then he sighs impatiently.

"We have to play games when the others are around because that's how *you* wanted it to be. But when we're alone, let's not pretend this isn't uncomfortable."

Even as I nod in agreement, I feel my heart sink. There's no mistaking the disdain in his tone. I usually don't give a flying fuck what other people think about me, and I'm still not sure what makes Jake so different…but he is different. And I *hate* the idea that he might hate me.

I'm saved by the return of Izzy with the champagne, and she immediately launches herself into rapid-fire chitchat about the meal. Everyone else returns soon enough too, and at first, I figure the tension between Jake and me will dilute, at least a little, as we settle into the company of our friends.

But I'm wrong about that too. Jake is polite enough to ignore me in conversation, but tense enough to narrow his gaze at me every time our eyes meet.

CHAPTER TWO

Jake

HERE'S THE THING: I'm a nice guy. I'm a healer by trade—an oncologist, actually, which is a pretty unsexy profession and not one you choose unless you genuinely care about people. I do care about people. I donate money to charity. I help little old ladies cross the street. I rescued a dog last year. Her name is Clara and she's the ugliest fucking thing you've ever seen—as far as I tell, a cross between a pug, a Brussels griffon and that ball of hair and gunk that clogs up the bathroom sink after a while. I found myself at the shelter just before closing time on what happened to be the very last day before Clara was due to be "put to sleep." She looked up at me with her one remaining eye and for some reason I just couldn't bear the thought of the shelter staff putting such a young dog down.

Well, Clara may be young, but she's not exactly healthy or even cute. In addition to that missing eye, she has a terrifying overbite, she's an odd shape, her fur is patchy and the shelter staff told me they suspected she was abused by a previous owner because she has severe anxiety. I pay more for her monthly medication than I did to adopt her, and I let her sleep not just in my bed but on my pillow. Sometimes I wake up and she's actually lying on my face. No matter what I do, her endlessly dirty ears always wind up smelling awful, and whenever I have guests, they always say the same thing—some variation on "Holy shit! What is that smell? Argh! Is that a dog?"

Right at this very moment, I'm paying a dog behaviorist to act as dog-sitter, which is costing me a stupid amount of money. The woman actually has to sleep at my house with Clara because my dog can't go to a kennel and she has a very bad habit of shredding everything in sight if she's left alone overnight.

And despite all of that, I love Clara, because that's the kind of guy I am.

A nice guy. A tolerant guy.

And yet, I'm sitting here staring at Jessica Cohen, and I'm struggling to find *any* goodwill toward her whatsoever.

I've had a lot of time to think in the two and a half years since our breakup, and I've come to a few hard realizations about our relationship. I desperately want to confront Jess, and I plan to do just that— *after* the reception. I'm due to fly out for a hiking trip on Sunday night, and I'm pretty sure Paul and Izzy aren't going to fuck this marriage business up again, so there's a very good chance tomorrow night will be the last time I'll see Jess in our lifetimes.

I'll say what I need to say, and then I'll finally be able to let her go.

Izzy hands me a bottle of champagne and I pop the cork. I pour some for Marcus and myself and then Izzy and Paul. Abby returns to the table, so I offer her some too, although I know she won't drink it. She points to her water with a sigh, then I flick a glance at Jess. She already has a flute in her hand, but just as I look at her, she avoids my gaze, lifts her glass and drains it.

I should offer her a refill.

I mean, I *should*. But I can see she desperately wants a refill, so I don't. Jess has always had a way of drawing out aspects to my personality I didn't even know were there. It turns out, she can even inspire me to petty childishness.

"How's things for you?" Paul asks me, when I've finished sharing the champagne around. "How's Clara?"

I feel Jess's eyes on me, and just for a minute, I let myself enjoy the possibility that she might think Clara is a girlfriend rather than a particularly high-maintenance pet. It was Jess's decision to end our relationship, so I'm sure she's not jealous, but I really do like the idea that she might be. It's ridiculous, and maybe I'm not such a nice guy after all, because I'm deliberately ambiguous as I say, "Clara is great," then I smile broadly. "Sure makes life better having someone to come home to each night. But I don't need to tell you lovebirds that—how long have you been back home, Izzy?"

"A few months," Isabel says, then she just beams

at me. I glance at Paul, and he's wearing the same stupid grin. I chuckle.

"I can't wait to officially welcome you back to the family tomorrow, Izzy."

She sighs happily.

"Everything is just perfect, isn't it? I'm so glad you could be here. I know the timing wasn't great…"

I wave her apology away.

"Even the timing was perfect. It was easy to push my trip back a few days—much easier than moving patient appointments if I hadn't been planning a break already."

"Where are you off to, Jake?" Marcus asks from across the table, where he's sitting right beside Jess.

"I'm hiking the John Muir Trail—doing an ultralight trip, so taking minimum supplies and walking it as fast as I can. I was originally thinking Paul might join me… I thought he'd want to be distracted when his first postdivorce wedding anniversary rolled around." I glance at my brother, then wink at him. "Turns out he had a better idea."

Paul laughs softly.

"I forgot all about that."

"Well, I decided to do it alone anyway. I'm flying back Monday morning and I'll start the trail on Wednesday. I expect to finish in about eleven or twelve days, depending on how I'm feeling as I go."

"How far does this trail go?" Abby asks with visible horror. I laugh at her expression.

"About two hundred and twenty miles. I'll try to

average twenty-two miles a day so I can have a few rest days along the way."

"You do realize you're completely insane, right?" Abby shakes her head at me and I grin at her.

"Maybe when the twins arrive, you guys can plan a hike with me. Marcus and I can carry the babies in backpacks."

"That does sound like fun," Marcus murmurs playfully.

"You know very well that it sounds like my worst nightmare." Abby scowls at him, and I laugh again.

"There's nothing like it, Abby. Fresh air. Silence. Disconnecting from all of the noise of modern life is the best way to nurture your soul."

"Clara doesn't mind you leaving her, then?" Paul asks, and he's teasing of course, but this time I have no doubt at all that anyone who hadn't made my terrifying pet's acquaintance would hear this and assume he was referring to a partner. I flick a glance at Jess. I'm both delighted and instantly irritated to see that she's visibly jealous. In fact, she's close to incandescent green.

"Clara is incredibly loyal," I say slowly. "It's one of her best qualities."

"She'll greet you at the door when you get back, and she'll be humping your leg—" Paul says, and I cut him off hastily.

"Classic Clara. So what's the deal for tomorrow?" I ask Izzy.

"The food is just about ready," she tells me. "I'll run you through our plans when we're done eating."

WE SPEND THE next hour gorging ourselves on the incredible four courses the caterers have prepared for us, and just as we finish with dessert, Paul hands me another bottle of champagne. While he and Izzy rise, I quickly top up another round into everyone's glasses. I studiously ignore Jess, then set the bottle on the table between us, so unlike *everyone* else, she has to fill her own glass.

Yeah. I might not like Jess anymore, but I definitely do not like the guy I've become tonight.

"Firstly, I'd like to thank you all for coming here tonight, especially on such short notice," Paul says. "I never dreamed that I would get a chance to do this again, and it means the world that you'd all be here again to witness it."

"Don't worry," Isabel assures us all. "Tomorrow is going to be very low-key."

She gives us the basics in about thirty seconds: Marcus and I are to meet Paul here at his home, Abby, Isabel and Jess will meet at a suite at a hotel for hair and makeup and whatever else it is that women do on wedding days. Truth be told, I tune out of the details after that because I'm pretty sure it's all I need to know. Instead, I busy myself staring at the roses in the center of the table, just so my eyes are pointed in Jess's vague vicinity, but my staring contest with the roses doesn't last long because my gaze drifts automatically toward her. She catches me and we both scowl, then look away, just as Paul and Isabel take their seats again. As best man, it's only appropriate that I make a toast, so I reach for my glass.

As soon as I'm on my feet, Jess snatches her own glass up and stands too. We stare at each other just as we've been doing all night, only this time, the moment is nothing like fleeting. It's still painfully uncomfortable—but neither one of us looks away.

I'm all too aware of the confused gazes fixed right on us right now.

"I was going to make a toast," I say carefully. I *am* Paul's brother, after all, *and* the best man, and traditionally a toast would be my responsibility. The polite thing for Jess to do is to sit down, or maybe even to apologize and *then* sit down.

Jess is anything but polite.

"I was going to make a toast, too," she says pointedly, and she remains stubbornly standing. Her gaze is pure challenge. *I dare you to make a scene.*

I try to wait her out, but we end up standing there in an awkward game of chicken. The moment stretches and stretches until I realize that no matter how long I wait there, Jess is not going to be the first to sit down. Given the opportunity, she'd stand and glare at me until the dinner finished, until the wedding happened without us, until we both starved to death and our bones decomposed. And as the earth crashes into the sun in seven or eight billion years, the last thing *my* ghost would see would be Jess's ghost, still glaring at me as we dissolved into a ball of fiery doom.

If I don't sit, either we're going to stay here literally forever, or one of our friends is going to have to intervene to break the stalemate. This leaves me very little choice but to be the one to say awkwardly, "Well, ladies first, then," and soon I'm the one taking my seat while Jess makes a very poetic, very touching speech about how wonderful it is to be in their wedding party for the second time, and how glad she is to see them back together.

The whole time I'm staring at my champagne flute, watching the bubbles rise, trying not to admire how eloquent she is, and trying to talk myself out of acting like a spoiled brat. It's been *well* over two years since Jess and I split, and we were together for only four fucking months. The woman should have no hold over me whatsoever, and the fact that she still does is actually kind of humiliating.

Jess finishes her toast, and everyone raises their glasses, then she says sweetly, "Jake, did you still want to add something?"

I glance up at her, and she flutters her eyelashes at me. I rise, lift my glass, tilt it toward my brother and his lovely bride-to-be-again as I say, "Paul, Izzy, I'm just so happy for you both. Not much to add to Jessica's wonderful speech, other than to say…welcome back to the family, Izzy. I couldn't be happier for you both. To Paul and Izzy."

As I sit, I glance at Jess and find her smirking. Yeah, she definitely won the "battle of the speeches." There's open triumph in her eyes. As the others start to chat again, she leans forward and whispers, "*That* was for pretending you didn't see I needed champagne."

"If that slurred, rambling word-vomit was any indication, more champagne is the last thing you need tonight," I whisper back. Jess looks like she's about to leap across the table and rip my face off, so I turn to Isabel and try to slip into her conversation. She's laughing with Paul about how "lucky" it was that they ran into one another at the vacation home six months ago. I catch the undertone but don't understand it, so I ask in surprise, "Was that not luck? Did you go out there to catch him on purpose?"

"Oh, no," she laughs, and then she flicks a meaningful glance to Jess. "It's a funny story, and you won't believe it—but it turns out it was all Jess's doing."

All roads lead back to Jess Cohen. Of course they fucking do. The woman has a finger in *every* pie.

"How so?" I ask, but my tone is resigned. I glance at Jess briefly and find she's smirking at me again.

And then Izzy tells me all about how Jess engineered for her and Paul to arrive at their vacation home for the same weekend away, and how they were both too stubborn to leave, and by the time Monday came around, they were in love again.

"Jess had a hand in us getting together, too," Abby sighs happily from across the table. "I was pretty determined that I wasn't in love with Marcus until Jess tried to set him up with one of the programmers from work. Nothing's quite so effective in curing self-denial as hardcore jealousy."

"Brave of you to intervene in your friends' life like that," I murmur to Jess, and she lifts one perfectly arched eyebrow at me.

"Brave?" she repeats.

"Either situation could've worked out very differently."

"I knew it was worth the risk in both cases," Jess says, then she leans back in her chair and begins to study her immaculately polished fingernails. Something about her lack of concern at my observation irks me even more, and I lean forward just a little.

"But either scenario could easily have turned to disaster," I say. "Did you ever think about that before you went about playing God with your friends' lives?"

"Playing God?" Jess repeats. Her tone rises just as her eyebrows disappear into her hairline. This is exactly the rise I was looking for.

I shrug and say casually, "Some people might consider what you did in both cases to be...manipulative."

I'm pretty sure no one was listening to us a minute ago, but in a heartbeat, all of the chatter in the room has stopped. Four shocked sets of eyes are now on me and Jess—and Jess is glaring at me with such intense rage that if I was just a little smarter, I'd be looking for something to hide behind.

Sudden, brutal regret grips me. I can't believe I let this escalate—but just as I'm trying to figure out how to undo the scene I've just made, there's a sudden shift in Jess's expression.

Holy shit. And now her big blue eyes shine with the unmistakable gleam of tears.

Jess turns sharply and reaches down for her hand-bag, which had apparently been resting below her chair. She withdraws her phone and begins to press the screen frantically as if she's texting. She's blinking rapidly, but a smidge of moisture leaks out anyway, and she swipes at it—accidentally smudging her heavy eye makeup in the process.

No one says anything. Perhaps the rest of our friends are in shock, just as I am.

"Izzy, I am so sorry," Jess says, raising her gaze. "I forgot I had a date."

The silence has been fraught, but in an instant, it becomes incredibly awkward.

"A date?" Isabel says hesitantly.

"A date," Jess says, as if this is the most normal thing in the world. She picks up her phone again and begins to madly press the screen. "But we're done here, aren't we?"

I suppose we are done. The plans have been discussed, the food has been eaten, toasts have been made. It might even be fine for Jess to leave now, if it weren't so painfully obvious that she's not leaving because we're "done."

The problem with revenge is that it's never as satisfying as you think it's going to be. I wanted to get a reaction out of Jess, to dig the knife in and to twist it a little, because she hurt me and I wanted her to feel bad. I got exactly what I wanted, but it feels disgusting. I just don't know how to fix this without embarrassing Jess even more…and an embarrassed Jess is likely to be a dangerously unpredictable creature.

There's a flurry of activity happening around the table. Abby and Isabel are trying to convince Jess to cancel this serious, last-minute, surprise date that Jess is now arguing she absolutely must go on. Paul and Marcus also appear to be trying to convince Jess that she should cancel her date, without actually telling her that she should cancel her date.

Probably because they're trying to avoid poking the bear. Paul and Marcus are definitely both much smarter than I am.

I'm silent, watching all of this unfold, also now trying to figure out exactly what I said that got such a reaction out of her. Was it the manipulation comment? The "playing God" comment? The whole night of awkward tension had built up and up. Did something just get to her?

Maybe she's sick?

Maybe she didn't know I was coming tonight?

Maybe she's been secretly pining after me for two years?

Well, that last one seems unlikely. It was her decision to end our relationship, not mine. I was all in—I had the fucking engagement ring in my underwear drawer, just waiting for the right moment.

I'm still sitting in useless silence right up until Jess leaves. And just as I suspected, the minute the front door closes behind her, all eyes are on me.

"What just happened?" Abby doesn't say the words, she growls them. I clear my throat.

"I didn't mean to upset her…" I say helplessly. I open my hands, because I read somewhere that if you expose your palms to an angry person, you're showing vulnerability and they'll go easy on you. The gesture does nothing to soothe the angry pregnant lady, who rounds on me like she's going to body-slam me.

Isabel approaches me from the other side and says sharply, "You upset Jess Cohen. I didn't know anyone *could* upset Jess Cohen. What did you do?"

"She didn't manipulate us," Abby says sharply. "She tried to help us, can't you see that?"

"I know," I say defensively, "I really didn't mean to hurt her. She's clearly oversensitive tonight—"

"Oversensitive!" Abby gasps.

"Jake, do you *want* them to kill you?" Marcus mutters, wincing. I stand, and I throw my hands into the air.

"She did manipulate you guys. I'm glad it worked out for the best, but what she did was pretty ballsy, and it all could have ended in disaster. I'm super glad you all ended up together, but what right does she have to interfere in other people's lives like that?"

"If you knew her like we know her," Isabel says, voice shaking with feeling, "you'd understand that her intentions are beautiful. She has a tough exterior, but beneath it, she's one of the most caring, loving people I've ever met. And you upset her tonight, Jake Winton, so you need to fix it before you ruin our day tomorrow. I don't know how you're going to do it, but *you are going to fix it*."

And there, shimmering in the eyes of my sister-in-law, are the second set of tears I have put in a woman's eyes tonight. I thought I could sit Jess down and have it out *after* the festivities tomorrow, but apparently, I lack the self-control to keep things civil until then. I sigh heavily, run my hands through my hair, and then I say, "You all know that Jess and I have always grated each other." That's the understatement of the century. We spent more than a decade clashing, four months fucking and now two years pretending the other doesn't exist. Apparently, Jess and I don't just run hot and cold, we can only exist in the same space as steam or ice. "I'll go see her now, clear the air and say sorry. And I *am* sorry."

"Thanks, Jake," Paul says before he sighs. "Jess can be difficult, but so can I. And you get me better than just about anyone, so I know you can handle her." He gives me a crooked smile.

"Sorry about this, Paul."

"I get it. If I had a dollar for every time I said something awkward, we'd be living in a castle of pure gold."

I slip my wallet into my pocket, scoop my phone off the table and load the app to call a ride share.

"Don't you want to know her address?" Abby says sharply.

"Uh…"

"She bought a condo. Two years ago."

Jess and I broke up *just* before she moved into that place, so she didn't invite me to the housewarming, but we were definitely together when she was house hunting. I helped Jess pick that fucking apartment, and she actually lived with me while the contractors were remodeling it for her. Abby just has no visibility of any of that, and now I have to pretend I need Jess's address, when I know it by heart because I actually figured I'd wind up living there with her one day.

That's the problem with lies. You tell one, and the next thing you know you're drowning in them. I never wanted to hide our relationship from these people in the first place.

But Jess was adamant that no one know we were ever together, and only in the last few months have I figured out why.

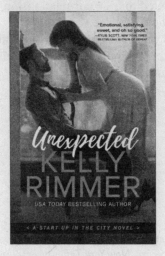

**Look for the third book in the
Start Up in the City series from
USA TODAY bestselling author**

KELLY RIMMER

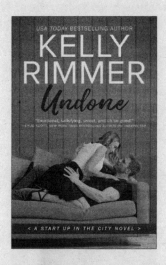

"Emotional, satisfying, sweet, and oh-so-good."
—Kylie Scott, *New York Times* bestselling author

Preorder your copy today!